# Death *on the* Thames

The Alexandra Raven Mysteries Book 2

Shiv Saywack

THE BOOK FOLKS

The Books Folks
A Joffe Books Company
www.thebookfolks.com

First published in Great Britain in 2025



This book is a work of fiction. Names, characters, businesses, organizations, places and events are either the product of the author's imagination or are used fictitiously. Any resemblance to actual persons, living or dead, events or locales is entirely coincidental. The spelling used is British English except where fidelity to the author's rendering of accent or dialect supersedes this.



ISBN: 978-1-80462-364-0

Death on the Thames

Also by Shiv Saywack

THE ALEXANDRA RAVEN MYSTERIES
Book 1: Death in Soho
Book 2: Death on the Thames

# Prologue

*April 1950*

She could have been sleeping, if she wasn't dead. It took two men to get her up to the deck. The narrow entranceway of the cabin cruiser and the steep stairs didn't help. An anchor was tied loosely around her waist, and petrol was splashed around and inside the cabin.

Then they waited.

At midnight, a car pulled up. The two men from the boat went to it, opened the boot, and lifted out the body of a man. They carried him to the boat and placed him near the woman.

One of the men glanced at his watch. He nodded to the other. The moon had risen, the sky was dark, and the river was gently slapping against the hull of the boat. A firm push with his foot sent the boat away from the jetty. The tide caught it and, as it slowly swung downstream, he took out a book of matches and struck one. Using the first match, he set the rest of the book on fire and flung it onto the deck. A few seconds later the boat erupted in flames.

A mile away, the chief of the midnight watch on the USS *Winfield Scott* saw the flames. He wrote it up in his log, his last entry, as the ship was readied to leave.

# Chapter 1

*Four days later*

I felt decidedly overdressed. Yesterday's creased frock and blouse would have put me more at ease. Hell, oily dungarees wouldn't be out of place. I saw what Mrs Geller's son meant when he called it a miserable hovel. Scaffolding supported the walls and extended into the street. The fact that the house was still standing surprised me. That it was inhabited surprised me more. That I was here at all… well, that was Mrs Geller's fault.

She'd hired me on behalf of her friend, David Blau. Knowing the woman, the power behind the throne of Messrs Geller and Goldmann, a firm of accountants with offices below mine, I'm pretty sure Blau wouldn't have had much say in the arrangement.

I glanced around again and reminded myself that not all of the East End was shabby, nor all slums. This part, however, had been, or still was – in its present state, it was difficult to decide which. The street had survived the worst of the Blitz. But only just. There were gaps all along, now just neatly stacked rubble of things that were once houses. Those that remained, like broken teeth, looked rotten. In the grand scheme of things, it wouldn't be long before they were consigned to the bulldozers. Not a bad thing. Five years after the war had ended, the city still wore its scars for all to see.

Maybe it was the look in my eyes that prompted Mrs Geller to say, 'The house isn't much to look at, not compared to what he had in Berlin, but it's his, and it's home.'

'There's no need to apologise,' I said. 'He lived in Berlin?'

'He loves Anna,' she said, having not heard me. 'He's making up for the six years they were apart… He lost everything in the war, Alex. Everything except Anna…'

*Until now*, she didn't need to add.

'He was in the camps.' Mrs Geller had already warned me several times and did so again when she knocked on the door. 'He's a bitter man, Alex.'

'He has every right to be,' I said, but she still wasn't listening.

We waited.

She could wear a soft face when the mood took her, but today's face was harsh and etched heavily with regret. Mrs Geller didn't try to hide it. Perhaps she couldn't. Some of her family never left the camps, either.

David Blau answered the knock. He was thin, grey-haired, and stooped. His face, like that of an apple kept dry throughout the winter, was finely creased, wrinkled and sunken. Devoid of sunlight, the colour had faded. Deep, drawn eyes flicked a gaze of curiosity at me. He looked old before his time. But then, who wouldn't, having survived hell?

Blau led us down an empty corridor to a warm sitting room. The single bulb that lit it created more shadows than light. The wallpaper was stained and peeled in places. On an old writing desk in a corner, there was a family photograph next to a menorah. A small dining table with two chairs stood on a threadbare carpet across from an open fire. The fire did little to dispel the dampness or the depression that hung in the air.

Having invited us to sit on a dilapidated sofa, he sat hunched like a busted spring in a worn armchair. An old coffee table stood like a barricade between us. A coffee pot and three cups rested on it. He filled each cup and took one for himself. He left it on the table as he reached for his cardigan. In the process of pulling it on, the left-side sleeve rose up his white, thin forearm. He drew it down quietly, covering the tattoo of a set of numbers. His eyes looked up at mine. They were lonely brown eyes, and when he spoke, it was in a soft, benevolent voice that took me by surprise and reminded me of an uncle I liked who always carried sweets in his pocket.

'You know what it is?' he asked. He'd not lost the German accent. At his age, he never would.

I nodded. He nodded as well.

He rose, stirred the fire around a little, and placed the fire guard back, then sat perched on the edge of his seat. He gave a nod to the fire.

'Miriam says it's an age thing,' he said.

'Miriam?'

'Madam Geller.'

The running joke was that Mrs Geller didn't have a first name, and in the four years I'd known her, I never dared ask. Now I knew, I wondered if I'd ever use it.

'When I was younger,' Blau continued, 'I never used to feel the cold. It was a different kind of cold in Germany. It was dry. Here it's wet. It sits inside your bones.' He massaged his arms with stiff, arthritic fingers. 'So, you are a private detective, Miriam tells me? A shamus, isn't that what they call them in the American movies?'

'I prefer a plain enquiry agent,' I said with a smile.

'Miriam speaks highly of you.'

'That's good to know. She's always telling me to give it up and get married again.'

'When doesn't she?' He flicked his eyes to the ceiling. 'And I am not to mention that you are a woman,' he whispered loud enough so Mrs Geller could hear.

I smiled. 'Isn't she cute.'

He broke out in a coughing laugh, then reached over and took my hand in his. Callous, old fingers scraped my skin.

'So tell me about this woman, Alexandra Raven, that she becomes a shamus.'

'The good bits only. Let's say I know what I'm doing most of the time. The agency belonged to my father. I think he wanted a boy and got me instead. Not that he ever complained. So when he died, it became mine, and I'm bloody-minded enough to want to do what he always knew I could do. Yes, I'm a woman, Mr Blau, but I can look after myself. I learned how to during the war. But that was another life… for both of us, I suspect. You can hire me if you wish, or not as you choose, but if you do, I won't let you down. It's your choice.'

He released my hand and, taking a photograph from beside him, handed it to me. 'This is my Anna.'

The photograph was of a smart-looking young girl, maybe eighteen, perhaps a little older, hatless, with a bright face framed by dark, wavy, shoulder-length hair. She was picnicking. A hot summer's day, judging by how she was dressed. She was on Hampstead Heath, sitting on the top of Parliament Hill. I recognised the ponds behind her. Anna Blau looked happy, smiling without a care in the world.

'She's pretty,' I said. 'Mr Blau–'

'David, please.'

'David, when did Anna go missing?'

'Four days ago. She'd left work for home.' His eyes rose to meet mine. 'She never arrived.'

'What did the police say? Inspector…'

'Jarrow.' He said it as if it were a dirty word, shook his head, and muttered an expletive in Yiddish under his breath. 'He said some bad things about my Anna. Bad things, Miss Raven. Do you know what I mean? He does not know her, yet he is prepared to judge her. Bad things about her and the boy she worked with. She's not that type of girl. He would not listen to me. He'd made up his mind already.'

'Then *you* tell me.'

He studied my face for a few seconds – looking for what, I wasn't sure. I knew it wasn't pity. I suspect pity died in him in the camp.

'Do you know how many girls go missing each year, Miss Raven? I know, because he told me. Do you know how much time the police spend looking for them? Or what the chances are of finding them? Do you know what a waste of police time and resources means? I know, because I was told. Just as I was told to not expect anything to happen soon. Wait, I was told. She'll turn up, I was told. Do they, Miss Raven? Just turn up? He never told me how many *just* turn up.'

'Then tell me what you think happened.'

Blau clutched the coffee cup between his hands, spying us over the rim. His face had darkened and hardened.

'Miss Raven, have you heard of Goel Hadam?' he asked.

I shook my head. I'd heard the name and no more.

'It is where my Anna works,' Blau said. 'It is an organisation that traces war criminals living in Britain – those that escaped Germany and somehow came here. Some even came at the government's invitation. Did you know that, Miss Raven?'

I knew.

I recalled the shock of seeing Otto Grunwald, Hauptmann Otto Grunwald in another life, smiling and laughing, surrounded by Special Branch men, enjoying after-dinner coffee at the Savoy. He hadn't changed much from when I'd last seen him, driving away in a staff car several hours before French forces liberated Paris. Perhaps he was laughing because he knew I knew who he was and knew there wasn't anything I could do about it. Or perhaps he was laughing because the local mayor raised a toast and called him a splendid chap. He'd lost the war and won the peace.

'Anna is privy to some of Hadam's sensitive information despite being a secretary,' Blau continued. 'There was a break-in where she works. No one thought much of it except a friend who works with her, a boy named Saul. He confided in her that he thought the Fascist League was responsible.'

'The League?'

'You know who they are, of course?' He couldn't hide the anger in his face.

'Oh, yes,' I said, nodding. 'A throwback to the bad old days. Affiliated to Mosley's Blackshirts, aren't they?'

'They are independent of each other but share the same sentiments. They wear black like Mussolini's fascists. The Nazis wore brown. Do you think the colour matters?'

'Not when their hearts are diseased. Didn't they put up a candidate at the local election from around here?'

'The League got a hundred or so votes.' He clucked in disappointment.

'Anna's route to and from work took her past the building occupied by the League,' Mrs Geller interjected. 'There is always trouble there. They are always intimidating people they don't like or think are against them.'

'Then they must get pretty busy. You think they were involved in her disappearance?'

Blau shifted uncomfortably in his chair as if to say yes.

'Did Anna ever talk about her work?'

'Talk, yes. Facts only.' He became agitated. 'About this or that Nazi they had uncovered or were investigating. But she has nothing to do with the investigations. She is just a secretary. She takes notes and dictation. She types them up. She told no one – *no one* – about what they did.'

'Except you.'

He nodded.

'Perhaps this League found out what she was doing?' Mrs Geller said. 'Maybe they think she knows things about them and their friends…'

'Is this what you believe?' I asked Blau.

He said nothing, but his face said yes.

'You told Inspector Jarrow your thoughts?'

He nodded.

'I suppose he did nothing about it?'

I needn't have asked; even so, Blau shook his head slowly.

'Why would they kidnap or hurt her? There must be others far more knowledgeable they would target first.'

'I don't know,' he said simply.

'How did Saul know it was them that broke into Goel Hadam?'

'Anna did not say.'

'Do you know what the police said about the break-in?'

'They were not informed.'

'Why? Did Anna know?'

He shook his head. 'What would they have done, especially if a man like this Jarrow investigated?'

He had a point. I wanted to tell him they weren't all like Jarrow. He'd tell me one was enough. And he'd be right.

'Is Saul her boyfriend?' I had to ask, even though Mrs Geller had already confided to me that Anna had no boyfriend.

'No,' he said defiantly.

'Have you considered she might have run away?'

'I know my daughter well, Miss Raven.'

'Perhaps you don't know her well enough.'

'Miss Raven, speak plainly to me,' he said angrily. 'I know what murder is. I have seen it often to know.'

'No, David, Alex doesn't mean that,' Mrs Geller said.

I placed a placating hand on her shoulder to stop her speaking. 'Mrs Geller might believe Anna has been kidnapped, David – you might too – but kidnapping makes little sense. Unless you have money stuffed under the floorboards, it's plain to see you are as poor as the proverbial church mouse. She's been missing for four days. Don't you think it's a bit remiss of the kidnappers not to send a ransom note?'

He did not say anything, but his eyes did not leave me for a second. As for the League being responsible, secretary Anna would be a cog, and a small cog at that. She was hardly worth the trouble when there were others higher up and more important.

'It might just be that, plain and simple, she may have just run away with Saul. I don't know much about your daughter, David…' I glanced around at the dilapidation and the ruin that was the house and left the rest unsaid.

'David–' Mrs Geller, understanding my glance, began, but Blau spoke over her.

'No, what Miss Raven means is true. What life is this for a young woman – looking after a broken old man? No, do not apologise for speaking the truth, Miss Raven. It is a rare commodity these days.'

'Then tell me about Saul,' I said.

'It is true that I don't trust him. He spends money he doesn't have… He is arrogant. He would lead her into bad ways. But Anna had the measure of him. He's…' He fell quiet, and his eyes dropped as if ashamed, and he took a deep breath. 'She is just a secretary, Miss Raven,' Blau repeated. 'Look. See.' He reached for an old newspaper – the anger had returned. 'They give more credence to a kidnapped Russian than to my Anna. Why's that? Why does she deserve a whole police investigation, and my Anna gets a tired old man who couldn't care less for her if he tried? Why, Miss Raven? Politics. That's why. Not justice. Justice? What is that?' He sat back, staring into space, unable to conceal his disgust. 'Maybe if you find out, you will tell me.'

I wish I could.

'Will you help me?' he asked

'That was always my intention,' I said. 'May I search her room, David? Just in case there is something there that will help me.'

He indicated I should follow him.

It was a small, quiet room – a bed, a dressing table with a mirror up against the window, and a wardrobe and chair. *Homely* would be an apt description. He left me, and I searched the drawers, under the bed, under the mattress, and inside the wardrobe for anything that was unusual. I found nothing. The room was what it was – the room of someone who'd left it one morning expecting to return to it that evening; even down to the small box that contained a pound note and some change on the mantelpiece.

He was seated when I returned. Mrs Geller had prepared more coffee and we sat, drank, talked, and then I read the newspaper reports he'd shown me.

They were straightforward reports. Natalia Popov was some kind of Russian scientist attending a symposium near where Anna disappeared. That caused a stink between Whitehall and the Soviet Embassy.

Maybe that's why Anna Blau only got a mention on page five, all thirty words, if that, and only in the local rag. She wasn't anywhere near high politics to warrant more. I would be surprised after that single report if she didn't vanish from the papers altogether, just like she vanished from the face of the earth. The disturbing thought that she might be under it once more came to mind.

I wanted to tell Blau that was the way of the world, but he knew that already. He was no fool. You don't live a life like his, go through what he did, and not know it.

# Chapter 2

Mrs Geller drove me back to Soho. She was unusually quiet; and so was I, for that matter. We were both preoccupied with our thoughts. I had a few jobs that could wait. The most urgent, I'd farmed out to two close friends of mine. When we reached our building, Mrs Geller vanished into her office; she looked a little broken, and I continued up the stairs to mine on the top floor.

I made the usual phone calls, the desperation of a drowning man at the start of any investigations of this sort. You sort of hoped the local hospital or a private clinic would have your answers, and in the same way you hoped they wouldn't. No one had any new intake matching Anna's description.

I called the local newspapers and a few reporters I knew that might be useful, but no luck. So, it was the turn of the local police station. I knew they wouldn't give out any information, but I had to try, and they didn't.

Chief Inspector Latimer held the highest-ranking office in the Metropolitan Police Force I knew – *when in doubt, go to the top*, so my old dad used to say.

During the war, for the two or so years I was in military service, Latimer was my commanding officer running a clandestine group operating in France. He was the quiet, intellectual type who played his cards close to his chest, making it impossible to tell what he was thinking. It served to make him seem untrustworthy. Some of that distrust might have been well-deserved. As far as those two close friends of mine were concerned, it was.

'This better be important!' Latimer barked as soon as he picked up the telephone.

'Well, good morning to you also, Chief Inspector. But seriously, is that a way to talk to a woman?' I said it with a definite smile in my voice.

'Raven!' he said in surprise. 'What the hell do you want? Let me guess. Help. What with?'

'A missing-person case.'

'And?'

'I'd like a look at the files to see what's been done or not. It looks as if the investigation's been shelved.'

'So, what do you want me to do about it?'

'Have I called at a bad time, Chief Inspector?'

'No, not really, Raven – no, I wouldn't say you have. Some might, but not me. I've just come back from seeing the Commissioner of Police, who just came back from seeing the sodding Home Secretary – Baron Chuter-Ede of Epsom, CH, PC, DL, and *bloody* JP. So, it's not a bad time at all if you know where Natalia Popov is; otherwise, yes, it's something of a bad time, and you're no bloody use at all. Call Dickens – he's your other pet detective, isn't he?' he suggested bluntly.

I allowed him a few seconds to get his breath back and was about to speak when the phone went dead.

Dickens was another *old friend.* I was about to call him when there was a knock on the door. Mrs Geller's son, Hiram, came in. '*Liebchen. Liebchen*,' he said in a delightful impression of his mother, a smile breaking apart his lips. 'Don't worry; I persuaded the witch to stay downstairs.'

He'd brought me a cup of coffee on a saucer. It was real ground beans, not Nescafé, and I sipped it gratefully.

'I understand that Mr Blau knew your family?' I asked.

He nodded, and his fingers clutched his goatee in thought. He looked less like an accountant and more like a… in his paisley-patterned waistcoat and bow tie, it was difficult to say. A happy, rotund accountant, anyway – assuming there is such a thing.

'Back in Berlin,' he said, 'during the bad old days, as she downstairs will call them.'

'She'd not be far wrong.'

'True. His house was three doors away from ours. Madam Blau could cook.' He licked his lips and kissed his fingers. 'Could that woman cook!'

'What happened to the Blaus? Madam Geller showed me a photograph of the family. I counted five.'

'Mr Blau, Madam Blau, their eldest son, Noah, the middle girl, Judith, and little Anna.' Hiram nodded sadly and perched on the edge of a chair. 'Noah and I went to school together. We were in the same year. Anna was – how do they term it? A gift from God. Judith, her big sister, was eight years older. So, Anna was very much the baby. When David decided to leave Germany with his family, it was too late. They went to Denmark just as the Nazis invaded. The family, with the exception of Anna, was rounded up during a raid and sent to the camps. She survived by virtue of luck and a kind fisherman who smuggled her on his fishing boat to England. David survived the camps only because he's a curmudgeon.' He smiled softly and sighed. 'The rest of the family didn't. I think his decision to delay leaving weighs heavily on him.'

'Wasn't it obvious how things were going? Your family left Germany in 1933. If you saw it as early as that…'

'He didn't.' Hiram looked down and slowly shook his head. 'Yes, we saw which way the wind was blowing. As soon as Hitler was made chancellor, we knew there'd be trouble. We tried to persuade David to leave. You can't reason with a mad dog, we told him. You either kill it or get as far away from it as you can. Some might say we took the easy option.'

'I wouldn't be one of them.' I knew just how the Gellers had suffered.

'What can I tell you?' Hiram hunched his shoulders. 'He fought for the Kaiser in the Great War, like lots of Jews – like my father. David was wounded at Verdun. They even gave him an Iron Cross. He showed it to me once. He was proud of it at the time.'

'Not anymore, I should think.'

'He thought it should count for something.'

'Like a lot of people, I suppose. What happened to Anna?'

'We didn't know she'd come to England until later; otherwise, we'd have taken her in. No, she was fostered off here and there. Then she was evacuated. You know what it was like. At some point, some kind person said she should change her name to Blue – the German is Blau – and not mention she was a Jew. I think that saved her a lot of bother. After the war, we discovered David had survived and brought him over. What a palaver that was. We made some enquiries and discovered Anna was staying with a family in Northampton, and they were reunited.'

'He lived in the same street as you in Berlin. He was wealthy. I've seen pictures of the house you and your brothers grew up in.'

'So why does he live in a miserable terrace in East London? The Nazis took everything, Alex.'

'Yes, Mrs Geller told me.'

'No, Alex. Everything.'

I understood. 'Except Anna. I get the impression he's a proud man.'

'Good and proud, and that's his problem. Like us, accounting was his profession back in Germany. Mama offered him a position in the firm. He said no. She offered to help set him up. Again, he said no. He said he and Anna could manage. He didn't want charity. Alex, it wasn't charity we offered; it was friendship. I don't think David saw it that way.'

I nodded. 'After spending all that time just surviving, trust must come hard.'

'I think so, as well. Over the years, he kept in touch, though it was more that Mama kept in touch. She treats Anna like the daughter she never had. Tell me, you know these things better than me, but so much time has gone…'

It was the same unasked question everyone asks, for which there is no good answer. No news isn't necessarily good news. Sometimes it's damn awful news.

'You're a good man, Hiram,' I said. 'And Miriam is a good woman. I know how important this is to her. I'll do a good job, and I promise not to fiddle the expenses.' We smiled weakly at each other. 'Four days is a long time. I believe you; she's not run away, but she's not been kidnapped either. You know, Hiram, for all the money in the world, she could be dead.'

'We are not foolish, Alex. We have considered that possibility.'

'That's good. When your mother asked me to look into this, I agreed to keep an open mind. I'll do that until I know different. We both know you don't kidnap a poor girl, but enough of them do get murdered… and for the oddest of reasons.'

'Just find her, Alex. Just find Anna. Money isn't a problem. You just let me know how much you need and when you need it. Find her, Alex. And if things turn out for the worse, then we will bury her.' His gaze never left me.

I made several phone calls after Hiram left. I called Inspector Dickens and then a friend of mine, Jack Brody, and arranged to meet him at his shop in Soho the next day. I wanted to go to where Anna Blau worked, and I wanted him with me. Afterwards, just to be certain, I visited the hospitals I'd only just called to be sure she'd not been admitted. I didn't need to double-check, but it made me feel good to do so.

# Chapter 3

I woke early the next day. I was meeting Inspector Richard Dickens later that morning. He'd agreed to let me have sight of Anna Blau's files. I'd know then where the police were in their investigations. Before meeting him, though, I had a few things to do.

I had an appointment at the county court to give evidence in a messy divorce case I'd been working on. I was told to dress appropriately. Perhaps going to Jimmy Durban's boxing gym in Covent Garden wasn't the best idea. A few years back, I helped Jimmy's son out of some bother with the law. Jimmy repaid me by making sure I got fit. Fit enough to do my job. It'd been a while since I was last there, and his phone call saying he missed me was his way of reminding me that it's easier to stay fit than get fit.

The usual light-hearted circus was there when I arrived. I knew most of them and didn't mind the wolf-whistles that greeted me – I could give as good as I got – but for those new to the establishment, if they were going to say something, Jimmy's eyes silenced them. Today's treat was Gus Brown, an old heavyweight, to whom I was giving away at least one hundred and fifty pounds. Three rounds of avoiding him were guaranteed to get my heart pumping and leave me exhausted. Generally, the boys were kind and didn't land their punches, except once when Gus caught me by mistake and I saw stars.

Afterwards, I showered in a private cubicle in Jimmy's office. When I stepped out dressed in a Christian Dior copy – a payment for another divorce case I'd been involved in last year – it brought a hoot of laughter and another round of wolf whistles. I bowed theatrically to the boys, and that only increased the volume of the whistles.

The tight-cinched waist, billowing blue skirt, small jacket with unpadded rounded shoulders, and dark-blue cape made me look trustworthy, or so the prosecuting barrister claimed. They made me look less like a private investigator and more like someone about to attend evening services and then cocktails with the vicar and his wife. Trustworthy! Clutching a copy of the King James Bible would have completed the outfit. He knew what he was doing. I just had to make sure I minded my Ps and Qs.

When I finished at the courts, I had a mid-morning snack. I'd worked up an appetite by then. Afterwards, I went back to the office to wait for Dickens, or Dickie, as his friends called him.

When my father was in the police force, Dickens had been one of his closest friends. They'd walked the same beat together and been promoted to detective in the same year, and before the war, I'd spent many a happy Sunday afternoon with him, his wife, Carrie, and their four children. But like everyone else, the war changed him. He was still married, but losing two sons, one in Europe and the other in Burma, weighed heavily. That's when the drinking started. I knew enough, though, not to interfere. Drunks needed to come to terms with their drinking before they needed a nanny.

I heard his footsteps shuffling up the stairs, scraping against the battered linoleum in what seemed to be a slow, tortured climb. The rap on the door was sharp, and before I could say anything, it opened.

He was a barrel of a man, and little of it was muscle. Fried breakfasts, lunches, and dinners, not to mention downright indolence, meant Dickens had gone to seed. He wore a jacket whose sleeves were too short and a scowl that was too long, and his crimson capillary nose brought back my worries about how much he drank. He was red-faced and breathing heavily. It wasn't quite climbing the Eiger, and I wasn't looking forward to giving him mouth-to-mouth resuscitation. That job would fall to the younger, fitter man who came with him.

'When are they going to install a lift in this place?' he grumped.

'When someone dies from climbing the stairs. Care to help us and oblige?'

He cleared his throat noisily and stared at me unsmilingly, then looked around the office.

'Take a good gander, Brown; this is how the other half lives,' he panted between breaths. 'Don't you ever clean up this tip, Alex?'

'What month is it, Dickie? Not May yet, surely?'

'Look at my face. See it laughing?'

He gave me his best deprecating glare. He never approved of me taking over the Raven Enquiry Agency when my father died; he'd seen too much to do that. That, and the fact I was a woman. But he knew little of what I did during the war, and I don't think he'd have approved of that either. He stood back, hands on hips, surveying me with a sarcastic grin on his face.

'So, is this how a private investigator dresses these days? Fancy, wouldn't you say, Brown?'

'At least my jacket fits,' I said. 'Nice to meet you, Sergeant Brown,' and I held out my hand towards him.

Brown, a lithe man, a vivid contrast to his boss, had a firm handshake. His features were chiselled with angles. Smoke-coloured eyes gazed out at me from deeply sunken pits. There was a dimple in his chin below lips that were made for smiling.

'I guess you're Raven,' he said.

'Can't fool you, Sergeant. Did you figure that out all by yourself?'

'I think I saw it painted on the door.'

'They've given you one who can read, Dickie. Does he do card tricks, as well?'

Brown grinned.

Dickens huffed and scowled, then he twisted around a chair and sank into it. The chair squeaked in surprise and groaned in complaint. He mumbled something under his breath. I only caught the words *Aunt Fanny*. I looked up as he shuffled to get comfortable, feeling sorry for the chair.

'Let's get something straight, Alex. You didn't save my life, and you're not pulling one in. You try that guff with me again and see if I don't arrest you.'

My jokes when I called him had obviously fallen flat.

'You're doing it out of the goodness of your heart, then. Thanks, Dickie. I appreciate it.'

He fished inside a small leather case and dropped a file on my desk.

'You won't think that way in a minute.' He pushed the file over to me.

I opened it, scrutinised the contents, and wondered why I'd bothered to waste my time. It looked decidedly thin, it felt decidedly thin, and that was because it *was* decidedly thin.

'No witnesses statements, not even proper interviews with those from her work, no theories – nothing,' I said after a few minutes. I closed the file and let it drop to the desk. 'A big, fat zero. Someone gets paid for this, I suppose?'

'Inspector Jarrow is the officer in charge.'

'That's meant to mean something?'

'It means I'm treading on toes – that's something you don't appreciate.'

'Remind me to thank you.' I gave him my smarmiest smile. 'What did Jarrow think happened? He hasn't exactly left any clues here, has he?'

Dickie firmed his mouth and took a deep, calming breath.

'It's hardly a kidnapping now, is it? It's been four days; where's the kidnapper's note? Lost in the post, was it? Or maybe they forgot where to send it. She ran away. She don't want to be found. It happens to skirts every day, especially when they get themselves knocked up.'

'Is that what Jarrow thinks – she's pregnant?' I rolled my eyes. Dickens didn't like that. I didn't mind. 'Did she indicate she was leaving to her friends – I mean, she has some, hasn't she? What did they say? What about the ticket collector at the Tube station? What about the bus conductors? What about–'

'It's been checked. She didn't board her usual bus. And no, she's not pregnant – at least as far as I know,' Dickens said. He sighed loudly. 'Look, I'd agree with you, Alex… it's shoddy. Jarrow's due to retire in a few months.'

'That's an excuse, is it?'

'No, it's not.' Dickens grunted as he stood up. The chair exhaled a sigh of relief. He leaned his considerable weight on his outstretched arms on my desk, making it tremble, and pressed his puffy red face into mine. 'Be grateful you're getting this much for free. If I thought you were going to make trouble, Alex, I'd be taking you across my knees. Or do you think Bert Raven's daughter's too old for me to do that?'

'You can try. *Bert Raven* tried.' I pushed the file back to him.

'Not hard enough.'

'I'm just disappointed. I expected more.'

'Don't we all.'

'The problem with Jarrow, miss, is he's old school,' Brown said with a smile that quickly vanished when Dickens flashed an angry glance at him.

'Watch your mouth, son. He's a lot of things you ain't.'

'Sorry, sir.'

I knew what Sergeant Brown meant by calling Jarrow *old school.* My father had called several detectives the same. They solved crime by using 100-watt bulbs, rabbit punches to the kidneys, the occasional knee to the groin, and a clumsy suspect falling down stairs when the bruises became too apparent. Subtlety was never their thing.

'Now, where's the little boys' room, so I can have a leak and get out of here?'

'You passed it on the way up,' I said. 'Open some of the doors. Or I could draw you a map if you want. But you're a detective. I'm sure you'll find it.'

Dickens sniffed his nose at me and sauntered out of the office.

I spent a minute flicking through the file again, in case I'd missed anything. I hadn't.

'What else should I know about Inspector Jarrow?' I asked.

Brown tightened his lips, and his eyes drifted to where Dickens went. 'I really shouldn't be telling tales, Miss Raven.'

'Between you, me, and the bedpost, Sergeant, help me out a bit.'

He paused for a moment, then raised his head to the ceiling. 'Blau's a Jewish name, isn't it? From what I know, Jarrow has his… well, let's call it his sympathies.'

'Let's call him a fascist little bastard and save time, shall we? I thought we fought a war to get rid of them.' Brown gave a non-committal shrug. 'What about you? Any theories?'

'I asked Jarrow's bag man,' he said. 'There was someone at her work, maybe a boyfriend; no one seems to know if he is or isn't… a boy named Saul Greenberg. She never boarded her bus; that was checked, even though it's not in the report. By all accounts, she vanished after leaving work that evening and before she arrived at her bus stop.'

'And there's no unidentified body in the mortuary matching her description?'

'Not as of this morning.'

'What do you know about where she worked? Goel Hadam.'

'I can't say I know much. Only they give us plenty of trouble every now and then.'

'What sort of trouble?'

'Well… let's just call them fascist-little-bastard-head-breakers, shall we?'

Brown looked up. Dickens was standing in the doorway, adjusting his braces under his jacket. The WC door hadn't been closed, and I could hear the cistern filling up with water.

'Miss Raven wanted to know about Goel Hadam.'

'Why do you want to know about them buggers?' Dickens frowned.

'No real reason; I just thought I'd do some investigating. You remember what that is, don't you?' I said.

'The boys from West End Central are right – you do have a big mouth.'

'Some of them still wear handmade shoes?'

'Ain't you a laugh a minute.'

'Goel Hadam?' I repeated.

Dickens sighed loudly. 'Heard of Group 43? Rich Jews from Hampstead? Goel Hadam is their poorer cousin from Silvertown. Yes, apparently there are poor Jews.'

I shook my head in disappointment, making sure Dickens didn't miss it. His expression, though, didn't change and he said, 'Why do you ask?'

'Their name came up.'

'Just like that, did it?' He found his hat and placed it on his head. 'Like 43, they go around disrupting meetings by Mosley's bunch.'

'And the Fascist League – I've read that in the papers.'

'Then, if you know, why are you asking?'

'Anna Blau worked for Goel Hadam.'

'Did she.'

I picked up the file he'd brought. 'I can't see any mention of them in here.'

'Can't you.'

'Has Jarrow done anything to find her, Inspector?'

'Which part of *she's run away* didn't you understand?' He nodded his head in what could pass for a small bow, took the file from me, and turned to leave. 'I'm inclined to believe Jarrow – in this one at least. Next time you call, ask for Brown. Unless you find a body, I hear you're good at that.' He gave me a small Scout salute. 'A girl detective, well, there's a novelty for you, Sergeant. Add that to your education. You don't get too many of them to the pound. What do you reckon she's like when things get tough?'

'She'll do a damn sight better than you, I suspect,' I said, reaching out, and patting his stomach. 'When's it due?'

'Funny girl.'

'And I'm a woman, or hadn't you noticed?'

'I certainly did, miss,' Brown said.

'I think I like this one, Dickie. He's better than your last one.'

Dickens looked his sergeant up and down with a slow, deliberate, penetrating stare.

'I'll have him gift-wrapped for you, shall I?'

He left without saying goodbye. Brown turned to doff his hat and followed him. From my window, I watched Inspector Dickens step out onto the street below me. He walked between the traffic to the pub on the corner in as straight a line as he could manage. I smiled as the traffic parted before him like the Red Sea. The Rose and Crown was the promised land where milk and honey was beer. It wasn't yet midday, but I guess the pub would open for him.

# Chapter 4

I left soon after Dickens. I walked down Wardour Street and turned into Brewer Street. My mind wandered back to Jarrow. I'd managed to suppress my anger at his inefficiencies, and I'd stopped murdering him in my mind. By then, I was thinking about David Blau and his daughter. They weren't nice thoughts.

It was a short walk to the place I was going to. MacDonald Tobacconist. It was years since it last sold tobacco. Now it did a fine trade in other barely legal things – magazines for certain discerning connoisseurs, films that the actors needed no particular acting skills or diplomas for, various helpful items for the bedroom, and it served as an accommodation address for men who wanted letters and parcels delivered there and not to their homes where their wives might see what's inside. But then, that's Soho for you, along with the *French Models*, who weren't French and didn't model.

Jack Brody and Martha Evans owned the shop. My father knew them before the war; they were friends of sorts. I only met them after the war and not long after my father died. They just turned up. There were no explanations, no real introductions; they were just there.

I remembered my father calling Brody a rogue, but he never meant it in a romantic way. He hinted that Jack ran guns to the loyalists during the Spanish Civil War and, before that, to the Irish Republicans. How much of it was true, I really didn't know. Neither Jack nor Martha ever spoke about those days, except as far as my father was concerned. They liked Bert Raven, and for whatever reason, he liked them too. I suspected he could have arrested them a dozen times had he put his mind to it. Like Dickens though, I always thought Jack had made my father a promise to look out for me. Why Jack would ever keep such a promise, I didn't know; only in his case, being *old-school*, meant he would.

At a quarter to twelve in the morning, the shop was closed. Martha would open it around two o'clock, when all the other shops of a similar ilk in Soho open.

Jack Brody stood outside.

The Irishman was something of a bear, with a mop of unruly black hair. He was doing his best impression of Errol Flynn but without the moustache. He'd shaved but you wouldn't have thought so. The fawn raincoat he wore was tied tightly across his waist and his hat, a brown homburg, which he put on as I approached, was low on his face. For a man in his forties, he cut an imposing figure.

He was leaning on a loud car, both in looks and probably engine noise. The maroon, left-hand-drive, five-litre Buick Roadmaster looked somewhat out of place in this part of Soho and knew it. It was showing itself off to the dented black Austin down the street and didn't care that pride was a deadly sin.

'This should get us where we want to go,' Jack said, patting the bonnet of the car.

'And some.' I stared at the car. 'A gift, was it?'

'Oh, you do have a suspicious nose.'

'Oh, don't I just. Why do I smell Tony Marcello?' For some peculiar reason, the American mobster who owned a gambling casino nearby had taken a shine to Martha. It might be because she once pointed a gun at him. Small things like that, I think, impressed someone who didn't impress easily.

'Well, don't I feel a little underdressed?' Jack stood back and scrutinised me with his inquisitive brown eyes and a smile on his face. 'Nice clobber, if I might say so. Where are we off to, lunch with the Archbishop or Lady Smut?'

'Just to see some fascist-head-breakers.'

# Chapter 5

We drove east, heading to the offices of Goel Hadam. As we passed through grey streets on a grey morning, it began to rain, a steady drizzle making everything even greyer. Five years after the war's end, London was recovering. The bomb sites were being cleared, and tall residential buildings were sprouting up in their place. Despite austerity, there was optimism in the air. There was money to be made, legally or illegally. But old habits die hard. Despite the war we'd fought, there were still a few who wanted to preserve the good old days. Like a cancerous growth, pockets of them existed in all strata of society. You'd have thought the world would have had enough of the Mosleys and the Fascist League. Goel Hadam, like a few others, stood as a bastion against them.

There were no signs showing that we had arrived at Goel Hadam's offices. From outside, it exuded all the charms of a Victorian workhouse. Next to it stood an abandoned church with an overgrown graveyard from where grass lapped the pavement. The iron railings that once surrounded it were long gone, taken away, and melted down in aid of the war effort. For some reason, I expected guards to be stationed at the entrance, scrutinising visitors with suspicious eyes. Instead, a pair of double doors led to a simple reception where a nice old lady with a blue rinse was seated behind a small desk out of the draft. She was knitting a substantial scarf with needles that seemed a tad long.

I didn't have an appointment, so I explained why I was there. She gave a compassionate nod when I mentioned Anna, and out of respect, she placed the knitting in her lap. She motioned to a nervous young man, who escorted us up a flight of stairs, along a cold corridor lit by strip lights, to a room towards the back of the building. He knocked. Someone said, 'Come,' and when we entered, he left, closing the door behind him.

I'd seen Bruno Marx's picture in a newspaper. He was at the head of some men at some rally somewhere. Seeing him in the flesh, I could see it didn't do him justice. He was a square-jawed, cologne-scented man with a crew cut – an advertisement for healthy living. Under the loose shirt, his muscles must be rippling. The shirt was silk, his trousers were pressed with creases as sharp as blades, and his shoes were the type you get made in a small but expensive place near Piccadilly. He spoke English with a German accent, and, no doubt, he drank coffee, not tea, and drank it black. In the photograph, he and the men were wearing dark army jumpers, the type you'd go foraging in, or, if you add a balaclava, wear to go out at midnight for a fight.

'Her father was right, Miss Raven,' Marx said after I'd explained why I was there. 'Anna was a typist. She did some filing.' He hunched his shoulders. 'She made coffee.'

'Tell me about the evening Anna disappeared.'

'There is little to tell. She left us twenty minutes to six, and it is a fifteen-minute walk to her bus stop,' Marx said.

'She leaves the same time every night?'

'The same. Punctual. At times she must work late. Not often.'

'Not that night, then?'

'No. She and a friend of hers, Saul, left together, as they sometimes do. On occasion, I have walked with her. It is a long bus ride to her home, and she buys an evening newspaper from the agents near her bus stop.'

'How do you know that?'

'I have seen her do it. She mentioned it a few times. Small talk, you know?'

'You said Saul went with her.'

'That night. Yes. Saul boards his bus across the street from her stop.' He looked up at the ceiling as something passed through his mind. 'Leah, our receptionist, left with them that evening. Ask her if anything strange happened. I did, but ask her again. Time plays tricks with our memories. Her recollection might be clearer.'

'Anna's boyfriend, Saul, may I speak to him?'

Marx sat back straight, his hands resting on the table, his fingers spread. His face took on a questioning look.

'No, Miss Raven, to call Saul her boyfriend is perhaps a little too much. A friend who is a boy is perhaps more accurate. But did the police not tell you?'

'Tell me what?'

'Saul is missing.'

'I don't understand.'

'We told a Mr Jarrow… no, no, it was his sergeant… I can't remember his name – only he too was a most uninspiring man.' He nodded to suggest incompetence. 'Saul did not come into work the day after Anna disappeared – both are missing. We informed the authorities. We naturally assumed they were working on the information.'

I glanced over at Jack. He'd got out of his chair and knelt to tie his shoelace; at the same time, I saw his eyes wandering the room. I knew he was listening, even though his attention seemed elsewhere.

'What did you tell them?' I asked.

'That it was unusual for Saul to just leave and tell no one. Just as it was with Anna. But if you are asking, did he and Anna run off together? The answer must be no.'

'Why? That's what the police think happened. They hinted at a relationship.'

'I do not know from where they got that impression.' Marx shook his head. 'You have to know Saul, Miss Raven, or, for that matter, you have to know Anna. The things you are suggesting, but politely not saying, aren't the sort of things he or she would do. They have family commitments; they are very loyal to those obligations. Saul's loyalty stems from the camps; it's difficult to explain fully – such things are. But as far as I know, he was fond of Anna, and she of him. But fond only. They are not secret lovers who have run off together in some Shakespearean pact.'

'But it's an unusual coincidence – two people missing from the same place of work at the same time.'

'Indeed,' he agreed. 'I considered at first that maybe Saul went looking for Anna.'

'If that's the case,' I said, 'why hasn't he left a message to say what he's doing? Anyway, he wouldn't have known she was missing at the time.'

'That was my conclusion, too.'

'Tell me, Mr Marx, what do you do here?'

'Apart from fighting fascist bastards? I think you already know, Miss Raven.' He reached for a file on his desk and pushed it towards me. 'This is what you mean, is it not? But Anna had nothing to do with this part of our business. That belongs to myself and a few others.'

'Maurice DuPont?' I peered at the name written on the file.

'We found him working in a hotel in Knightsbridge.'

'He's French.'

'The people in Pas-de-Calais knew him by a different name.' He opened the cover, and the cream-coloured front sheet showed a photograph of DuPont in an SS uniform with the name tag, *Klaus Frasch.* 'He's due to be deported next week.'

'You have more names you are following up?'

'Several. But why do you ask?'

'Mr Blau thinks the Fascist League may have had something to do with Anna's disappearance,' Jack said. 'He was hinting at your other activities. He mentioned a break-in.'

'Our bête noire – the League, not Mr Blau.' It brought a smile to Marx's face. 'The break-in, yes? Maybe it was them, maybe it wasn't. There are plenty who would, including the local louts. We don't keep money here except petty cash, and that was the only thing missing.'

'Where's that kept?' I asked.

'At the reception desk.'

'And nothing else was touched?'

'No. They broke a window when they came in.'

'What did the police say?'

Marx gave a dry laugh. 'And have them trample all over the place, making a mess, poking their noses into our business? Then there would be the endless questions, and, in the end, over tea, they'd agree that there was nothing more they could do.'

'Yes, but they'd agree ever so nicely,' I said. 'Money isn't the only currency of importance in this day and age.' I nodded at Maurice DuPont's file. 'You sure nothing went missing?'

'I am, Miss Raven. Our files are kept secure and locked away, and that is another reason we don't want the police here. They get our reports, but only when we are ready to give them. And we like to give them personally, so they don't go missing.'

'Are they likely to?'

'It is not unknown.'

'So, you give them only after you've informed the press, and make a show of it.'

'It works better that way. But I understand what you are saying regarding the break-in. A lot of people would like to get our files, but, as I said, only petty cash was missing – a few pounds, no more.'

'When exactly did it happen?' Jack asked.

'We discovered it two, maybe three mornings before Anna and Saul disappeared. You think their disappearances and the break-in are connected?' Marx asked.

'No, it was just David Blau who mentioned it, and we're just crossing *t*'s and dotting *i*'s. But as you say, just petty cash was taken. Whoever broke in probably expected to find more than that.'

Marx nodded. 'But as far as the other activities are concerned, Anna was not privy to them.'

'She's a secretary, Mr Marx. In my experience, secretaries are privy to everything.'

'Yes, maybe you're right,' he agreed with a smile. 'Now that you know Saul is missing too, will you also include him in your investigations?'

'I think I should.'

'As do I.' He glanced at his watch and then me. 'I'm afraid I have an appointment I must keep.'

'We may need some more information–'

'Of course. I am always here if you need to talk again.' Marx half rose, hesitated, then stood up completely. 'Ask Leah at the front desk for Saul's address. You may want to speak to his mother, Ruth Greenberg. When you do, you will understand a few more things. If you can shed any light on his disappearance – and Anna's as well – I'd be grateful. You need only ask for any assistance in this matter.'

'Thank you for your time.'

I liked Marx. It was difficult to dislike a cultured and polite man, the sort who'd tell you his word was his bond, and it wouldn't be mere platitude.

As we shook hands, Jack crouched down once more to retie his shoelace. He spent a while doing it before running his fingers across the floor and skirting. He stood up, and his gaze drifted around the room, taking it all in before returning to Marx.

'Tell me, Mr Marx,' he asked, 'how often does your cleaner come in?'

'Our cleaner? I see, yes, we're a bit dusty at the moment,' he said. 'Saul cleans for us… He needed the extra money… but…' He shrugged.

I turned to leave, then stopped and turned back.

'Mr Marx, I wonder, just for my curiosity, have you any records on an Otto Grunwald?'

He thought for a few moments, his brow furrowed, before shaking his head slowly and pouting his lips theatrically.

'The name is not familiar. Is he someone we should know about?'

'Perhaps.'

'Perhaps, then, we will look into him.' He wrote the name down, pronouncing each syllable as he did. 'Why do you mention him?'

'He was having lunch at a fancy restaurant in town. The local mayor was toasting him. I knew of him in Paris when his rank was Hauptmann.'

'I see.' His eyes rose to meet mine. He, too, was curious. 'And why were you in Paris when the gentleman was there?'

'I'd like to say I was on holiday.'

'It must have been an interesting place to visit during the war.' He'd cocked his head, watching me curiously. 'Then let's see what we find out, shall we? By the little you say of him, he might be one of the chosen few.'

'Chosen few?'

'Those precious few that officially do not exist – those that lunch in fancy restaurants and are toasted. But, Miss Raven, as far as Anna is concerned, this business is separate from our other activities. They do, however, include these *gentlemen.*' He shoved a leaflet across to me, one of several on his desk.

*Keep Britain Pure* was the headline. The leaflet was an advertisement for a meeting to be held at a nearby park by the Fascist League. They would gather there and hear some stirring speeches about the good old days before marching to Whitechapel. The rhetoric wouldn't come as a surprise, but it wouldn't be confined to the Jews. I looked at the word *pure* and wondered what it meant. How far had they intended that purity to go back – to the Anglo-Saxons or the Celts? Not that far back, I suspected.

I passed the leaflet to Jack. He looked at it for a moment, totally expressionless, folded it, and slipped it inside his jacket pocket.

'Come along and support us,' Marx said. 'We will be *meeting* them in Victoria Park. Let's see if they have the stomach for a fight.'

There was something dark and wild in his eyes.

# Chapter 6

My father once told me that at the start of any investigation, you do the simple things first. The complicated ones you leave for later. Get the simple ones out of the way, and the complicated ones become simple. I'm not sure I ever believed him, but I had enough sense to listen and more than enough to try it in the hope that he was right. 'Life's never that complicated,' he said. 'It just suits our ego to think it is.' That, I did believe.

The simple thing was to walk Anna's route to the bus stop she used to go home. I would have wished to do the walk nearer six o'clock, the time she disappeared, rather than early afternoon, but I didn't want to wait that long. Whatever happened to her happened on that walk, and I believed Brown when he told me Anna hadn't boarded her bus. I wondered if Jarrow did the same walk. Somehow, I doubted it.

Before leaving, I took up Marx's invitation and spoke to Leah. The night Anna vanished, it rained heavily. She confirmed they left later than normal and it was already dark.

'I insisted we waited for the rain to lessen,' Leah said. 'We did for a while, then Anna said she needed to get to the butchers near where she lived before they closed. He was keeping two lamb chops for her evening meal. He'd open for her, but she was that kind of girl and didn't want to inconvenience him more than was necessary. Anyway, we all left together – me, her, and Saul.'

'You went all the way to her bus stop?'

'Oh, no, only about halfway. I live just off the high street, so I left them then.'

That at least narrowed it down a bit. Halfway through her walk, whatever happened, happened.

I started out with Jack in tow, down an empty street towards a busier one a couple of hundred or so yards away, where a bus crossed the junction. We'd only gone a few dozen steps when Jack stopped. His face lit up with a grin.

'Did you just swallow a canary?' I asked

'What's that thing you women have – intuition, isn't it? How's it doing today?' He reached towards me, holding something between his fingers. 'Here, a present for you.'

He dropped a small piece of plastic tubing into my open palm, no more than an eighth of an inch long. I looked at it and then at him.

'I picked it up by the skirting in Marx's office,' he explained.

I gave it back to him.

'You better ask Martha's permission if you intend to swap jobs and clean for Marx.'

He frowned thoughtfully. 'Why would you break into Goel Hadam's office?'

'I wouldn't. But if I did, it might be to steal their files on the people they're investigating.'

'But they're under lock and key where no one can get to them, says Marx. Can't say I believed him.'

'I can't say I did either.'

'That leaves another option.'

He pointed to the plastic tube again. I looked closely at the object between his fingers and noticed the shine of the copper wire it enclosed. One of the edges was crimped by the pliers that cut it.

'It's a piece of electrical flex.' I stopped, glanced towards Goel Hadam's building, and felt Jack smiling. When I turned back, he was.

'That's right, someone bugged him,' he said. 'A professional job. It took time and effort. And therein lies the mystery.' Jack flicked the plastic tube into the gutter. 'There are probably several bugs. It's a long-term job, so they've wired them up to the mains. There's one in his office, behind that drinks cabinet, I'd say. There were some scratches on the floor, barely visible, where it had been moved out and back again. Someone did a hasty job with a piece of cloth to hide the marks.'

'And a longer job to wire up the bugs. The mystery?' I asked.

'Didn't they teach you anything in spy school, Alex?' He pushed his hands into the pockets of his raincoat. 'Or was it a holiday in Paris, after all?'

I wrinkled up my nose and kept quiet for a few seconds, casting my mind back to another life.

'You always break in for a reason,' I said. 'If it's not to steal, then you steal to hide the reason, like stealing the petty cash.'

Jack gave me a soft, annoying clap. 'Whoever did it knew how to wire the bugs, had enough time to do it, and knew to leave broken glass so no one would ask any questions other than the obvious.'

'Why didn't you tell Marx about the bug?' I asked.

'Why don't we find out who's playing the game first? You never know when you might need a favour.'

Jack turned to look in the direction of Marx's office. That was several streets and a few turns away and too far to see, but I knew that's where he was looking. Who would he collect the favour from? Marx? Or whoever did the bugging? That was the thing about Jack, he liked to keep his options open.

'Which leaves two possibilities of who bugged Marx,' he said. 'Them or the cops.' He nodded to the building across the road from where we were standing.

I hadn't noticed where we were. The banner hanging between the two first-floor windows above the main door proclaims it to be the headquarters of the Fascist League. Their logo, a white lightning strike zigzagging across a black circle with red lettering, was a prominent display of arrogance.

From one of the upstairs windows, a man wreathed in cigar smoke looked down at the street below. His head turned to acknowledge someone with him in the room. I'd seen him before, but I wasn't entirely sure where.

Jack took out a packet of Gauloises, flicked one out, and lit it. He took a deep drag and puffed out the smoke, making a show of it. 'Smile for the camera; now there's a good girl,' he mumbled to me.

He was watching a blue decorator's van park badly across the road from us. There was a small window on each of the van's back doors. Were it not for condensation on the window that shouldn't have been there, the van would have appeared empty. Behind it was a house where scaffolding had been erected.

'Before the day's out, they'll be screening us in some dark room at Scotland Yard,' he said. 'Now, where's the other camera?'

Jack eased himself around in a circle, looking up to the sky like someone assessing the weather, wondering if it would start drizzling again. Halfway around, I heard him grunt something, and he continued turning. He gave a slight flick of his head.

'That house, with the scaffolds, I bet it has a grand view of the League through the upstairs windows. There's probably a camera in the van, but the one in the house is doing the real work.'

'Think they have footage of Anna's walk home?' I asked.

'Why don't you ask them?' Jack answered. 'Maybe Mr Chief Inspector Major General Latimer, your good friend and confidant, would help,' he said sarcastically.

There was little love lost between the two, and it was always best to keep them apart. One day, I will have to ask him what their problems were, if I thought either would answer truthfully.

I crossed the road, leaving Jack with his thoughts. I took a leaflet from a dispenser by the front door. It was similar to the one Marx showed us in his office and the one Jack had in his breast pocket. I could understand David Blau's concern, that his daughter had to walk past this building twice a day.

A military-looking gentleman stood behind the glass panel at the front door, watching me. He was dressed in black and wore knee-length black boots that shone. A Sam Browne belt extended down and across his chest to a holster on his left hip; the flap enclosed whatever was inside. It was as if he'd stepped across a divide, and we were back in the thirties.

I was tempted to go inside, but Jack thread his arm through mine and steered me away. As he did, he gave the military gentleman a tight, nasty stare. I glanced over my shoulder and back to the building.

'It won't be the cops looking, but Special Branch,' I said.

'They're just cops.'

I wanted to tell him they weren't just cops. Jack, though, rarely made a distinction. Cops were cops, as far as he was concerned.

No, the League would fall under Special Branch's remit. If what he said was true, it'd be more their style.

We carried on walking until we reached the bus stop on the main road, the one Anna would have used. The thought that Anna was dead weighed heavily on my mind. Call it a premonition; and intuition, if you wish, but as we walked Anna's route, I couldn't shift the feeling. I knew Jack well enough to know he'd had the same thoughts. Where I had hope, he was a pragmatist. More so than I.

We crossed the road to the newsagents Marx had mentioned, the one Anna visited each evening on her way home. It was the only one we passed. Jack bought a packet of cigarettes, and I spoke to the agent. He was a thin man with weedy hair of an indeterminate colour, not strong enough to be brown, not enough life to be blond. Behind his glasses, his eyes seemed to bulge. He had to think for a while, counting back the days in his mind and filing them away, to arrive at the day Anna vanished.

'No,' he said in his slow way. 'She didn't come in that evening. She normally does and buys the *Standard*. Regular, like clockwork, that one, but not that day.'

'How can you remember?' Jack asked.

'We chat. She always chats. Come to think of it, I ain't seen her since, either. Nor that boy she walks home with.'

'She's missing,' I said. 'Been missing for a few days now.'

He was silent for a few seconds, then he rubbed his jaw pensively, nodding his head as he did so. He took off his glasses and squinted at Jack.

'It was the car… that's why I remember.'

'What car?' I asked.

'It had a flat tyre.' He pointed with his chin to somewhere across the road from the shop. 'I remember because I noticed it when I was closing up. I didn't see it properly, mind, not with all the rain and my specs getting wet. I was busy with the awning. It gets stuck, you see. It's a devil of a job to sort out the kink to close it. It's sort of bent back–'

'Across the road?' Jack interrupted him.

'Aye, just over there.' He nodded and made more affirming noises, watching where several houses once stood. All that remained of them were shattered walls; their roofs had gone, and ceilings had collapsed into the rooms below. Like a lot of the bomb-damaged buildings in and around London, especially the East End, they were waiting to be cleared away when the developers finally decided it was time. For now, though, it was a playground for the children, who we could hear screaming and shouting happily.

'Now, there was a girl there…' He nodded again, searching his memory. 'No, no, wait… there were two girls. One by the car, and another I couldn't see properly just behind it. She had her umbrella up.' He shook his head slowly and deliberately. 'My glasses,' he explained. 'I mean, it could have been Anna…' He shook his head again. 'But she'd come and see me if it was, wouldn't she? She's in shortly before six, before I close. I always keep a paper back for her. The one she likes. There were also three men. I remember them because of the commotion they made hurrying to change the tyre. I thought for a second they were having a bit of a drunken barney.' He gave a small laugh, as if remembering something else. 'It was pouring down, and they looked soaked.'

'Can you describe the car?' Jack asked.

The man shook his head. 'Black. Big.' He hunched his shoulders. 'It was raining, you see, and my glasses…' He shrugged again.

'Did you mention this to the police?' I asked.

'Well, no… I mean, no one asked… I didn't even know she was missing until you said.'

'An Inspector Jarrow; he didn't see you?'

He shook his head, then fell quiet for a moment, before saying, 'You know, I thought it was strange. The people with the car seemed to know what they were doing, but they took so long changing the tyre.'

'How long?' Jack asked.

'I don't know exactly. Over half an hour, that's for sure. What's that saying? Too many cooks? One of the men, the drunk one, must have gone into the car, because the other two made light work of it after. I never saw him again.'

Jack flicked his eyes towards me. I knew what he was thinking.

# Chapter 7

I stood outside the newsagents, staring blankly across the road. Between where Leah parted with them and here, Anna and Saul had vanished.

Like me, Jack was also gazing across to the bomb site.

'Let's face it, we're having the same thoughts, aren't we, girl?'

I wondered when he first had those thoughts. Probably when I called him last night for his help. As I said, he was always the practical one.

The bomb site was something to tell Jarrow about, of course. Then get him to do the work of searching the place. That would have been the sensible thing to do. But it was just a hunch. He'd already moved on in his simple thoughts, and it wouldn't please him if I was right and showed him up to his superiors. That, and it'd be no use speaking to him anyway. For a moment I thought about calling Dickens. I suspected his reaction would be the same as Jarrow's.

We stepped across the rubble and into the shattered ruins. A few of the children gave us curious stares before continuing to play what they were playing.

'Once you're here, you're screened from the street,' I said, looking back. The street could still be seen, but half-walls and rubble obscured and obstructed the view from every angle. If someone wanted to hide what they were doing, it could be easily done. 'The houses over there that back onto the site are too far away. Those trees between them conceal whatever is going on.' I kicked a few bricks across the floor. 'If her attacker was strong and caught her off guard–' I picked up one of the bricks and held it firmly as if it were a weapon. 'It'd be simple enough to do the job and drag her here.'

'She was with Saul, remember,' Jack said.

'I've not forgotten.' I let the brick drop.

'It was dark and raining heavily that evening. There are few pedestrians on this road. There's little traffic on it, even now.'

'Except the car that night the newsagent saw.'

'Except the car,' Jack agreed.

'How do you know she didn't leave in the car?'

'Why should she? I've just got a bad feeling, that's all. Even at that hour and despite the weather, no one would pay attention if she screamed. The racket these kids are making… they'd just assumed it was them playing.'

'Even if they weren't playing there that evening.' I spun around in a slow circle. It was a sizeable area to search, but manageable. 'There's no time like the present, I suppose.'

'If we must. You start at that end.' He gave a nod to the gardens. As I moved, he placed a hand on my shoulder. 'Trust me. After this long, the cats or the dogs would have found her first, if not the rats.' He sniffed the air. 'And I can't smell a thing.'

He was being kind, and no more.

'It's as cold as a fridge.' I stabbed my chin out. 'There's enough rubble here to bury anyone safe from the cats and dogs. And when did London air smell fresh?'

I began searching in the gardens of the houses. It was empty open ground, and a cursory glance told me nothing had been buried there recently; at least there were no mounds of disturbed earth. The idea that whatever happened was opportunistic came to mind, so that ruled out anyone coming armed with a spade. I went back into what would have been the houses and picked my way through the rubble.

The bricks and beams, scattered all around, had been exposed to the elements and were grimy, dark, and greasy with growth. Anything that had been recently moved would be easy to see. The few areas that looked promising, I dismissed when I came closer. It was clear nothing had been disturbed. There were several grey corrugated iron sheets laid on top of each other. No one had yet taken them for scrap. I lifted the edges up and peered under them. More bricks lay on a concrete floor, along with a few rusted pans and bits of wood and glass.

We searched for half an hour and received curious looks from the children. They'd stopped playing. Some shifted away, whispering and looking at us through suspicious eyes. A boy in short trousers, standing across from me, came closer.

'Wot you looking for?' he asked.

I gave him a short smile and turned away to another pile of rubble stacked against a wall.

'Your friend's not very friendly,' he said, looking across to where Jack was, and came to stand beside me, peering at the rubble that I was searching through. 'Said he'd give me a thick ear; he did.'

I moved a few bricks out of the way and realised that this too hadn't been disturbed. I walked to the opposite side to make sure.

'You from the council?' He perched on his haunches near me and moved a few bricks, imitating what I was doing. 'I can help. Wot we looking for?'

'Shouldn't you be in school?' I asked.

'Nah! It's Easter, innit. We're on holiday.'

'This is your playground, is it?'

'The one on Sheldon Street was. But we can't go there anymore because the council's clearing it. You from the council? You gonna clear here as well?'

'No, I'm not from the council.'

'Wot you doing here then?'

'It's private business. Go on, run along.'

'Private business? Wot's that then?'

I sighed in resignation and continued looking, and he continued following. It was all much of a muchness, and my bit anyway, hadn't had any major disturbance for years, probably since the night the bomb did its work. I looked over to Jack. He was standing with his hand on his hips and a scowl on his face. He glanced my way and slowly moved towards me. His face was grim, and when he began taking off his coat, my heart sank.

Jack knelt beside the boy, grasped his thin arm firmly, and showed him a small folder he'd taken from his breast pocket. The boy's mouth dropped open wide in horror, and he wrenched himself free of Jack's grip. He was off, running, shouting, 'They're rozzers!' in his shrill voice, panicking the others who took off with him.

Jack watched them go before slipping what I knew was a police warrant card back inside his jacket. If I didn't know Jack so well, I'd have wondered where he got it. More to the point, I'd have wondered whose it was. I had my suspicions. He then walked back to where he was a few moments ago.

There was a wooden trapdoor over a cellar. The children hadn't found it yet because a heavy tarpaulin had been thrown across it. Some bricks and rubble had been scattered on top. Only when I was standing over it did I become aware of the odour. It was faint and ripe, softly turning the air sickly. I could hear the buzz of flies. Jack peeled back one edge of the covering; a plank was missing from the trapdoor. He grasped the edge of the sheet firmly and heaved it away. A cloud of dust rose around us. He levered the trapdoor up. Immediately, a nauseating, rotting smell enveloped us. I stumbled back, my nose buried in the crook of my arm.

I had a small torch in my handbag and came back to the edge of the opening. The steps down to the cellar had completely collapsed. That left a ten-foot drop. Jack was about to climb down, and I stopped him.

'Me, not you,' I said. 'I can't lift you out afterwards. Lower me down.' I took off my coat.

'You'll mess up your best clothes.'

'There's a good dry cleaner in Kilburn.'

'It might have to be.'

Jack grasped my hand and held me as I climbed over the edge. He crouched and leaned forward, supporting himself on his other outstretched arm, as he slowly lowered me down. When there was a twelve-inch drop, he released me.

In the airless, enclosed space, the chemistry of death was overwhelming. I gagged, placed a handkerchief across my nose, and swallowed back the sickness. I washed the torchlight around. The shadows danced and slid out of the way, and the rats became statues, staring at me with red, indignant eyes at having their lunch interrupted. I picked up a brick and hurled it at them, and they edged away, unafraid, prepared to wait until I left.

I've seen dead bodies before, and the one curled up in the corner looked no different from the others. This one, though, would have had rats for company. I stepped around the crawl marks on the dusty floor and crouched beside the body that was lying on its front. The flies buzzed around, crashing into me occasionally, and I brushed them aside as best as I could.

I shone the torch on the side of the face and stiffened as I forced myself to look at the mutilated body. I searched quickly through the pockets and found an identification card. I knew it was Saul Greenberg, even though I'd never seen him before.

I flicked the light around the entire space. He was the only occupant. It seemed callous to be grateful that Anna wasn't there. But where was she if Saul was lying here dead?

The drag marks on the floor intrigued me until I realised Saul had crawled four or five feet to die in utter darkness. He wouldn't have known which direction to take to get out, not that it would matter. With his leg twisted the way it was, he wouldn't have been able to get out without help. As it was, I'd need Jack's help, and I was uninjured.

As for shouting for help, I reckoned he could have shouted and shouted, until the proverbial cows came home. Poor Saul died here alone.

I went back to the trapdoor, and Jack extended his arm. A slight jump, and I grasped it, and he easily hauled me up and out. I sat against a wall, leaning forward with my elbows on my knees, fighting the nausea and pushing away the image of Saul and all the other thoughts that vied for purchase in my mind. I wanted a bath. I wanted to wash away Saul Greenberg, the rats, the flies, and the cellar. I wanted to be clean.

Jack swung the trapdoor shut and dropped it. It rang out like a gunshot, clean and loud, echoing off the shattered walls around us. Then he drew the tarpaulin over it to half-cover it again. He walked towards me, brushing any dust and grime off my coat, and wrapped it around my shoulders. He lit a cigarette and placed it between my lips. I drew on it, and he took it back after a minute.

'Saul Greenberg,' I said. I showed him Saul's identification papers and leaned back on my straight arms, looking up at the sky. The clouds were solid grey and suited my mood.

'Anna?' he asked.

'It's just him. I'd say he was pushed or thrown in. It's not pretty. His leg's broken. The rats found him. Yes, you were right, Jack – it's the perfect place to hide a body if it wasn't for nosy people like us.'

Jack dusted his hands together. 'That answers some things,' he said drily, drawing deeply on his cigarette.

'But not where Anna is. She didn't run away. So, why kidnap a penniless girl?' *Apart from the obvious*, I thought and chewed my lip. Jack didn't answer, but I could tell we were thinking the same thoughts.

Suddenly, my staple diet of divorce cases sounded welcoming. There were no dead bodies to worry about, no breaking bad news that wasn't expected, just a few indignant people to deal with, some smutty pictures to laugh at, a judge and the occasional barrister to be obsequious to, assuming it ever went to court, then a nice pay cheque, and nothing else to care about. Divorce cases are about as close as I get to what would pass as a regular nine-to-five office job, and they seldom hold any surprises.

The children had returned. Curiosity got the better of them; they knew something was up. A silent grey bunch watched us from the far end of the bomb site. They'd have to find another place to play for a week or so. The next time they were in school, they'd be the centre of attention in the playground, telling taller and taller stories of what was found here.

# Chapter 8

It had taken me twenty minutes and several phone calls to find Dickens, when a 999 call would have sufficed. I wanted him here, not some duty officer who happened to be around, and more so, not Jarrow, who I didn't know but had nevertheless managed to form an opinion of quickly. Dickens arrived with Sergeant Brown, with the bells of the police car ringing out for all to hear. From across the road, curtains twitched, and a few faces peered at us from behind the grimy panes.

'It didn't take you long, did it?' Dickens made a show of glancing at his watch. 'Must be some sort of record.'

'Don't start with me, Dickie,' I mumbled.

'Don't start with you… now you know why I don't want you in this business.'

'I've seen dead bodies before.'

'Not like this one, I suspect.'

'Maybe if Jarrow had done his job, he'd have found him.'

'Him? What do you mean, him? Isn't it Blau down there?'

I gave him Saul's identification papers; he looked at them with slight interest and mumbled distinctly, 'The boyfriend.' I would have corrected him, but it seemed pointless.

He walked to the entrance of the cellar, peered down, and then turned back to me. His face creased like an old, worn leather glove.

'Welcome to my world,' he said in an admonishing way. I missed the rest of the words that accompanied it. I held vague hopes that they'd be complimentary. 'Brown,' he shouted.

Dickie wouldn't go into the cellar. He was too old and too fat. That'd be Brown's job. The sergeant did it gingerly. He was lowered down by the driver of the car they came in. The driver had volunteered to go instead, but standing over the trapdoor, he'd visibly paled. He must have been glad he was refused, because five minutes later, Brown emerged in a hurry. The detective sergeant regurgitated his lunch behind a wall and then sat, ashen-faced, on another. He wiped his mouth with a handkerchief. He said enough to confirm what I'd seen – that there was only one body inside.

By now, the rain was falling in a slack drizzle. There was scant shelter under the ruins. I managed to find an overhang along with Brown and waited.

He gave me the sullen, if ill-tempered, look of someone who thought a trick had been played on him. I wanted to tell him it wasn't by me. He sported the same scowl as his boss. By some peculiarity of osmosis or proximity to him, Brown had inherited it. The conspiratorial smile he shared with me only that morning had vanished like a morning mist in the sun.

'His face…' Brown stumbled over his words. 'He'd been severely beaten.'

He couldn't bring himself to say the rest, just as it hadn't surprised me how Saul looked; it was the stuff of nightmares. But he hadn't been beaten. For the best part of a week, Saul was breakfast, lunch, and dinner to East

End rodents – and that's not to mention all the in-between snacks and the occasional cat that dropped by.

I pointed with my chin to the houses on the other side of the street. 'Why don't you start by questioning them? Also, question the newsagent; he saw something that you'll want to follow up on.' He needed something to do – something to take his mind off the sight he'd just seen.

Brown just sat there instead, feeling sorry for himself, so I left him to his misery.

Dickens, seeing his sergeant otherwise occupied, went to his car to call it in.

An hour later, the bomb site was filling up. The forensic people arrived and brought with them some more rain, along with several uniformed constables from the local station. The pathologist arrived in a small, unobtrusive car, followed by a mess of obtrusive press photographers – a little too many for my liking. The requisite crowd had gathered by the time the ambulance came. Then, to add to the mix, Hugo Latimer drove up in a shiny black car, looking important.

It was a good thing Jack Brody took the opportunity to leave before he arrived. He was oil, and very volatile oil at that, to Latimer's water. For all concerned, it was best he was elsewhere. There was nothing he could add anyway, so he'd tipped his hat, giving me his very best Jack Brody smile, and left.

I waited for Latimer to finish his conversation with Dickens. Neither looked pleased. Latimer's displeasure, however, mattered. Dickens, his face pure acid, pointed at me and made a comment. I was too far away to hear what it was, but I have a good imagination. Latimer looked over, and I gave him my best Alex Raven smile. He didn't return it; instead, his hand stabbed towards the houses across the street, and Dickens and Brown went there sheepishly with some uniformed policemen.

A couple more conversations later, he came over to me.

*'Bonjour, ça va?'* was Latimer's greeting. He doffed his hat in a friendly way. His face was slick with rain, and his shoulders were damp. He wiped his face dry with a handkerchief.

It had been several weeks since I had last seen him. We had lunch together, a no-expense-spared affair at Simpsons in the Strand. Despite the austerity, the restaurant was packed with City types and scrap-metal merchants passing themselves off as gentlemen. All in all, though, it made a pleasant change from the sandwiches made by Arnie at the eateries in the basement of my office building. I ate my share of veal and everything else that my budget barred me from eating and washed it all down with a fine claret, about which I knew nothing except that it didn't give me a headache the next day. I was thankful that the good major as he was then, Chief Inspector Latimer as he is now, wasn't shy about spending money.

Over dessert – strawberries grown under glass – he reiterated his desire to *help me out*, as he put it. The Raven Enquiry Agency was solvent again, in no small part thanks to Latimer. Since then, he'd passed me a constant trickle of cases, mainly legwork, through several solicitors he knew, with whom his recommendation carried weight. They paid well and on time, and they were satisfied enough to want to keep using me. Generally, what they wanted was as boring as dishwater, but I wasn't about to complain.

'Well?' Latimer asked.

'If you make any cracks about me finding bodies…' I left the threat unsaid.

'Where does this leave you with Anna Blau?'

'Dickens tell you about her?'

'Did he have a choice?'

'Then you tell me where I am. It's a case of murder, now.' I flicked my nose to where Saul lay.

'You're a private citizen, Alex. Miriam Geller hired you to find her friend's daughter. Nothing's changed as far as that's concerned.'

'Tell me, was Inspector Jarrow following up on a missing person report on Saul Greenberg?' I asked.

Latimer looked at me morosely. 'I've just found out. No.'

'Jarrow knew about it. So did his sergeant.'

'How many different ways do you want me to say no?' He said it irritably.

I looked at him as if to say that once was sufficient. Latimer shook his head in apology for barking at me. He cupped his chin as if wondering whether he needed to shave again, his mind elsewhere, before he forced it back into the present once more.

'They were *getting around* to booking it in,' he said wearily, keeping his annoyance in check. 'He hadn't done so because he was unsure that it was a disappearance.'

'That's a polite way of saying he didn't much care. What the hell did he think it was? Saul had gone on holiday? Two people were missing from the same place of work at the same time. Maybe they both went on holiday.'

Latimer snorted, and I took a deep breath.

'For some bizarre reason, he didn't make a connection between the two vanishing together other than the obvious,' he said.

I gazed at the sky, looking for an answer. There wasn't one.

'And I guess he has a new theory now: pregnant Anna lost it with Saul, who wouldn't marry her, so she shoved him down a cellar to die, then ran away. Didn't Saul's family report him missing?' I asked.

He looked over to me with cold eyes, a clear enough warning that he'd had enough. Latimer was picking up the pieces. He didn't know what was broken, how it got broken yet, or, I suspect, how to fix it. It was plain from my conversation with him yesterday, the little there was of it anyway, he had other things on his mind.

'It's this Popov thing, isn't it?' I asked.

He grinned at me sourly, then his mouth drew taut with anger.

'A Russian scientist kidnapped off the streets in broad daylight, and no one saw anything?' he said after a few seconds of silence. 'Where was Special Branch? They were meant to be looking after her? The Russian embassy's creating merry hell. The Home Office seems to think it was the Special Branch's responsibility. Special Branch is busy pointing fingers our way. And the good old press is asking who'd kidnap a Russian scientist.'

'As if they couldn't guess. The Americans. The French. The Canadians – even the bloody Russians if they thought it'd cause trouble,' I said. 'Let's not forget us. I sympathised, but only a little. I don't suppose the Home Secretary will raise a single worried brow at Anna's disappearance.'

There was even a time limit on how long Anna would stay in the newspapers, and that had expired a good few days ago. Maybe Saul's death would bring it back. At least the papers were interested; they'd sent their photographers, and Saul's death had upped the ante.

By now, they were taking Saul Greenberg out of the cellar with a block and tackle. It was a little unseemly, but I didn't think Saul minded. It was better than being left there if he had not been found. Thankfully, he was completely covered by several blankets, leaving the morbidly curious to wonder what was under them. Latimer took out his pipe and filled the bowl with tobacco. Ignoring the drizzle, he lit it and watched the work in hawk-like silence.

'You do know Anna worked for Goel Hadam?' I asked.

'I didn't, until Dickens told me just now,' he mumbled. 'And the League is just down the road. Is there a connection?'

'Between a Jewish anti-fascist organisation and a fascist one? One's not going to invite the other to a bar mitzvah, are they? Are either of them of special interest to you?'

'Just the usual. We keep tabs on them, or, more to the point, Special Branch does. It falls under their remit more than ours. There's a march coming, which is what we'll be policing; that's the main area of our responsibility. Why do you ask?'

'Curious, that's all. Are you expecting trouble?'

'When hasn't there been trouble?' He chewed the stem of his pipe, added a match to the tobacco to relight it, and sucked it into life, nodding his head as he did. 'I'd keep out of Victoria Park if I were you,' he mumbled.

His gaze was fixed on the scene as they lowered Saul to the ground and loaded him onto a stretcher. The bearers carried him to an ambulance as if he weighed nothing.

'I'll get the autopsy rushed through,' Latimer said. He tapped his watch with the mouthpiece of his pipe. 'Meet me tomorrow; say, ten.'

'You're not locking me out?'

'Tomorrow at ten.'

'Are you taking over the investigation?' I asked, confused.

'I have my own worries and you're working for Miriam Geller, aren't you? What's your plan?'

'I'm going to see the Greenbergs,' I said. 'I want to find out about Saul and Anna and whether they had a relationship. I don't think they did, but I have to ask.'

'Just to discover if pregnancy resulted in murder?' he said.

I would have smiled if I hadn't grimaced.

That wasn't my only reason for going to see Saul's family. There are plenty of things women do better than men, and more so than men like Dickens and Brown, and that's breaking bad news, especially when the news is this bad. Emotions are the problem. Women just seem to have more control over them in these situations. I knew Dickie well enough to know he'd be sympathetic. I just didn't know Jarrow.

Maybe I'd become cynical but I felt old at thirty-one. Or maybe I was just arrogant.

# Chapter 9

The Greenbergs lived in one of those Peabody Trust buildings that dot the East End. This one was in Hackney, and when the sun touched the wet red bricks, they glowed warmly. There were no lifts. The stairs and corridors were cold and austere, but they were swept and washed with pride. The sweet, tarry smell of carbolic soap claimed each floor and clung to my skin as I walked up the stairs.

I exited the last flight on the top floor. An open walkway extended ahead of me, the front doors of the flats on one side and the spread of London, grey under a grey sky, on the other. I paused beside a plain four-panel door and waited. The muffled sounds of classical music came from inside the flat. Steeling myself, I knocked. When the door opened, the music wrapped itself around me like something warm and inviting.

Ruth Greenberg, the woman who opened the door, had a tired but kindly face. She looked old before her time. Her smile was tight, and her black hair, streaked with grey, was tied up in a loose bun. I explained who I was, and the smile slowly slipped away. At that moment, she had the look of someone who already knew my news. She knew it when she opened the door, and I think she knew it before then. She looked like someone who was just waiting. There was an immense sadness in her face that she could not hide, so she said nothing, not in the hope that she was wrong in her assumption but simply because there was little to say that would make a difference. I knew that look all too well.

A cosy corridor led to a small, well-proportioned living room.

Solomon Greenberg was sitting in a low armchair as if he'd been stuffed into it – for, indeed, he had been. A lean and angular man, his creased skin a pallid white, clung to his face thinly, giving the impression of a living skull. An immense hollowness surrounded him, into which he was about to be sucked. He looked as if he was in his nineties, but he must have been younger. Solomon Greenberg had the look of someone not long for the world. His eyes, though, were like drops of dew; they were the only thing alive in his silent, bloodless face. They studied me guardedly as I studied the room.

It was a plain room, neat and tidy, well dusted, and warmed to the point of being tropical by a healthy coal fire. I slipped off my coat and wiped a trickle of sweat from my forehead. We were in a garret, and the ceilings sloped. Two big windows inset into the walls gave an uninterrupted and smoky view southward towards the river. Peace lilies, basking in the heat, bloomed in pots on the wide sills, each with a fleshy, creamy white bulb and fat, glossy leaves that shone a vibrant green. There were several paintings on the walls – nothing to write home about – just pleasant views of the countryside and sea that brightened up the room, and a few recent photographs dotted the tops of various pieces of furniture. A large, ostentatious radiogram laid claim to a wall, from where Dvořák's *New World Symphony* was playing.

'This is Miss Raven, Solomon,' Ruth said.

The man did not speak; he did not nod. He could do neither. Just his eyes moved in his frozen face.

'Speak,' she said simply to me when we sat down. 'Six months ago, Solomon had a stroke. It has left him, as you can see. He survived the camps, Miss Raven, but this he will not survive. He cannot move. He cannot speak. But he understands what you say.'

I told them that their son was dead. I didn't mention the particulars; I only said that he was dead. I told them that the police would ask someone to identify his body. Ruth listened quietly, knowing it would be her. I didn't envy her that prospect; the body was mutilated, and she would see it like it was because there was no other way to see it. At some point, she reached across and grasped Solomon's hand. All the time, his heavy, silent stare did not leave me, and it was unfathomable.

When I had finished, she stood. 'Please, have some coffee with us.'

In truth, I wanted to leave. I rued that charity, that devil of good intentions, had prompted me to bring the bad news to them. The excuse that I didn't want it to be Dickens or Jarrow and that I could do it better than them was a conceit I now regretted. The reason I gave myself, that I had things to ask the Greenbergs, could wait.

'I'm intruding,' I said, hoping they would believe it.

'Please, Miss Raven. You have come out of your way to tell us something dreadful; it cannot have been easy. Stay just a little longer.'

'You're remarkably calm after hearing such bad news.'

'Calm? No, Miss Raven, not calm. Just used to hearing such bad news. That is all.'

I was embarrassed by her matter-of-factness, her kindness, and her courage. I think she understood that and the cowardice I'd feel if I left, and she'd made the decision for me that staying would be the better choice. I nodded, ashamed of the thoughts, and wondered if guilt made me remain.

'Speak to Solomon,' Ruth said as if reading my thoughts. 'He will not answer. Tell him something. It does not matter what. He will like to hear your voice. He hears mine too often. When we were first married, he said it was a nagging voice, ideal for keeping him on the straight and narrow.' She leaned over and kissed his cheek. 'Do you still think that, you old wasp?' She went to the gramophone. 'Enough of the Bohemian. We can visit America another day.'

She left us alone.

It took Ruth fifteen minutes to make the coffee. In that time, I told Solomon about my father. I told him he was a Metropolitan Police officer until he was invalided out of the force. I told him about the Raven Enquiry Agency and how I inherited it. He never wanted me to enlist during the war, and not with the group I did. But I spoke French fluently, and I knew Paris intimately, having stayed there many times with my aunt, his sister. I was clever, and all in all, that made me an ideal candidate for what they wanted me to do. Anyway, I told him I was too much of a tomboy to make tea and give out sympathy with the aspirins. Eventually, my father said our nature couldn't be denied. I never knew if that was a compliment or not, and he never chose to explain.

Solomon Greenberg listened to every word, his eyes smiling at me, or so I imagined. All the time, I wondered how Ruth Greenberg would cope on her own. Solomon needed everything done for him. We were at the very top of their building. He'd probably never left it since he'd been brought home after his stroke. Something told me the next time he'd leave it, he'd never return.

When Ruth came back carrying a tray of coffee and cups, her eyes were dark and red, but her face was expressionless. Whatever emotion she shed while in the kitchen remained where she left it.

Coffee was served in an expensive bone china service – a good shilling, even one and six for each piece. They were very unlike David Blau's, which were, by and large, old and cracked, their lustre gone with age. These were new. The spoons were silver. The coffee itself was ground beans, not Nescafé.

'He cannot drink coffee anymore,' Ruth explained as she placed a full cup beside her husband. 'But there is no rationing the smell. We are allowed simple pleasures only.'

She talked about Saul. By some miracle, they had all survived the war. 'God was good to us,' she said. I wanted to ask why he wasn't good to the rest, but it wasn't the sort of question you ask at a time like this.

They had hopes for Saul. He was studying at night school to become an electrician, a thing for which he had an aptitude. Between working full time at Goel Hadam, the extra cleaning he took on for them, and helping with his father's condition, I wondered how he found time to study. He did, and for that, she was proud of him. That was why she showed me his room. It was small, and despite the volume of things inside, it was tidy.

He'd taken apart radios and reassembled them. Bits of speakers, valves, and such were neatly contained in boxes on the floor or the table he worked at. There were manuals dotted here and there, along with various testing equipment. Everything appeared to be brand new. Various magnifying glasses sat on a desk; one was on a stand with a built-in light to make working easier. A neat box of compartmentalised electric tools was beside it. Saul's ambitions reigned beyond those of a simple electrician, judging by the work he was putting in and the books on his shelves. There were books on higher-order mathematics, logic, and syllogistic reasoning. I was impressed and curious to know where he'd picked up his education. Not from the camps, I was sure.

Ruth said how Saul doted on her and his father. The dress she wore wasn't the cheapest, and she opened his wardrobe to show his clothes that were worn and a little shabby. He'd spent his money on his family and his passion.

'He repaired radios,' Ruth said in answer to my unspoken question. She was already speaking in the past tense; she'd crossed the boundary from the living to the dead with little or no effort. It was a journey she was familiar with. 'Anything electrical – irons, gramophones. Saul had an aptitude for such things – an innate understanding, as Solomon called it. He attended lectures on electronics, the last one only a week ago. It was a passion. He was hungry for knowledge. Look, his pride and joy.' She uncovered a television set. 'He was taking it apart. Saul said there would be as many of these as there are radios in ten years' time. If he knew how to repair them… then… then… It was something he was good at,' she ended quietly.

'Surely getting a job at a radio repair shop would pay more than working for Goel Hadam?'

'He considered it. But he felt the work there was important. And he could always make extra with his repairs. It paid well to repair things, and that's how he could buy all these things.'

I wondered if Ruth knew how much *these things* cost. I certainly didn't, but I knew none of them were cheap. The notion that he'd got it all on the never-never didn't appeal; there was far too much here for me to believe it was bought on credit. That left few other choices. But from what I could gather, Saul didn't strike me as a thief.

'How long had he been working at Goel Hadam?'

'Six months. He was so pleased he'd got the job.'

'Were he and Anna walking out together?' I asked.

'God forgive me,' she said, and horror turned her face ugly. She reached out and took my hand. Her calloused fingers were rough against my skin. 'I'd forgotten about Anna. Where is she? Was she found with him?'

'No. She's still missing.'

'But she's alive?'

'I don't know.'

'Poor Mr Blau, what he must be going through.' She sighed as she let go of my hand. She turned to gaze at Saul's room and took a deep breath to compose herself. 'No, Miss Raven, they were good friends only.'

'I think she and Saul were together when he died.'

Her look was one of curiosity, of not understanding what had happened for Anna to have been there and to have seen Saul die.

She bit back on her questions and said, 'Saul liked his own company, Miss Raven. He was shy around girls. He did like Anna. I think he'd have liked to ask her out. I wanted him to. I think Anna likes him.'

'I was told he was loyal to the family.'

'Devoted. That is so.' She flicked her head towards the sitting room. 'But that is no life for a young man, loyal or not. The young need their freedom, not to be burdened with such responsibilities at their age. That's for us older people who are nearing the end of our lives. But no. Saul felt it was his duty; he would not leave him. Solomon will be dead before the year is out. Then Saul would have been free.'

She'd said it with little regret, more relief that it would be over, not for her but for Solomon. After all, what sort of life did he have to need everything done for him?

'How will you manage?'

'Like always.' She smiled as she gave her answer to me.

Ruth, stoic, would weather the storm of the loss and the loneliness to come and tell her sorrows to a man who couldn't reply. So, I said goodbye to Solomon Greenberg. His eyes blinked, and I took that to mean his farewell. I felt as if he wasn't looking at me, but it wasn't a blank stare either. He was seeing something only he could see.

As I left, I glanced back, and I couldn't help but think that Saul was living beyond his means – the radiogram, the good china, the expensive coffee – and I wondered if that would not come back to haunt Ruth now that his salary was no longer there. The extra cash he made with his repairs would only ever be pocket money. The next knock on the door, after the police came to inform her officially about Saul, would be that of the debt collectors.

'Let me know if there's anything I can do for you,' I said.

I walked down the stairs and back into the open street, glad to be out and annoyed with myself that I'd offered help, since I'd done it more out of guilt than anything else. Shame's a cruel emotion, especially as Ruth Greenberg knew how I felt and was being polite when she said I was not to worry. She understood.

Rain had fallen while I was with the Greenbergs, and the pavement was awash with puddles that I stepped around. A cold wind added to the misery. It had been a bad day, from seeing Dickens this morning to being in Hackney this afternoon. I hadn't expected things to move so quickly, and it was all something of a mixed blessing.

I wasn't too sure where I was with finding Anna. It's surprisingly easy to vanish in a crowded city, by choice or otherwise, and to stay hidden if that's your wish. But why would Anna want to do that? Saul's death came to mind. I wondered cruelly, did he try something on and she reacted? Perhaps the pathologist would shed some light on things. Maybe Saul wouldn't give up any secrets about Anna's whereabouts.

But right now, I needed to be home – somewhere familiar for a while – where I could gather my thoughts.

# Chapter 10

I spent the evening listening to Dvořák. My downstairs neighbour, Jeff, told me all about his music. Since I didn't have any records of his symphonies, I borrowed Jeff's. He advised me that to get the best out of Dvořák, I needed a better record player than the cheap one I owned. His HMV model, apparently, was ideal for reproducing the great man's music. He spoke gushingly about the movement's middle section, how the passage in C# minor evoked a nostalgic mood that leads eventually to a funeral march, made more poignant by the pizzicato steps in the basses. Despite the advertisement, I declined his kind offer to discover it on his machine. That night, I dreamt of America and didn't have to wonder why Jeff never married.

It was a grizzly April morning to wake up to. The sun was hiding, and Dvořák was still in my head. Despite the dreams, I'd slept well, and I left my flat soon after breakfast. The tube journey was unpleasantly crowded, and I was grateful when we reached Charing Cross.

I'd scoured the papers for a paragraph, if that, about the body discovered on a bomb site in East London. There was nothing. I'd expected a little, judging by the nosy photographers that were there. I guess no one wanted to be reminded of the war and the Blitz, and I guess that would have been the editor's assumption – the body of some poor bloke, killed during an air raid, finally being recovered, wasn't going to make the nationals. It would only make the local rag if the rumours about the Rotary club wives weren't true. No one had bothered to hang around long enough to learn there was flesh covering the bones.

The pigeons looked well-fed as I passed Trafalgar Square. Some early-rising tourists were busy contributing to their diet while having their photographs taken. Their daughter, her dirty blonde hair enclosing a peach-shaped face, held out a pigeon-covered arm and smiled at the camera. I wanted to tell her they may look cute, but you can catch something pretty nasty from them as well. At least it was a short walk to the hospital if she did.

I skipped away from the square towards the main entrance, crossing the road just as the lights turned green and earning the annoyance of a taxi driver. We exchanged pleasantries.

The last time I was at the hospital, I had a letter of introduction from Hugo Latimer. It opened many doors, including the one to the Charing Cross Mortuary. I didn't need it this time. I walked past the receptionist, who barely acknowledged me, and I didn't bother announcing myself to the officious Mr Barrows, in charge of this part of the building.

Chief Inspector Latimer was pinching the bridge of his nose as I entered the mortuary. He stood next to a sheet-covered corpse. I can't say he looked pleased. Neither did the man he was standing with, the pathologist, a tall man with an ageing, saggy face. I stood back, not wanting to intrude.

The man's mouth was turned down and he was shaking his head in a forceful way. His sallow skin looked unhealthy under the greenish tinge of the fluorescent lights. One of them was flashing intermittently on and off, flicking the shadows around and buzzing like a fly.

'And no chance of prints?' Latimer asked.

Farmer lifted back the sheet, exposing the top half of the corpse. I was startled. It was blackened, blistered, and bore all the hallmarks of a fire. There was not an inch of it that wasn't burned. I swallowed back the nausea and told myself the lie I'd seen worse. I turned my head away as Farmer lifted one of its hands, blackened and claw-like. He was shaking his head. 'What do you think, Chief Inspector?'

'But you are certain about the height, weight… age?'

'I will be more certain if I have some time. If I knew you wanted her done first, I'd have left the boy for later. However, as a result of a preliminary examination only, I am certain.'

'How long had she been in the water?'

Farmer drew in a deep breath. With a certain reluctance, he said, 'Less than a week. But I will tell you this: It wasn't a propeller or some such thing that did this damage to her face.'

'What then?'

Farmer sighed. 'Just what I said.'

'And?' Latimer asked tiredly, knowing there was more.

'The marks around the waist suggest a restraint was applied to keep her under water. A weight. My guess is that the fire damaged the ropes and weakened them sufficiently for the current to do the rest. It was shoddy work.'

'So, she broke free and floated to the top? What about the other body?' He flicked his head to another sheet-covered corpse next to them.

'I'm not a magician, Mr Latimer. He's as badly burned as this one. It'll be just as difficult.'

'Well at least we know it's a he. When can I have the report?'

'Later this afternoon.' When Farmer realised I was in the room, he turned towards me. His face hardened into a *this isn't a place for a woman* expression. 'Can I help you?' he barked.

'She's with me,' Latimer said. 'Alex, Dr Farmer. Farmer, Alex Raven. She's here for the boy.'

'I see.' He said it slowly and curiously while replacing the sheet over the corpse. 'Is she a relative?'

'She isn't. Now get on with it.'

He moved silently to another table deeper inside the room with another sheet-covered corpse. He pulled back the white linen from the head to the shoulders. The beginnings of the Y-shape cut were visible. Saul had been thoroughly cleaned, at least of the dirt and grime. The wounds inflicted by the sharp teeth that feasted on him, however, were prominent. Under the strip lights, he looked washed out, bluish-pale, and bloodless – an odd sight with his feet sticking out from the bottom of the sheet, a toe tag dangling his name, resting on the sole of one foot. I wondered what Ruth had made of it all and this somewhat austere, impersonal, and unfriendly space when she came to identify her son. I knew she'd seen worse, but I didn't think that would have prepared her for this sight. I didn't think anything could.

'Where shall we start?' Farmer asked us.

'I haven't all day,' Latimer said brusquely. 'Hurry up.'

It didn't please Farmer to be told to hurry, but small delicacies like tact never bothered Latimer.

'The boy was alive when he was placed in the cellar,' Farmer said. He was wrapping Saul up, since he didn't need to display him. 'The point is, Inspector, I'd hazard a good guess that it was the fall that broke his leg. Shock killed him. Had he been found earlier, only a few hours earlier from when he went in, he'd be alive. Here, look.' He'd picked up some photographs that showed the drag marks in the cellar. 'This is the boy trying to find a way out. He dragged himself a few feet, then probably passed out, and if he awoke afterward, it would have already been too late.'

'The cellar door was covered up,' I said to Latimer. 'It was to hide the body, that's obvious. But if he were still alive, he wouldn't have been able to get out. It would have been pitch black inside.'

Latimer thought a while, pouted, then nodded as if in agreement. 'Was the bruise on his head post-mortem?'

'A product of his fall?' Farmer shook his head.

'Detective Constable Brown said he'd been severely beaten – his face had been battered, or so I gathered,' Latimer said, and that prompted a deep sigh from Farmer. He used the opportunity to once more shake his head forcefully, as if he were a teacher about to tell a student he'd got it wrong.

'Hypostasis, livor mortis,' he said, 'post-mortem lividity – well, you know, Mr Latimer. You may not, Miss Raven. He was found face down, and the gravitational settling of the blood vessels after circulation had ceased caused the blotching. That's what gave it the look of bruising – hence the purple discoloration. It's easily mistaken. However, Brown should have known that. What do they teach detectives these days? Shocking. Truly shocking.' He tutted.

Hugo Latimer was about to say something, but decided it would be better to give Farmer a hard stare instead.

'Of course, the rodents had had their way.' He was looking at me. 'They go for the eyes first, did you know? And for the bits that protrude, like the nose and cheeks? And he'd been there for nearly a week.' He smiled, and he turned back to Latimer. 'However, they did not destroy the bruise on his forehead.'

'That's significant because…?' Latimer asked.

'Something struck him, of course, before he died. It may well have resulted in a concussion. Perhaps he was in a fight? Then there is the bruising under his arms…' Farmer left the thought standing in the open air for a few moments. He appeared to be thinking. 'Well… it suggests he was assisted… somewhere… rather forcibly…'

'Into a cellar, perhaps?'

Farmer hunched. 'I would say there were two helpers, but that is just a guess.'

'Apart from that, anything else?'

'Lunch was sardines and bread, but otherwise he was healthy. No medical problems I could find. A healthy specimen as they come.'

'So, he was alive when he was put into the cellar,' I said.

'I believe that is what I said. Would he have bruised otherwise?'

The contents of Saul's pockets and all his clothes were laid out on a small-wheeled trolley. There were only two things remarkable about them. Saul's well-kept and highly polished shoes had two scuff marks, suggesting he'd been dragged somewhere – probably to the cellar – and his wallet, which contained twenty pounds in various notes. It was a lot of money for someone employed at Goel Hadam, where none of them earned that much.

'Did Dickens find out anything?' I asked Latimer.

'Someone remembered a car parked opposite the bomb site the night Anna and Saul vanished,' Latimer said. 'It tallies with the newsagent's sighting. The car might have broken down; they didn't know. It was raining, and it had darkened. And no, due to good old English reserve, they didn't get the number.'

'I'll have a chat with them.'

'No need. Brody has. Talk to him.' He said it with disdain, ending our discussion without telling me how he knew Jack had been with me.

It amused Farmer to see Latimer's reaction, but I gathered he knew better than to show it openly. A slight curling of the corners of his mouth was all he allowed himself.

'And the other bodies?' Farmer asked and motioned with his chin towards the burnt corpses.

The policeman sucked on his empty pipe, then viewed it thoughtfully, considering it for a moment, before breaking it apart. He blew through each section, then reassembled it and added tobacco. From somewhere, Farmer found a match, and Latimer used it to light the pipe.

He walked over to the first body. His eyes fixed on it, and he chewed the stem of his pipe. The somewhat theatrical silence he'd fallen into conveyed the impression he was thinking. Maybe he was. Latimer was a difficult person to read.

'German? You are sure?' Latimer asked quietly.

'I don't make mistakes, Chief Inspector.'

Latimer's eyes flicked up in disbelief.

'I've checked it several times.'

Whatever they had been speaking about when I'd entered the mortuary, they were doing so again. Farmer gave me the *should she hear this* look, and Latimer made a quick motion with his pipe to say *hurry up*.

'I can't comment on wartime dentistry,' Farmer said, 'but pre-war, I can. There are sufficient clues to say it's German.'

Latimer nodded his head, more to himself than to Farmer.

'There are enough teeth to make an identification?'

'Only if records exist.'

'Unlikely.' Latimer slipped into the coat he'd been carrying across his arm. He slipped on his gloves, flexing his fingers to make them comfortable. 'And the face was deliberate?'

Farmer plucked at his lips. 'I would say yes.'

'Can I say a hammer?'

'You can say what you like.' Seeing Latimer's narrowing stare, Farmer smiled fawningly. 'But it would do the trick nicely, I'm sure.'

'Confirm her height, weight, and build. Whatever else you can – hair colour, scars, operations – as soon as you can. It'd be too much to ask if she's got her name tattooed on the left cheek of her arse, I suppose?' Latimer poked

Farmer in the belly with the mouthpiece of his pipe. 'Leave your thoughts about her dentists out of your report. Is that clear?'

'But–'

'Is it clear?'

Farmer nodded, none the wiser but unwilling to disobey.

'You'll want this.' Farmer found something and placed it in Latimer's open hand. A small, blackened wedding ring. 'It was on the female corpse. There's an inscription. But I can't read Russian. Do you want me to include it in the report?'

Latimer took it, squinted at the writing inside the band, and handed it back. 'Give it to my sergeant. For the moment, leave that out of your report as well.'

# Chapter 11

As we left the hospital, Latimer paused on the pavement. Several street photographers were busy at work. One had just taken our picture. Perhaps it was the grump on Latimer's face that stopped the photographer from giving us his business card, should we wish to have a print. Or it could have been when the Chief Inspector growled, 'Do we look like bloody tourists?' that did the trick. Whichever it was, the cameraman turned tail and began following a family of four, catching up with them as they crossed the street. They looked like Americans as nearly as I can imagine Americans looking, and they looked as if they would pay him for his trouble – he'd get no change from Hugo Latimer.

'Who's she?' I asked and indicated with my chin the direction of the morgue. Few things worried Latimer, and those that did, he seldom showed. I'd noticed his dismay in the mortuary and was intrigued by the fact that he hadn't tried to hide it.

'Haven't you been reading the newspapers,' he said sharply. His face went through a series of expressions before settling when he added, 'Natalia Popov.'

'The Russian diplomat?'

'Scientist,' he corrected me.

'And the other one?'

'Yes. The other one.' He pursed his lips.

'I read a diplomatic note was raised.'

In the highly purified air of diplomacy, that spelled trouble, especially for Latimer, as he was in charge of the investigation. He said nothing and started walking to his car, then he stopped, turned, and came back to me.

'Tell me, is Saul Greenberg connected with Anna Blau's vanishing act?'

'Only that they were together when it happened.'

'You're sure of that?'

'Pretty sure.'

'She didn't kill him?'

'Personally, I don't think so.'

'But you don't know her and he's dead.' He nodded in answer to his own statement. But it was also because of what he hadn't asked, the same question Jack Brody had been asking: If Saul's body was there, why wasn't hers? That left the hope that she was alive. Something else, though, troubled him. He was good at keeping secrets – annoyingly so at times. 'Then there's this car…' he pondered, again to himself, as if I weren't there.

I risked his displeasure and mentioned the van outside the headquarters of the League, the one Jack and I had seen. It'd occurred to me they might have a photograph of the car that had broken down.

I was met with the stony silence of someone who didn't know Special Branch was there. It rankled. For one thing, they were operating covertly on *his* streets without *his* knowledge, and for another, he'd have to go cap in hand to them. It was not the sort of thing Hugo Latimer was good at doing. He couldn't very well send Dickens or Jarrow either. Such matters necessitated the weight of rank. With recent events and everyone blaming everyone else for the Russian's disappearance, and him, Latimer, bearing the brunt of it, I doubt it endeared him.

'What you saw and heard in there,' he said, flicking his head again, to where he imagined the mortuary was, 'stays in there. Am I making myself clear, Alex? There was a reason you signed the Official Secrets Act all those years ago. You don't un-sign it.'

He tipped his hat politely and again made for his car. I turned towards Soho, and the sound of grinding teeth faded.

# Chapter 12

Martha and Jack's shop was closed. I was about to rap on the door when I saw Jack through the glass panes. He motioned me in. The door was ajar, and I entered. I told him about my visit to the mortuary, and he took it all in silence. When I finished, Jack said thoughtfully, 'He was alive before he went into the cellar.'

We were in a small kitchen – cosy, neat, and easily warmed by the gas oven, its open door allowed the heat to suffuse the room. By the time Jack made coffee, Martha Evans had entered.

The busty middle-aged woman had the dishevelled hair of someone recently risen. She pulled her dressing gown tighter, greeted me with a surly nod, and lowered herself into a chair. Her elbows found the table, and her hands supported her head, holding it as if it were likely to fall off at any minute. She yawned. Mornings were never her best time.

I spooned a second heap of sugar into my coffee. Martha, watching me with dispassionate eyes. 'Why don't you ever put on weight?' she mumbled.

'I live clean, eat healthily, get my eight hours with the sandman each night; and I find exercise helps.'

'Wait a minute; let me write that down so I can remember it.' She sniffed at me and pinched her stomach with both hands. Then she pouted at Jack.

'Of course, that means there's more of you for me,' he said.

Martha flicked her eyes up. 'Ape!' she said, less than impressed. 'Don't stand there. Get yourself a coffee.' She sipped his. Jack grinned behind her back. Turning to me, she handed me a neatly typed note with some figures on it. 'Here is your bill for our time.'

A week ago, I'd engaged them to follow an elderly gentleman, Patrick Fernley, a retired captain from the Coldstream Guards. His wife suspected him of conducting military manoeuvres away from home, and the smell of divorce was in the air. His wife wasn't far wrong, and it wasn't much of an effort to discover the truth. I would have been the one following the captain had I not bumped into him as I left their house. Since he'd seen me, I needed someone else to keep an eye on him.

'You pick 'em, don't you, girl,' Martha said to me between yawns. 'She's eighteen, and he's sixty if a day, with the face like the arse end of the number 38 bus.' She yawned some more and pressed the hot cup against her cheek. 'I ask you, shagging in the back row of the cinema and making me miss Katharine Hepburn. *Adam's Rib* – she's good in that. What's the world coming to?' She twisted her head in profile, lifting her chin theatrically. 'After you shot your husband… how did you feel?' she quoted. 'Jack says I look a bit like her – I've got her nose.' She tapped her index finger against an entry on the bill. 'The price of the tickets – and two cornets as well. Vanilla, if you want to know. We had to blend in, didn't we?'

I took the bill, and folded it into my handbag.

'Make sure she gets it back,' I said and her brow furrowed. 'Hepburn. Her nose.'

'Oh, ha, ha, I'm sure.' She rolled her eyes. 'Here's the dirty old sod!'

I smiled at the rather comical thought of Martha Evans, the morally outraged owner of a shop in Soho that sold dirty magazines and various items for the bedroom, as she pushed a glossy ten-by-eight-inch print towards me.

An elderly man and a young girl were staring through the corners of their eyes at the person with the camera. The brilliance of the flash had picked out every detail. His startled eyes. Her startled eyes. The slight smudge of her lipstick on his cheek. The darker patch of it on his lips. How close and comfortable they were. The impossibility of sliding a single sheet of paper between them. The detail that mattered, though, was his hand inside her blouse.

'And no cheques,' Martha said. She patted the chair beside her and flicked her eyes at Jack. 'Come on, park yourself, lover, and don't make faces behind my back. I can see your ugly mug reflected in the kettle. Now, Alex, girl, what's this all about? What's Jack been telling me?'

I explained again. At the end of it, Jack was drumming his nails against the Formica tabletop.

'Latimer mentioned you'd talked to the people across the road from the bomb site,' I said.

'And how did he know that?' he asked, but didn't wait for a reply. 'Your Inspector Dickens went at them like a bull in a china shop–'

'He's not mine,' I said. 'But if you want him–'

'Got right up their noses, quoting King's Regs and the Riot Act. They said, politely, that he wasn't in a good mood.'

'But did they see anything?'

'A black, officious car, like a limousine. It had a flat, and the driver was changing it. There were four people. Mrs Jenkins couldn't make them out.'

'Bit of a nosy bint, is she?' Martha chimed.

'So, it confirms what the newsagent saw,' I said.

'One was a woman,' Jack said. 'Mrs Jenkins remembered because the woman was in the back, like she was being chauffeured. She got out and caught jip from one of the men. She didn't seem to care because she was giving back as much as she got. Anyway, she returned inside the car with another woman. I'm thinking that was Anna. Something was happening on the pavement, but the car blocked her view. At that point, hubby had a coughing fit, and she had to slap his back. Something had gone down the wrong way. Then Arthur Askey was on the radio, and she never misses him. So, she, hubby, the cat, and a cup of Horlicks sat down to listen. When she looked again, the street was empty.'

'So, what happened?' Martha asked. 'How come she gets in the car and her friend ends up dead?'

I guess it was what we all wanted to know. I couldn't imagine Anna getting into the car voluntarily, not if something was happening to Saul.

'I've taken your suggestion,' I said to Jack. 'Latimer's going to see if the van has any pictures of Anna or the car.'

Jack grinned. I could see he was amused by the prospect of the Chief Inspector going cap in hand to Special Branch.

I left them. It was a short walk to my office. I was at a loss for what to do, but at least I had the rundown on Mr Patrick Fernley, captured by the chemistry of light on photographic paper.

The guards had seen action at Walcourt, Waterloo, and Inkerman; Mons, Loos, and the Somme; and most recently, one of its troopers in the back row of a cinema near King's Cross. It wasn't destined to be the regiment's finest moment. On the technicality that he was retired, they'd probably not enter Captain Pat's recent engagement into their battle honours.

Mrs Fernley wouldn't care either way. From what I knew of the erstwhile lady, she'd not be taking prisoners; she didn't look the type, and I knew she wanted the house. If that meant having the kids as well, she was prepared to make the sacrifice. They were all grown up, after all.

I waved at Arnie, who ran the sandwich bar in the basement of my building, exchanged a few pleasantries, and walked up the stairs to my office. A smattering of mail had been placed against my door, probably by the office boy who worked for Geller and Goldmann.

I should have reported my progress to Miriam, but I had little to say, so I avoided her.

There were a few circulars in the mail. I filed them in the bin. There was a cheque from a client for fifteen guineas. I liked those who thought in guineas, they were always prepared to pay a little more. It took my mind off any thoughts of tidying my office and making it fit for any future visits from Inspector Dickens.

I called the hospitals near where Anna went missing once again to make sure they hadn't made any mistakes, even though I was confident they hadn't. Then I typed out an invoice for Mrs Fernley that I intended to hand-deliver that afternoon.

As I left the office, I took a last look around. Yes, Dickens was right; it did need a tidy.

On the way to see the captain's wife, I deposited the cheque into my bank and got a welcoming smile from the cashier, along with a friendly wave from Mr Henderson, the manager.

# Chapter 13

Mrs Fernley lived in splendid fashion in Queen's Park, a nice residential area in North London. The house, a three-storey semi-detached affair, sat proudly back from the street in front of a small but neat garden. It had taken more than a few minutes for my knock to be answered, and I took time to cast my eyes across the quiet and pretty street. A highly polished black, two-door Bentley was parked outside the house, one of three cars in the street, and they were its poorer, twice-removed cousins. It stood out like the proverbial sore thumb.

The lady herself answered the door. She was small and compact, wearing an expensive gown and scent, and had her hair up. Her carefully applied lipstick couldn't disguise her indignant face, which changed with magical simplicity into a pleasant one when she recognised me. She knew I'd brought good news.

She introduced a thin, badger-faced man in tweed jacket and grey flannel trousers as Mr Cramer, her solicitor. Two things struck me about him. His tie made him out to be an alumnus of Millfield – I knew the tie as I once dated a Millfield boy who drove an Alvis at ridiculous speeds – and the gold monogrammed cufflinks. They sat alone and forlorn on the coffee table. Cramer quickly picked them up and stuffed them into his pocket. I had the impression I'd interrupted the solicitor and his client in the middle of an important meeting.

The children, apparently, were visiting friends in France, and the captain was living elsewhere, having moved out suddenly. I suspected he'd confessed his indiscretion in the hope of forgiveness. He obviously didn't know his wife as well as I did, and I had managed to acquire that knowledge in less than a week. Tomorrow, the locksmith was coming to change the lock on the front door. I guess that meant she thought it an ideal time to consult her legal representative about her forthcoming divorce.

The photograph of her husband, therefore, was of distinct interest to both of them, and it warranted a generous sherry. She surveyed the wall, picked up the print, and held it up in a free space between two pretty seascapes, asking if this would be a good place to *hang him.*

'Really, Nancy,' he admonished her, as if he actually meant it.

Little fuss was made with my bill; only a promise that the person who had taken the photograph would, if necessary, appear in court to validate its authenticity. I knew Jack would hesitate over what Martha would relish. All things being equal, which they seldom are, the divorce would be uncontested. Mrs Fernley held all the trumps.

I walked away with another cheque. Two in one day, things were looking up. At this rate, I wouldn't know myself.

* * *

It was nine in the evening by the time I arrived home. I'd treated myself to a meal and a couple glasses of wine in celebration at a local restaurant. As I walked up the front steps, the door opened. Jeff, my downstairs neighbour, was leaving to walk his dog, an elderly terrier.

'Your messenger service called.' He used his thumb to point to the hallway where the telephone was, tipped his hat, and carried on.

I knew then that my plan to spend the evening curled up on the sofa with Grieg was in jeopardy.

I dialled the service and slipped in tuppence when Polly answered. I never met her, but she always sounded like a ditzy blonde – a high-pitched nasally voice in a cockney accent; wearing a figure-hugging skirt and a tight sweater; and painting her nails a pillbox red while she talked on the phone crooked between her neck and shoulder.

'There you are. You're bleedin' late, ain't ya? Been dancing?'

'Stewart Granger picked me up, and we went to the Ritz.' I sighed loudly. 'I do wish he'd stop buying me champagne.'

'Has he been cheating on me again? Just you wait till he comes home, I'll give him champagne.' She giggled loudly and happily. 'Know a Mrs Greenberg, lovely? She called three hours ago. Knickers in a twist. Give her a bell, darling, before she has twins.'

# Chapter 14

Ruth Greenberg was in a state when I returned her call. There had been a break-in, the details of which she wouldn't go into, and she'd left to stay with family. By she, it meant Solomon as well. Something serious must have happened if she'd moved him.

I said I'd come. At that, Ruth became composed, more so than I suspected when she called Polly three hours earlier. When she said the morning would be better, I could feel her anger mixed up with a myriad of other emotions that I couldn't comprehend. I guess she needed time to work through them.

Early the next morning, I caught a taxi to an address in Brick Lane, where the Greenbergs were staying. I knew of the lane because of Jane Windlass, a favourite teacher of mine from school. She was active in her fight against fascism. The rumour was that she'd been involved in the Battle of Cable Street, when anti-fascist demonstrators, British Jews, and other socialist groups clashed with Oswald Moseley's British Union of Fascists. They said she'd felled one of the Blackshirts with a right cross. I never did find out if the rumour was true, but it left a lasting impression.

The address was a doorway next to a small greasy spoon eatery. I knocked. The person who answered was Sarah, a middle-aged woman with loose black hair, Ruth's youngest sister, I found out. We ascended a narrow stairwell to her flat. Once inside, I was introduced to Sarah's family. The children were sent away, and her husband, Oscar, remained with us.

On the way to the kitchen, I passed Solomon Greenberg resting on the mattress of a single bed placed near the fire in the living room. He lay there, stiff and unmoving, his blue eyes bright in the firelight. I didn't ask how they had managed to get him here, down the many flights of stairs of the building where he lived, across the few miles, and up the narrow passageway.

Ruth looked drawn and tired. A deep anger lived in her face that she was keeping under control. Coffee was welcomed, and we all sat huddled in the kitchen like refugees seated in a railway station waiting for a train.

'I went out, Miss Raven,' Ruth said. 'Solomon was asleep. He naps after lunch, often until four o'clock, so it's an ideal time for me to go shopping, see neighbours, pay bills.' Tears appeared. She took a lace handkerchief from inside her sleeve and wiped them away. 'I stayed a little too long with Mrs Spills. She's lonely, and we have tea together. She always shows me her family photographs. It was late when I left, so I hurried back. The front door was open, and…' She stopped and burst out into tears as her sister hugged her. Her body heaved, and she sobbed silently, not wanting Solomon to hear.

'Someone had broken in, Miss Raven,' Sarah continued for her sister. 'The things they did.' She shook her head in dismay. 'The things they wrote were disgusting things. And all the while, Solomon was there and could do nothing but watch them. It's a mixed blessing that Ruth was late coming back–'

'I should have been there–'

'Who knows what they would have done if you were.'

'I would have killed them,' Ruth said defiantly, and she balled her fist around the handkerchief with the menace of someone who would have done exactly that.

'What did they do?' I asked.

Ruth shook her head, unwilling to speak about it.

'You need to see it,' Oscar said. 'It's not pretty.'

'Hooligans?'

'No, Miss Raven. Nothing so simple.'

'Do you want me to look into it?' I asked Ruth.

Ruth swallowed and sniffed back her tears. 'I don't know, Miss Raven – yes, but only if you can. It was… you were the only one I could think to ask.' She hesitated, unsure of my reaction. 'I would not ask, but I do not know who to turn to. But if David Blau trusts you–'

'You told the police, yes?'

'Ruth saw a man from the local station.' Sarah sighed heavily and didn't need to finish her sentence.

'I'll talk to them. How's Solomon?'

'He does not complain,' Sarah said. I understood what she meant – even if he could, he wouldn't. 'He will stay here.' She grasped Ruth's fist and squeezed it firmly. 'He can't go back there. Not now. Not after what they did. He stays here, and so will you. Isn't that right, Oscar?'

'Solomon will have more company as well, Ruth,' Oscar said.

'At a time like this, you shouldn't be alone,' Sarah said. 'I will speak to the policeman about Saul as well. We will bring him home. Oscar will talk to Rabbi Bavli and make the arrangements for the funeral.'

'The boys will not mind you and Solomon here. We'll make another bed beside Solomon for you. So, it'll be tight, so what?'

'They broke his records…' Ruth said and fell quiet.

Oscar reached across and hugged her.

'Well, it's high time the old bastard heard some jazz,' he joked, pinching her cheek.

'Give me the keys, and I'll have a look around,' I said. 'I'll talk with the neighbours; maybe they saw something.'

'It is not something a woman should see,' Oscar said, dropping his head apologetically.

'Don't worry, Oscar, there're many things a woman shouldn't see. Whatever there is, that will just be another one.'

I left them and stood for a few minutes in the living room. Solomon was asleep. They'd have to live cheek by jowl for a while, but he'd be well taken care of until they could return. He should be in a place where he could be looked after, with the medical help he needed, but I couldn't imagine Ruth wanting him to be amongst strangers.

Ruth had cleared her eyes of tears and was her calm self again. She was holding several pound notes and fiddling with her purse. I placed my hands across hers, closing them.

'I'm being paid by Miriam Geller. Saul's death is a part of it as well.'

There was enough truth there for me to believe it too.

# Chapter 15

I caught a taxi to Hackney, where the Greenbergs lived, and trudged up the several flights of stairs to their flat. I spent ten seconds fiddling with the key in the lock before realising that I didn't need to. The lock had been forced, probably with a crowbar. A firm push was all that was needed, and the door swung back easily. The small hallway looked the same as I remembered it, which didn't prepare me for the living room. Once there, I stood in the doorway and gazed around in utter disgust.

Someone had turned the place upside down. I was walking across clothes, books with their covers ripped off, broken ornaments, and the shiny remains of black recording discs, all scattered across the floor. Sugar crunched under my feet. The expensive china set that I'd drunk coffee from left a trail towards the kitchen. On the walls where the gramophone leaned, a bright red Star of David had been painted. The word *Jew* had been scribbled across it, with paint dripping across a set of descriptive prose beneath it. Solomon's chair had been gutted. The smell of excrement was in the air, along with a faint whiff of rotten eggs. I stood in silent disbelief, feeling angry. In the distance, I heard a train and then the click of metal on metal coming from the kitchen.

I picked up the leg of a chair and cautiously approached the door. It was half open. I swung it back, weapon raised. The figure kneeling in the corner with his back to me jumped in fright. Losing his balance, he slumped against the wall, and the small wrench he was carrying clattered to the ground.

He was a stocky, grey-blond man with a soft face, dressed in a neat suit under a fawn raincoat. He looked at me in surprise. 'Whoa! Whoa!' he shouted, and raised his hands in surrender. 'Who the hell are you?'

'Who the hell are you?' I shouted back.

I pointed the end of the broken chair leg towards him, and his hand quickly dived into his jacket pocket. Pulling out a small cardboard folder, he opened it and showed it to me.

'Just keep your hair on, love,' he said. 'I'm from the gas board. Can't you smell it?'

The smell of rotten eggs was stronger in the kitchen. I could make out the gas pipe and the stop valve in the corner where he'd been crouching.

'Since when do gas men wear suits?' I asked.

'Since I smell gas.' He rose tentatively, still holding out the identification to me, his grey eyes urging me to look at it. 'Come on, love, if you can put down the head basher, I'd appreciate it.' I lowered the chair leg onto a cupboard, and he exhaled in relief. 'I can turn a stopcock as well as anyone else. Only this one was stuck. It's off now. Luckily, they had some tools in the cupboard.' He rubbed his fingers together as if they were hurting and then sniffed the air. 'Glad you don't smoke; otherwise we'd all be for it.' He placed the identification folder back into his pocket, seeing I wasn't going to take it, and held out his open hand towards me. 'Charlie. Charlie Mathers. That's me. Now, who are you?'

I ignored his hand. 'I was asked to drop in.'

His eyes roamed across me, up and down, and something of a rakish smile widened his cheeks. 'Well, if asking's what it takes, love, maybe you can drop in at my place?'

I crooked my head to one side and glanced at him with a pained expression. His pert smile became a wide, full-bodied grin that creased his face and narrowed his eyes. He held his hands up again, palms outwards in appeasement. He glanced around the kitchen, which was in the same state as the living room.

'What happened here?' he asked.

'What do you think, or can't you read?'

'Yeah, that's not what I meant,' he said apologetically. 'I mean… well, you know what I mean.' He squatted down beside the cupboard under the sink, opened it, and reached inside. 'I'll turn off the water as well, just in case. What a mess.' He was struggling to turn the stopcock and gritting his teeth with the effort. 'Almost… bloody rusted… in place.'

'How did you get in?'

'The door was open.' He'd risen and was massaging his hand as if it hurt.

'And you just happened to be passing by.'

'Blimey, you're a tartar, ain't you? The local nick asked us to come and see what's what. I was meant to be here with an engineer, but he must have got delayed. It's only a minor leak, but if gas accumulates and someone flicks the light switch, then it's goodnight Vienna.' He slapped the wall with his palm. 'The good thing about these flats is that they were designed for just such a thing. They built them like blockhouses back then.'

He rose and dusted his hands together, then wiped them on a tea towel hanging near the stove. He looked me up and down in an approving way, smiling as he did, ignoring my frown.

'Is it a nice job?' he asked as he gathered up his folder that was leaning on the wall where he'd been crouching. I gave him a curious stare as we left the kitchen. 'Working for the Housing Estate? That's where you work, don't you?'

'Oh, yes. It is,' I lied quickly.

'Jews, were they?' He stared at the Star of David.

'Bloody stupid question,' I snapped.

He shook his head. 'Sorry, yesterday's brains. You'd think we'd have had enough of this sort of thing during the war, wouldn't you?'

'Apparently not.'

He fidgeted for a moment, placed his hat on, and drew his coat tighter, flexing his shoulders to get comfortable. He gave me a beaming smile.

'So, how do I know you ain't a burglar?' he asked.

I held up the keys Ruth gave me to the flat.

'I can do that,' and he delved into his trouser pocket and brought out his keys, jingling them in front of me.

'Except mine will fit the locks. Anyway, do I look like a burglar?'

He paused for a moment, took a step back to take me in. 'Not unless you're one of them lady burglars,' he said. 'You know, sort of a female Raffles. Now, if you are and care to burgle my gaff, I wouldn't complain.'

I should have rolled my eyes. 'Fresh, aren't you? Who was it from the local nick that told you?'

'Can't help you there, love. I just get a chit that says, go here, go there.' His hands went inside his case and came out holding a pad. He flicked through a few pages to find an address, which he showed me. 'See? We'll have to come back later to check things, but we'll drop a note in to say when.'

'Until then, you done?'

'Well, there's a nice programme at the Hackney Empire this Saturday, if you're free?'

'I'm washing my hair, and then I have something trivial to do. Now are you done?'

He grinned at me. 'I guess I am. Done and sunk. Better make sure the door's locked as best as you can when you leave. We don't want the estate kids playing here. Oh, and if my mate turns up, tell him I've turned off the gas, but it'd be good if he could check that I did it right. I did; don't worry – I used to do his job.'

I escorted him to the door and closed it when he left, then went back to the living room. Finding an unbroken chair, I sat amongst the filth and looked around me again.

Maybe I was born with a suspicious mind, but what nagged me was the timing. That, and how it looked too neat and staged, from the big Star of David to the pithy message scrawled under it, and the way they set about reconstructing Kristallnacht in a flat in the East End.

Why choose the Greenbergs? There were other Jewish families living in this block and any number nearby. If someone wanted to make a statement, then why restrict it to them? The coincidence of Saul's death wasn't entirely lost on me. Nor the convenience of Ruth being away while it all happened. It had the hallmark of being well planned, with the knowledge of Solomon's disposition foremost in my mind – and foremost in theirs, whoever they were.

Mrs Grant lived next door. I asked her if she'd heard anything of the break-in. She showed me a photograph of her dressed in a thick woollen jumper and wearing a tin hat while carrying a bucket and stirrup pump. She had been a fire-watcher, sitting on the roof of the publishing company she worked for during the Blitz. Little scared her and little impressed her. She reminded me of Martha Evans. We had tea, and there the resemblance ended.

'I saw two men walk past me when I was taking out the rubbish, but, sorry, dear, I didn't pay them any notice. I told the police that, not that they cared. Kids, they said. They had more important things to deal with than vandalism. I ask you? But if you're asking me, would I recognise the men I saw again' – she shook her head – 'not in a month of Sundays.'

'Who do you think they were? Any thoughts?'

She puffed out her cheeks and shook her head.

'Debt collectors, maybe? Charity people?' I said. 'Peabody people?'

'No charity people will climb those stairs, dear – they're not that bleedin' daft; just us who live here. The Greenbergs weren't in debt, either, so it won't be the tally boys.'

'What about all the stuff in their flat? The gramophone? Saul's equipment?'

'Saul!' she blew out a long, sad breath. 'I'd forgotten about Saul. And now this. How's Ruth? Poor Solomon. He was there when it happened? Stuck there and couldn't do anything? Bastards!' She spat the word and became calm again. 'If I had my way…' She made a face to suggest what she had in mind, and it wasn't pretty. 'No, dear, all that stuff Saul bought. Nothing's on the never-never. No hire purchase. They own it all.'

'But Saul couldn't afford those things on his salary.'

'Well, he couldn't, could he? I asked the same question; I was concerned – that was all, you understand – that he was at it, nicking stuff. But not Saul. He's too nice a boy to be thieving. The last thing you want to be is in debt with some of the rats around here. Saul come into some money; an aunt left him a legacy, he said. Good luck, I say. Spend it now while you have it.'

I nodded dumbly and stared into my cup of tea as if reading the leaves – I didn't like what they were telling me.

I tried a few neighbours, and no one saw anything of significance. What surprised me was that no one heard anything either. With the quality of the mess in the flat, it suggested a lot of noise, yet no one heard anything. But as Charlie Mathers had said, they made the flats like blockhouses.

The smell of gas had dissipated from the flat when I returned, but the smell of excrement remained. I glanced around. What nagged me before nagged me again. The slogan, scrawled on the wall, looked tired. The mess contrived. Saul's bedroom had the same treatment, but more so. This wasn't the work of kids. The flat looked like it had been searched.

There was nothing about Ruth and Solomon Greenberg that suggest they'd warrant such attention. Two refugees with nothing to hide. Saul was a different proposition. His death wasn't an accident. And now the place he lived in was turned over and made to look like vandalism. I wandered through the flat and ended up in Saul's bedroom. Whatever it was about, it was about Saul. I looked at the electrical equipment and still wondered how he could afford them.

I knelt on the floor and began a methodical search, looking for loose floorboards. None. I wasn't sure what I was looking for, something that looked out of place. Something that didn't belong. I lifted up the corners of the carpet, rolled it back as far as I could. The same. I peered under the bed, ran my hand across the underside of the bedstead. Dusty and no more. Nothing under the mattress. Each drawer of his dressing table contained no more than what they should. I went through each book. Flicking through the pages, shaking them and nothing fell out. I considered searching the rest of the flat, shook my head, and came back to Saul's bedroom. All the other space was occupied by the family: the bathroom, the kitchen, the hallway, and such. If Saul wanted to hide something, then it would be in his room. This was the place to look.

Two possibilities occurred. First, whatever it was had already been found, in which case I was wasting my time. And second, there was nothing to find, in which case I really would be wasting my time.

Even so, it felt crazy, but so did the feeling that I was right. I'd considered a number of ways Saul could afford those things, and somehow, a dead aunt's legacy seemed a tad too convenient. That, and I wondered how many aunts Saul had who weren't dead a while back and in Germany as well.

So, I began again. I took down each picture from the wall and checked the back; they'd been taped against the frame.

An hour later, I sat on Saul's bed, doubting myself. The expensive magnifying glasses, the other electrical testing equipment, the gramophone, and the tea and coffee set, all bought according to Mrs Grant, and none of them cheap, were all telling me a different story. Even Ruth's mention of how hard Saul worked to buy them didn't ring true. The money from the odd repairs to radios and such and his salary from Goel Hadam, supplemented by some cleaning work, just didn't add up.

I was about to leave when I noticed it. A corner of a cream-coloured sheet peeked out from under the wardrobe. It wasn't on the ground, but floated a few inches above. I pulled the corner of the paper. It wouldn't budge and I risked tearing it. I worked the wardrobe forward several inches and leaned it back against the wall, enough so I could see under it clearly.

A foolscap manila envelope was taped to the underside of the wardrobe; the mouth of the envelope was open at the front so that things could be slipped inside and out of sight. The sheet had snagged on the gummed edge of the flap that had become wet, and that held it firmly. I pried it loose. There were puncture marks at the top, showing it had been attached by staples to other sheets. I'd seen such a sheet before when Jack and I visited Goel Hadam. Bruno Marx showed us the file on Klaus Frasch, alias Maurice DuPont. The name, typed neatly in the middle of this sheet, was Julia N Hildebrandt.

The firm knock on the front door startled me. I was still holding the sheet when I answered it. A swarthy, middle-aged man, dressed in black and wearing a cap, carrying a canvas workman's bag, stood there. He gave me a long, almost surprised look, taking me in completely from head to toe, then smiled, showing me his teeth.

‘Looking for Charlie,’ he said, looking at the name of the piece of paper I held. ‘Miss…’

‘Raven,’ I informed him, and he touched his cap, nodding.

‘Bit late, I’m afraid. There was an emergency I had to deal with first. Is the bugger still here?’

‘No, he went about an hour and a half ago.’

His smile vanished into disappointment.

‘Missed him, have I?’

‘He’s turned off the gas–’

‘Turned it off? Cheeky! Let me check he’s done it right and pray the union don’t hear about it,’ he joked, and I allowed him to pass to the front room. ‘Bleedin’ hell, what’s happened here?’

‘The estate’s got big rats,’ I said.

‘Looks it. The things I see. Never this before, though. Cor, what’s that whiff?’ He looked around with wide eyes and a scrunched-up nose before returning his gaze to me. ‘Where’s he done the job? The kitchen?’ He went towards it without waiting for a reply. I heard a crash and the clinking of tools as he dropped his bag, and a few minutes later he came back. ‘Yes, he’s turned it off all right. It’s safe. He used to be one of us until he got ambitious. Okay, miss, that’s me. Give us a call when it’s all decorated again, and we’ll come back and fix it and turn it back on for you.’ He took one last look around the room, then at me, doffed his hat again, and went to the door.

‘Not gonna fix it?’ I asked.

He took out a piece of paper from his breast pocket, scrutinised it for a few seconds, and then shook his head.

‘Turn off gas is the job.’ He shook his head once more. ‘Nothing here about repairs.’

# Chapter 16

I had to run to catch the bus outside the Greenbergs' flat. The conductor urged me on and caught my hand when I finally bounded up. He laughed as he directed me inside.

'I'll have a shilling on you if you're running the three-thirty at Kempton Park,' he said. Bowing, he found me a place on the bench seat.

I spent a few fruitless minutes looking at the name on the paper I'd picked up in Saul's room. I thought about asking Marx about it since it came from his office. Then I wondered why Saul should have it. Then I wondered how Saul got it. Whoever Hildebrandt was, Saul at one point had the entire file on her. That explained the mess in Solomon's flat, not why she was important.

I sat back, reading a newspaper left on the seat beside me. Amongst the usual stuff – floods, changes of government, a house in Littlehampton that could be mine for under two thousand pounds, a US Navy Privateer that had been shot down over the Baltic Sea. A map showed where.

The front page was about Natalia Popov. Her body had been identified. Daniel and Billy McCabe, bargees, had found her drifting on the Thames, burned and blackened. In a photograph, they were posed rather stiffly at the wheel of their barge, the spread of the Thames behind them. 'It was filthy,' Dan said, and whether it was the river or the body he meant was unclear. The Soviet government was up in arms. I could already see tomorrow's headlines in the *Daily Mail.*

How the news of Latimer's corpse made it to the papers was a mystery. Such things were designed to get right up the Chief Inspector's nose. I knew he wanted it kept under wraps. Someone at the mortuary was about to lose their job.

The body was too mutilated for a visual identification, the report went on. It had been severely burned in a fire of some proportion – I could attest to that; the burns, not the fire – but some jewellery, a ring in particular, was sufficient to say who she was. Teeth weren't mentioned. The Russians were clamouring to have the body released to them – more so than seemed in good taste.

His Majesty's Government had yet to comment.

The Russian government wanted to know why an American destroyer, not so far from where the body was found, left in such a hurry. And was the rumour true that it met up with a submarine twelve hours after its departure?

Good luck with finding that out.

In the middle of it all was Chief Inspector Latimer. No doubt his wartime career in military intelligence was the main reason he was involved in policing this issue. I understood why he was behaving like a bear with a sore head, and I decided to avoid him for a while. The powers that be would be leaning on him heavily.

The bus dropped me off at Fleet Street and I walked back to the office. Miriam Geller was waiting, arms crossed, seething. She'd heard about the Greenbergs and wanted to know what I knew. I wasn't going to tell anyone what little I knew until I'd made sense of it. I asked her whether Saul came into an inheritance – she knew the family and would know. He hadn't. None of his aunts had survived the camps. I wasn't surprised and avoided her questions of why I wanted to know.

When she left, I made some phone calls to find out who Julia Hildebrandt was. I called some of my father's friends at Scotland Yard. Nothing. Then some old acquaintances who'd moved seamlessly from the secret things they did during the war into nameless, undefined offices somewhere in Whitehall. Serious nothing. What I found out was the name Hildebrandt was Old High German and Old Norse, and *hilde* meant battle and *brandt* meant sword, and Hildebrandt killed his half-brother in Norse legends. A friend of mine, AB Pringle, told me that. For the time being, I didn't want to speak to Bruno Marx until I knew why Saul had something he shouldn't have had. So, I was none the wiser.

That had taken several hours, and afterwards I made several attempts to do some work, mainly admin, before giving up. I surveyed the office and felt it could wait another day before it was tidied, and I went home. I managed to beat the rain by a minute and heard it drumming the windows by the time I opened the door to my flat.

I had a feeling that the flat had been broken into. It was no more than that, because when I checked, I could find nothing missing, just the odd sense that I didn't leave the drawer to my writing desk open, and a few things looked rearranged. Then, maybe I did leave the drawer open and did move something around. I couldn't be sure what kind of mess the flat was in. It's a fair bet, paranoia is a common complaint amongst investigators.

I filled the bath and had a long soak, steaming up the windows and mirror, the condensation dripping off the tiles. I arose limp, rested, and weak as a kitten. Still, I washed my hair, wrapped a towel around it and a bathrobe around me, and wandered aimlessly around the flat for a while. Several things troubled me, and I sat down and counted them off in my mind.

Latimer had asked, 'Is Saul Greenberg connected with Anna Blau's vanishing act?' and I'd said, 'Only that they were together when it happened.' I didn't like the thought, that she was dead anyway, and though I shook it away, it came back.

At least she wasn't the body in the morgue. Anna had been an infant when she left the country. Too young to have German dental work.

But if she was dead, why take her somewhere else to kill her or dispose of the body? Where Saul was found was an ideal place; the only people buzzing around there were the kids playing there. They'd have eventually found Saul. But *eventually* could be weeks, if not months, and by then a cold trail would be icy.

There was something else I didn't like: the haphazard nature of Saul's death. I didn't understand why he'd been thrown alive into the cellar. If he hadn't broken his leg, he would have found his way out, and where would that leave things with Anna and what happened to her?

Saul had become an enigma. He had more money than he should have and no likely way to earn it to buy the things he had in the flat. He'd clearly lied to his neighbour about his finances, and he wasn't the person described to me by several individuals. The break-in at the Greenbergs' raised more questions. It clearly had more to do with Saul than the daubing of anti-Semitic rhetoric on walls.

Then there was Julia N Hildebrandt.

I held the cream-coloured paper with her name and wondered who she was. Nothing was missing, Bruno Marx had said of the break-in at his offices. I wondered if that was the case, and if there was something missing, would he tell me? Apparently not.

And then there was Chief Inspector Latimer's sour face outside the mortuary when I told him about the surveillance of the Fascist League's building. His relations with Special Branch were strained, but I had the notion there was more going on. Of course, that was always the thing about Latimer – even when he was a major in intelligence, he always knew more than he was willing to share. But then his job was to keep secrets, and he could do that well.

I'd changed into pyjamas and was about to settle down to read when I heard the telephone by the front door ring. Half a minute later, Jeff's slow footsteps sounded as he climbed the stairs. His self-appointed task, for which everyone was really grateful, was to answer the telephone, as he was the nearest. He had one of those annoying, rhythmic, and happy raps when knocking on doors, and I could at least console myself in knowing who was doing so. There was a call for me from Virginia Bright, someone I didn't know, who wanted to speak to me urgently.

'Hello, Miss Raven,' a rather prim, well-spoken voice sounded at the other end of the line that wouldn't have gone amiss broadcasting programmes on the BBC. 'I have a request from a gentleman you met some time ago. He'd like to meet you. Do you recall a Mr Ash?'

I did. I was surprised, and I replied yes, and I allowed her to make an appointment. It's rare you get to meet a dead man; at least, that was the belief, unconfirmed as it was.

I wasn't told why he wanted to see me; only the enigmatic response spoken in countless movies since the invention of talkies: 'I'd hear something to my advantage.' Since the only thing that I might hear to my advantage concerned Anna Blau, I readily agreed. I didn't bother to ask how the voice knew my home telephone number; people in her profession didn't need to be bothered by such trivialities.

# Chapter 17

The next day, I arose early, breakfasted, and left for Liverpool Street train station and the seaside. I arrived at Ipswich by mid-morning and caught a bus to Orford. Wilfried Ash lived on the outskirts of the village in one of those houses that seemed to typify English village life – ivy growing up the walls of a beautiful gabled property, neatly pruned fruit trees in the garden, the promise of endless summer days. From the back garden, there was a view across the River Alde and the island of Orford Ness. Beyond that, from where an icy wind was gusting and stifling summer's promise, rolled the grey North Sea.

A lychgate stood at the start of a small gravel path that led to the front door. A yew tree grew on one side of the path, and what I knew to be an ash tree was on the other side. I wondered if it was a joke on Wilfried Ash's part, and he'd planted the tree.

A well-presented lady in her early fifties answered my knock. She was blousy with an apron around her waist and was drying her hands on a tea towel. Her face had a healthy glow, giving her a certain outdoorsy quality. When she spoke, I recognised her voice as the person who'd called me the night before.

'I'm Virginia, but everyone calls me Ginny,' she said.

She led me into a room with wooden panelling, memorabilia strewn about, and a welcoming atmosphere. Ash was as I remembered him. A tall, thin man with a careworn face and sad brown eyes. Despite the ravages of the gas in 1917 and the wrinkles, his natural good looks had survived the years. He was seated in an armchair that faced a window overlooking the garden. He rose in a polite and gentlemanly manner when I entered, leaning on a walking stick to do so. Ash was that type of gentleman who'd stand when a woman entered the room.

Wilfried Ash went by quite a few nicknames, and he quite happily answered to any of them – Mad Dog, the Dashing Major, and Dorian Grey. Most of them, with the exception of the last, he'd earned during the Great War. He'd been invalided home after having lived through the hell that was Passchendaele. Then he vanished, in the sense that very little was known about him after he left the army. Rumours of his death abounded, and he did little to contradict them.

I didn't know any of this until I met Ash on a drunken night out with a reporter friend of mine, AB Pringle. The next day, after Ash left, AB told me of one of the greatest secrets of the Second World War and Ash's part in it. How AB knew, he never explained, but I suspected Ash must have told him. It was also never explained why AB told me. I suspected that since it was a thing he'd never be able to print, he wanted someone to know that he knew. I'd never heard of the place he spoke about, and I had to look on a map to find Bletchley Park.

'Sparrowhawks, not Ravens,' Ash said. A pair of heavy navy binoculars was in one of his hands, which he used to gesture towards the garden. He placed it down. The smile was mischievous and very young. He took my hands in his and gave them a firm squeeze rather than a shake. Picking up the binoculars, he gestured with them again to the garden, where his eyes returned. 'There's a pair nesting in that copse of trees just beyond the fence. They're very early.'

'They're a bit far from home, aren't they?' I asked. 'I thought they bred in more covered spots, with lots of trees around them.' I looked to either side of where they were, though I couldn't see their nest. 'Not many trees about… no, not sure. It's a bit exposed, if you ask me.'

'Good, good,' he said approvingly, not looking at me but still out to the garden. 'Did you hear that, Ginny? She knows about birds. What else do you suppose she knows?'

Following his eyes to the garden and beyond, I said, 'They eat woodland birds, don't they? Is that why your garden's empty of them?'

'The sparrows and robins know better than to hang about here.' He used the binoculars to point somewhere to his right. 'The woods over there are where they'd nest. You saw the work that's going on there when you came?' I'd seen some building work; it seemed as if some trees had been felled. 'Disturbed them.'

'So, they've graced your trees.'

'They have to find a home. They do what they must, as does nature. Though I think this is something of a *pied-à-terre*, they will move on to someplace more suitable.'

I looked up at the large, leaden sky over the sea.

'Definitely not enough cover for them,' I said, and Ash nodded.

'I wonder what Darwin would make of this,' he said. His laugh was small and indistinct. The slight cough that followed it carried an air of illness. 'Tricky fella, Darwin – observant about bird beaks, though.' He turned away from the window and eased himself into his chair, inviting me to sit in the one opposite. 'Where does this knowledge of birds come from?'

'My first client was an ornithologist,' I said. 'Before him, I wouldn't have recognised a pigeon from a peacock.'

He laughed, and that ended in a splutter. I was going to go to him, but he held up his hand to keep me back. Then he twirled his hand, indicating that I could continue speaking.

'Small birds of prey were his specialisation. He had several stuffed specimens in his house that he lectured me on. A sparrowhawk was one.'

'Sad that such a beautiful bird should end up gassed and stuffed.' Ash shook his head slowly. 'I've never understood why. To what end do you think people do that?'

I wondered then if Ash was speaking about himself and his experiences.

'I don't think Miss Raven has come all the way from London to listen to you discuss taxidermy, Wilf; or Darwin; or, for that matter, sparrowhawks at the end of the garden,' Ginny said.

'And what has she come to discuss?' He said this as a grin spread across his face. 'Now, will it come as a surprise if I were to say you've come to my attention recently?'

'A lowly peasant like me?' I said.

'You do yourself a disservice. I'll get to the point since it'll please Ginny if I do. There are two names that interest you. One I may be able to help with; the other I cannot. Julia N Hildebrandt and a certain Hauptmann Grunwald.'

'You're well informed,' I said.

'I am. Always. But not always why, and this is where most problems arise.'

I was unsure of what he meant. He extended his hand to me. I knew what he wanted; though how he knew I had it, I didn't know. I took out the sheet of paper I'd found in Saul's room and gave it to him. He studied it for a while, nodding his head.

I spent the next while explaining my commission and what had occurred these past few days. He listened, interrupting only to add a comment here and there. I felt I should not keep anything back, so I mentioned Latimer's bodies. When I finished, I wondered just how much of what I told him he already knew.

Smiling, he rose and tottered out of the room. I stood to go with him. Ginny said I should remain. She'd make some coffee.

'Give her some of that cake,' Ash shouted from somewhere in the corridor beyond. 'But keep her away from my whisky. Especially if she's brought Pringle with her.'

I sat and waited.

The room was comfortable, more like a large study than a living room. The bookshelves were populated with volumes about ornithology. Bird prints and paintings hung from the wall, and a few of the ornaments were bird-related. A painted plaster duck swam across the tabletop as curlews dipped their long beaks into solid oak. On a writing desk, I saw he had been making notes with some crude drawings of birds next to them. His handwriting was small and neat. Ten minutes later, Ginny came in with a tray and poured coffee.

'Mrs Bright?' I said, and she shook her head.

'Ginny, please. Miss Bright is far too formal,' she said. 'And no, Ash and I are not married. And I shall call you Alex.'

'Mr Ash didn't explain just how I came to his attention. Or that I might need help.'

'He says you and he met once. Knowing Wilfried, he'd have formed an opinion about you then. But I suspected he'd have asked AB.' She laughed. 'Wilf makes assumptions, and he's usually right. The first is that you don't know anything about her, Hildebrandt – which, of course, you don't. I suspect he knows your connection with Grunwald. You were one of Latimer's lot, weren't you?'

'You know the major?'

She raised her head slightly, thinking. 'Paris for a while, I believe, until they moved you. To Northern France, wasn't it? Spring '44, till the Allied army moved into the Netherlands. Eight months was a long time to be in the wilderness. At least you weren't in Holland,' she added sadly. 'Yes. We and the major have had dealings.'

'And where were you?' I asked.

'Here and there,' she said enigmatically. 'Like Wilf. Here and there.'

I shouldn't be surprised that she knew so much about me if what AB told me about Ash was only half true. She offered me a slice of Battenberg cake.

'And the second assumption?' I asked.

'It is the one you've just come to: Hildebrandt's more to do with Ash.'

I nodded. The cake tasted delicious, so I complimented her.

'The whisky?' she asked, spying me from under her brow. She already knew the answer and was just being a good host.

'In my defence, that was AB's fault,' I said.

'Oh, my dear, I think I know whose fault it was.' She flicked her head to where Ash had gone. 'He can be incorrigible. Whisky and birds are his few pleasures. I don't suppose you know a reasonably priced bird illustrator? He's writing a book on the birds of Suffolk and is determined to have it illustrated, not photographed.'

'I don't, I'm afraid.'

'There's no reason why you should.' She grinned at me. 'Ask Wilf anything to do with the war – the important things, what went on behind closed doors, by whom and to whom – and he will talk the hind legs of a donkey. But ask him to do something simple, like find an illustrator to illustrate a book that has been in the planning stages since the Ark, and you might as well be speaking Chinese.'

She pointed a finger towards the window. A large bird was sitting briefly on the bough of the tree before vanishing behind the new foliage.

We talked about more pleasant things after, and I didn't enquire too much about Wilfried Ash, and she didn't have to evade answering my questions.

We lunched on trout, sautéed potatoes, green beans, and a glass of very nice white wine. We walked a little after, got as far as the Alde before the blow, and a few minutes of horizontal rain forced us to find shelter back in the house. Later, we had afternoon tea while listening to the radio. She read a little, I read a little, and wherever Ash was, I didn't know. The house was silent, except for the wind gusting against the windows. In the pleasant soporific heat, I closed my eyes and dozed for a while. The light was just leaving the sky when Ash returned.

'Julia Natalia Meyer,' he announced triumphantly, and he sat wearily in his armchair. Ginny closed the curtains and poured him a cup of freshly made coffee. 'Born 1905 in Saxony, well educated, excelled in mathematics. One of the few women to study at Humboldt University in Berlin.' He tapped the side of his head. 'She has brains. Married Walter Hildebrandt in June 1932. His was a military family, and he was killed at Kursk. No children. Then, like magic, she vanished at the end of the war.'

He sipped his coffee, ate some cake, and sat back again, the colour returning to his cheeks.

'Why did she vanish?' he asked me. 'Because' – again he tapped the side of his head – 'she had brains. A few too many. The Russians collected her along with others and shipped them all back to the Motherland.'

'How much brains?' I asked.

'Ah, that is the question. Good. Good. Have you heard of electronic cryptanalysis, Alex?'

'I could make a guess at the individual words.'

'Put them together, and you get codes and cyphers. Or more accurately, in her case, how to break them using machines, programmable computers.' He looked across to Ginny and nodded. Whatever passed between them in that nod, I could not guess; only something did, and her eyes brightened. 'That is what she excelled at – designing them – the theory, at least.'

'Can machines think?' Ginny said. 'It was a question a scientist called Turing asked. He dismissed it as meaningless and contemplated a different question instead: *How do we know if a machine thinks?* It's all very abstract.'

'I never knew they could think. It seems fanciful,' I said. 'And what have thinking machines got to do with Hildebrandt?'

'The question, as Ginny says, is abstract,' Ash said, 'but it has relevance in Hildebrandt's work. She has published several papers concerning the problem. Mainly routine stuff, but hinting at more. It's not a case of proving a machine can think; it's more a problem in logic. The Soviets allowed her to continue her work – why wouldn't they? The German military hadn't taken her seriously when they had her. Even when she mathematically proved their unbreakable code could be broken. Teutonic single-mindedness should never be underestimated and should always be relied upon. In March 1948, she remarried. Then, in April 1950, she vanished again.'

He sat back and surveyed me with calm patience, along with a surreptitious smile.

'Natalia Popov?' I said in a hoarse whisper. 'Hildebrandt and she are the same.'

Ash clapped his hands

'Yes. She who has occupied the newspapers of late. Wife of Gregory Popov, a dying Russian physicist. Yes. The thought is her husband contracted cancer when he was accidentally exposed to radiation. Of course, the Russians deny it. The Russians' cavalier attitude towards his illness did not endear her, hence her decision to leave their employment.'

'She defected then – she wasn't kidnapped?'

Ash's face said a number of things, none of which I could read. Instead, he said, 'Ah, that is the question, isn't it? Kidnapped or defected. Or murdered. It's a curious game that is being played.'

'Much of it is in the shadows,' Ginny added.

'German dental work,' I mumbled. I shook my head.

So, Natalia Popov was dead after all. A Russian with German dental work was lying in the mortuary. Why? What went wrong? I looked at Ash for an answer, I suspected he knew what I was thinking, and I was met with a smile. I thought the smile said more than he would.

'Tell me more about this.' Ash held up the sheet of paper I'd given him. 'You mentioned Marx.'

'It belongs to Goel Hadam. I found it in the bedroom of one of their employees.'

'Ah, yes, the dead boy. I can see why Marx would have it. He is building up quite an archive. Only she would not have been tried as a Nazi criminal. She was not involved in that side of their activities, as much as that can be said. Her work was theoretical.'

'It's interesting, then, that Marx should have a file on her.' Ginny's frown accentuated her creased brows. 'It might mean he doesn't know who she is.'

'The file was prepared a while ago, before all of this news about Popov,' Ash said. 'And then the file was taken.'

'That would suggest someone knew who she was, or perhaps suspected she was Popov,' Ginny said. 'Marx would have asked questions about her. That would explain how it came to someone's attention. He knows how to stir a pot.'

'What do you know about that side of Marx's business?' I asked.

'Only that it makes for an interesting paradox that the British government does not want to engage with. More, I can't say.' Ash smiled a slightly reluctant smile with an equally slight shrug.

'Not that they would complain if Goel Hadam were to go away,' Ginny said.

'Now, Alex, tell me again, the rest,' Ash asked, and sat back with his eyes closed to listen.

I explained my commission once more. Hearing it again, I supposed, with his new-found knowledge, gave him different insights. Both he and Ginny were silent, nodding when they should, shaking their heads when they should, always in unison. When I finished, his face was hard.

'It sounds like a cock-up to me,' Ginny said to Ash. She wasn't speaking about my efforts, but about Anna Blau. 'If she's not dead, it sounds as if she should be,' Ginny added dismissively.

'Or she soon will be.' Ash spoke softly. 'But something went wrong.'

I waited for them to remember that I was with them in the room.

'The problem is Popov,' Ash said. It took him a minute to think before he spoke. 'Popov has been courting us and the Americans for a while,' he told me eventually. 'She wanted to defect. But such things we need to think carefully about – they shouldn't be rushed, and this one has been. There are so many games that can be and are played, and I won't go into them.' He grumbled as some thoughts went through his mind. 'She defected a week ago, hence the Russians' accusations of kidnapping – they wouldn't want it to be known that someone left their fold voluntarily. And now she's dead?' Ash stared at Ginny, a questioning stare.

'Alex said something about a car breaking down where the body of Saul Greenberg was found?' said Ginny. 'Do you think Popov was in the car?'

'Then how did her body end up in the Thames?' I asked. 'The car was heading north, away from the river.'

'Yes,' Ash said thoughtfully. 'The boy's death raises so many questions.'

'That Anna Blau hasn't been found dead raises even more,' Ginny said. 'So, Popov and Blau are connected?'

Ash rubbed his chin. 'Their disappearances, not them personally.'

'And Alex visiting us will not have gone unnoticed,' Ginny said. 'You do know that?'

Ash mumbled, neither to me nor Ginny. 'Things will move apace if that is the case.'

'Alex needs to find the car.'

'You might be right,' Ash said. 'Aren't there photographs of it? Isn't that what Latimer is asking about? Who has them?' It wasn't a question for me, but for Ginny. 'Yes, Alex, you need to discover the who to find Anna Blau. Unfortunately, we can't help you there.'

'But we will do what we can.' Ginny smiled at me.

I wasn't sure what they had just said or how they knew Latimer was enquiring about the possibility of photographs existing. That, I hadn't mentioned. But I knew then how I came to his attention. Someone I had spoken to in my enquires about Hildebrandt had spoken to Ash. Whatever was happening, he was already involved. I knew enough to not ask any more. I knew they would not tell me.

'And about Hauptmann Grunwald?' I asked instead.

Ash harrumphed. 'A nasty man, if half the stories are true. I don't know much about him, but I can guess; his recent history is all I have to go on. But you and Mr Marx have stirred up quite a hornets' nest as far as he's concerned.'

'I don't understand.'

'Some people can't be touched,' Ginny said. 'Best leave him be.'

'I'm not looking for him.'

'Even so, the damage has been done,' Ginny said. 'It's a brave new world, Alex, and he's been given a niche in it. Maybe Marx can do something.'

Little more was said. Ash looked pale. His tiredness was evident, and he retired early. Afterwards, Ginny and I chatted pleasantly before it was time to go.

She drove me to Ipswich and dropped me off by the train station. She waited with me until the train came, and as I boarded, she said, 'He'll never finish his book, Alex. He's dying. A few people who don't know him as well as I do might say he's found religion. But he cares that Anna Blau is mixed up with all of this, and he wants to do right by her before it is too late.'

'He seems to be able to make phone calls, and people jump. Why can't he do that with Anna?'

'It's not like the old days. When you're out of the game, you're out of the game. Ash's been sidelined and has been since the end of the war. They want a new breed of warriors to fight a new kind of war, but Ash knows it's the same old game, just packaged differently. The war has bred too many independents, as he calls them. There is an information problem he wants to deal with. Popov is part of it, but there are others he's more concerned about. It's his chance to contribute before he can't anymore. Call Wilfried if you need to speak to him – day or night, any hour. He's in bed but not asleep. He's a ferocious insomniac.'

Perhaps it was paranoia on my part, but there was a warning in her voice.

* * *

I was back in London a few hours later, and after a quick underground ride, I was back in my flat. I finished the remains of a bottle of wine and nibbled salty biscuits before going to bed, my mind a jumble.

The jumble was what Ash and Ginny didn't tell me. People like them like to play games. I played those games once, so I knew. I also knew there were no rules. In their profession, everyone had an agenda. Sure enough, Ash had one. Whether it'd help Anna Blau, I didn't know.

# Chapter 18

I awoke to sunlight streaming through the window. My mouth felt like sandpaper. I drank a glass of water and then a cup of coffee. After a bath, I fixed myself a fried breakfast and wolfed it down. Then I began wading through the dirty dishes. It had been a while since I'd had someone over, and I'd become lazy. The flat smacked of my office.

There was a stack of newspapers that I'd meant to take to the bin but forgot. I collected them, skipped down the cold linoleum floor in my walking shoes and bathrobe, and went outside to the bins. The paperboy, who was just climbing the front steps, eyed me with a smirk. I gave him my harshest stare, and he went red. He averted his eyes, mumbled an apology, passed me the newspaper, and hurried down the steps. His rush didn't stop him from taking one last glance over his shoulder.

Once I'd put the rubbish into the bins and closed the front door, I glanced at the newspaper he'd delivered. Natalia Popov was all over the front page. The Russians were screaming, and questions were being asked about whether the streets of London were safe. The photograph accompanying the article was an old one of Chief Inspector Latimer, taken on one of his better days. In the best tradition of Scotland Yard, he'd promised to catch her killer.

I flicked through the rest of the newspaper until I reached the city news and stopped. Not a single paragraph about either Saul Greenberg or Anna Blau. That's how the world works: you have to be someone to make the news, dead or alive.

I was about to put the paper on the small table by the telephone when Jeff's door opened a crack, then swung open further, and Jeff popped his head out. He glanced down at my walking shoes and grinned at me.

'Morning, Alex. Not going out like that, are you?'

'Didn't you know it's all the rage?' I handed him his newspaper and nodded at the telephone. 'Got a couple of pennies, Jeff?'

'Righto!' He popped inside, and a second later, he reappeared with two.

'Thanks.'

I dialled Whitehall 1212 and managed to get through to Chief Inspector Latimer's office.

'Are you sure you and Brody aren't seeing things?' Latimer barked as soon as he heard my voice. He sounded like a man who hadn't slept well.

'And good morning to you, Chief Inspector,' I said brightly.

'Well?' He grunted.

'What aren't we seeing?'

'A van parked outside the Fascist League?'

I waited to let him speak, and for a moment, neither of us said anything.

Jeff smiled at me, and I smiled back. He suddenly realised he was eavesdropping. He waved his newspaper at me and quietly shut the door behind him. I had a feeling he'd have his ear to the panels anyway.

I broke our silence and asked, 'So, what about the van?'

'There isn't one,' Latimer continued. 'And more to the point, Special Branch has not had the League under surveillance beyond the usual.'

'What can I tell you?' I said. 'We saw what we saw. Anyway, is Special Branch going to tell you what they know?' He and I both knew the answer.

'All right,' he moaned, followed by another painful silence. 'Good morning, Alex. How may I help you?' He said it politely, if somewhat forcefully.

'You can't. I've called to help you. Natalia Popov is German. That answers your question about her dental work.'

'What? How the hell did you know that?'

'I'm either psychic or I met up with someone who knew.' I wasn't about to tell him it was Wilfried Ash. Latimer knew him, or at least knew of him, and I was sure Ash wouldn't want his involvement broadcast.

'What's this *someone* got to do with her death?'

'Nothing, as far as I know. See if you've got any records on Julia Natalia Hildebrandt, née Meyer. The people you mixed with during the war will have them. If your bosses haven't told you, that'll explain who she is and why her wedding ring is in Russian.'

The silence seemed to last a year. He was putting two and two together and figuring out who the someone was, if not his exact identity, but what they did.

'Is this anything to do with Anna Blau?' he asked eventually.

'I think it is, but I don't know why.'

'You have some suspicions…'

'I have a thought.'

'But you're not going to tell me.'

'I have rumours only. When I know more, I'll tell you.'

He gave a grudging thank-you and said his goodbyes.

I spent the next hour tidying the flat and thinking about what Latimer had said. I was hoping to hear from Ginny

Bright but I also needed to find out why the van wasn't there.

I'd left late for work, well past rush hour, so the journey was comfortable. I picked up my letters at the street entrance hallway of my building, climbed the stairs, and surveyed the mess that was the office. I sat down with the newspaper I found when I travelled in on the Tube until the desire to do a spring clean passed. Then I called my messenger service, and Polly answered.

'Hi, lovely,' she said in her brightest voice. 'You're in demand today. Right. First call Mr Arnold; he's got a job for you. Says he's in the office all day, and it's not a divorce. A Mr Cramer called to say the Fernley case is being settled out of court, so he'll not need your man to give any evidence, and can he have the negative? Is the case a bit tasty?'

'Sixty-year-old man with an eighteen-year-old girl.'

'Sounds like my uncle Bert, the dirty old sod. Lastly, you're to meet a Mrs Bright in Victoria Park at one. She's got something to show you. She sounded very mysterious. You better get your skates on, lovely; it's nearly twelve now.'

'Anywhere particular in the park? It's a rather big place.'

'I'm getting there! In the pedestrian alcove. I asked!' she said quickly before I could say anything. '*The Pedestrian Alcove*, she said, as if everyone knew it. Looks like you're gonna have to put on your detective hat and find it. Oh, and you're to come alone. Very dramatic, I must say. If it's any help, she sounded nervous… At least that's what my detective brain said.'

Mr Arnold could wait; his jobs were never urgent, even though he made them out to be so. I'd get to Cramer after Martha gave me the negative. Before leaving, I telephoned a cab driver I knew, Theo Drakas. He didn't have a phone, but his next-door neighbour did. I left a message that I might need him tonight and would appreciate it if he could keep his diary free. Then I left for the park.

# Chapter 19

It was a little after half past twelve when I got to the park. I'd paid little attention to the few people I'd arrived with, but it quickly became clear that the few had multiplied. A crowd was gathering, sporting all the qualities of a mob. I tagged along behind them, heading towards the middle of the park. A few carried banners: *Freedom not Fascism*; *Civilization not Nazism*; *Remember Auschwitz*.

It was then that I remembered Latimer's warning to keep out of the park.

One of the wardens, an elderly man in dungarees and a flat cap, said there were two alcoves, and he proceeded to give me not only their direction but their history. He was talking nervously, all the while eyeing the gathering crowd with apprehension. In a fit of pique, he spat his disgust openly on the ground.

'My boy was captured at Dunkirk,' he said. 'The Nazi bastards are meeting at the fountain.' He looked around at the anti-fascist demonstrators gathering. 'They plan to march to Whitechapel. I don't reckon they'll get out of the park at this rate.'

I left him, and he retreated to one of the entrances. I thought he had good sense. I wondered about mine as I headed deeper into Victoria Park.

A deep murmur had arisen amongst the demonstrators that fell away to an unearthly hush. In the sudden quiet, I could hear the birds sing. Another crowd was approaching, and everyone's gaze was drawn to them. This one was disciplined. They were marching to the beat of drums. A big banner spanned their width with the sharp lightning logo of the Fascist League. Soon, angry voices began to rise around me, until they became a deafening roar.

A dozen mounted policemen waited patiently a short distance away, trailed by a swarm of others on foot. Three groups were about to converge at the site where an ornate Victorian fountain stood. The police, despite the heavy artillery of the horses, looked decidedly outnumbered.

I weaved my way past the crowd, heading towards one of the two alcoves at the other end of the park. It was away from the fountain, away from the trouble, I hoped. Ginny Bright would have to find me if I went to the wrong one. The knots of bodies in front of me soon became densely packed, making progress difficult. I backtracked and went to one side, skirting them. As I pushed past, a hand grabbed my arm, and I spun around in fright.

'Miss Raven, you came. Is Mr Brody with you?'

I was looking into the eyes of Bruno Marx where something dark and dangerous lurked. His mouth twisted into a fractured smile that wasn't meant for me. I could sense the anticipation it held; it was feral. He was dressed in a black sweater, trousers, and boots. Behind him were a dozen men similarly attired. A few were slipping on balaclavas. Several dour-faced women stood behind them, carrying soft handheld bags – like everyone else, their eyes were gazing towards the sound of the drums. I saw bandages inside one half-open bag. A fight was in the air, and Marx had come prepared.

I shook my head, I'd come alone.

'That's a pity, he looked like he could handle himself. I can't say you're exactly dressed for it. Best you keep out of the way.' Suddenly, he stabbed a finger towards the approaching group. 'Him. Between the drummers. Him!' He barked at his men, and their eyes mechanically followed where his finger pointed. 'There's going to be some blood today, Miss Raven.'

He'd said it with relish, and I didn't doubt him.

Bruno Marx was a big man when he was seated behind his desk and when he wasn't, bigger still. He meant business. He gestured to a few of his men like a general directing his troops, because that was exactly what he was and what they were. Some slipped away, taking up their positions. He did the same, moving as gracefully as a leopard dressed in black. Marx didn't notice me leave. He'd already forgotten I was there. His eyes were gazing across the heads of the crowd. Something cunning played on his face.

The Fascist League marched in four columns, with drummers at the head of each. An imposing man in what could pass for a uniform swaggered in front of them. Several others, dressed likewise, flanked him. The Union Jack fluttered in the breeze in their middle, along with another flag, the one with a circle and a sharp zigzag arrow striking through it. In ten minutes, the two forces would collide. In between them would be the police, who had started to move forward. They'd need reinforcements to deal with what was about to happen.

I edged away, moving quickly. The alcove, a semi-circular stone archway with benches inside against the walls, was a shelter from the rain, but not the type of rain that soon would be falling. I hoped Ginny Bright would arrive quickly; I didn't fancy being caught in the downpour, either for my sake or hers.

As I reached it, the two groups met with a roar. If the Fascist League thought they'd be making speeches today, they were sadly mistaken. Taken by surprise at the suddenness, the police moved forward with a charge. Soon, a battle erupted, spilling out everywhere I looked. It was easy to spot Marx. The big man had found his quarry, the uniformed man at the head of the League. Marx was raining blows on him. Around him, his men were busy clearing the way for his assault.

I looked around nervously. Five minutes passed. The fight was coming closer, and some people fled. The dusky-faced women were busy bandaging and patching up the wounded with makeshift field dressings, seemingly oblivious to the carnage around them. They carried the air of people well used to this sort of affair.

My worry increased as the battle drifted wider and threatened to engulf me. Where was she? There were two alcoves; was she in the other one? Why meet here, and today of all days? My head was full of questions, and my heart was thumping. My mouth had dried, and I felt exposed all of a sudden. Victoria Park was no place to be, not today. I just hoped what Ginny Bright had for me was important. Knowing Wilfried Ash, it would be.

Suddenly, a group of men broke away and started running in my direction. Another group pursued them from behind. Who was who was difficult to tell, yet somehow they knew. They caught up with each other just beyond where I hid and became a mix of fists and feet. Two mounted policemen turned towards them, intent on driving through them. The horses neighed nervously and foamed at the bit, their flanks glistening with sweat.

It was a glimpse – no more than that from the corners of my eye – of three figures rushing towards me. Even as I turned my head, they were on me. I was slammed back against the wall of the stone alcove. A tirade of anti-Semitic abuse exploded around me, followed by blows. I struck out, kicking and punching, only to be dragged deeper into the alcove. Suddenly, one of my attackers screamed, twisted around, and vanished out of sight. A heavy bellow followed. Two others had joined the fight, but on my side. I elbowed the person with his arm around my neck. As he fell away, I spun around, swinging my fist and striking him firmly – a right cross that Jane Windlass would have been proud of. I was about to do it again when, at that moment, I was sent sprawling to the ground. When I looked up, my attackers were gone. As soon as it had begun, it was over.

I glanced to each side, suddenly aware that someone was laughing – and laughing at me. I was about to snarl abuse when I saw it was Charlie Mathers. Grinning like some wild-haired madman, leaning back on his outstretched arms, legs akimbo, he was staring up at me. A dribble of blood ran from his nose.

'Blimey, it's the lady burglar. I thought it was you.' He wiped his nose on his sleeve, looked at the blood, and grinned even more wildly. 'Stone me, I ain't had a dust-up like that since God knows when.'

'What's so bloody funny?' I shouted. I was breathing deeply, from the very bottom of my lungs, trying to get as much oxygen into me as I could. My heart was pounding. I felt my head twitch with each pump.

'My pleasure, I'm sure.' He cocked his head sideways, but the inane grin remained. 'I knew you were a tartar; you certainly fight like one. You probably didn't need my help.'

He grabbed my arm and hauled me deeper into the alcove just as two mounted policemen rode past. The horses neighed in excitement, their hooves stamping the ground. Their riders pushed them forward and through another fight happening on the path. The weight of the animals scattering the men.

'Get up, you bleedin' cherub,' shouted Charlie's friend, the one who came to the Greenbergs' flat to turn the gas off. 'The rozzers are arresting people.'

Above the shouts, the sounds of police whistles echoed. People were being dragged away.

'Damn bad manners of them, what?' Charlie said it in a posh accent, almost falling backwards with laughter.

'Now. We have to leg it. She'd better come with us if she doesn't want to spend the night in the nick.'

‘Go on the run with her?’ His eyes gaped wide in mock horror. ‘No way, Pongo.’ He pointed at my legs. ‘Her seams ain’t straight. I ain’t going on the run with someone with crooked seams.’

Charlie Mathers was laughing as Pongo hauled him to his feet.

# Chapter 20

I tagged behind Charlie and Pongo as they cleared the way. I couldn't see Marx or his men, and I guessed they'd left, having achieved what they set out to do. That seemed to be busting a few heads. Or one at least. I could see where they left him, surrounded by a few battered supporters. The Fascist League gave all the appearance of being military, but it was all show. They weren't as well trained or as disciplined as Marx's men, nor, I reckon, did they have their experience. Not only that, they didn't seem as determined.

Little fights were erupting all around us. Along with Charlie and Pongo, I dodged and fended off bodies, carving a path through the throng while making for the exit. I nearly lost them on a few occasions, but somehow managed to find them again. We exited the park along with several others, escaping the melee. Behind us, by the fountain, the mounted police were driving through the ranks of protestors, fascist and anti-fascist alike, and swinging batons, cracking heads as they went.

We found Pongo's van and climbed in. I was sandwiched between them on the bench seat. Pongo drove. We left to the sound of ringing bells announcing the arrival of police reinforcements. Charlie was still grinning. He'd obviously enjoyed himself.

I swivelled the driver's mirror around so that I could look at my face. My hair was a mess, and I sported a slight bruise on my left cheek. Otherwise, I was fine. I heaved a sigh of relief and hoped Ginny Bright got out of the park unscathed. I wondered what she wanted to tell me that was so urgent. Surely, a phone call would have sufficed.

Pongo lived across the river in South London. Since it'd be too much of a diversion to go north to take me home, he said he'd go to Charlie's flat and drop us off there. When we arrived, Charlie and I got out, and he spent a few minutes talking to Pongo before giving him a proper, stiff army salute, complete with a stamping foot.

'Yes, sir, Carruthers,' Charlie joked, putting on his posh accent again. 'We gave the native a damn seeing to, what ho, old boy!'

Pongo rolled his eyes as he drove away, and Charlie turned to me, still grinning.

Charlie surprised me, not least of all because he lived in Pimlico and in a mansion block. The red-brick Edwardian building extended unapologetically sideways a considerable distance and was four storeys high. Gable windows at the very top gazed silently across the roofs towards Buckingham Palace. A flight of stairs led up from the street to a pair of ornately panelled doors beneath a stone arch. A polished parquet floor took you inside to a wire cage lift. The staircase wound around it. It was one of those places where your footsteps echoed, it smelled of nothing, and there were pigeon holes for your mail. Back in the day, it would have had a concierge to keep out the riff-raff.

'Slumming it, I see,' I said.

Charlie looked around, put on a down on my luck face, and winked. 'That's me,' he said, laughing.

We took the lift to the third floor, to flat thirty-three.

Inside, the small hallway had several doors leading off it. One led to the living room. I entered. It was almost thirty feet long, with wall-to-wall carpet and heavy, old-fashioned furniture that was darkly rich. Oil paintings hugged the walls. A weak sun had decided to reappear and was spreading its rays through the windows, leaving three amber rectangles on the floor and dust motes dancing in the air. Charlie nodded towards the cabinet of drinks in the corner.

'Fix yourself a snifter,' he said. 'Mine's a whisky and soda. Light on the soda. Put some music on while I sort out my face.'

'A new shirt would help,' I said, taking off my coat and laying it across the back of a leather settee.

'Light a fire as well,' he shouted.

'The maid's day off is it, or did you work the last one to death?'

He popped his head around the door. 'Sorry, wasn't that the job you applied for?'

There was a box of matches on the mantelpiece and a gas fire below. I kneeled, turned the gas tap, and struck the match. There was a soft pop, and the grating hummed.

I opened the cabinet, searched through the small army of bottles, found what I wanted, and poured two glasses and squirted soda into them. I flicked through the record collection, mainly classical with a smattering of jazz, before putting on a Mantovani album. Soothing, cascading strings filled the room. Then I eased into a chair. Five minutes later, Charlie came back in a clean shirt with cotton wool protruding from one nostril.

'Cheers, my dear,' he said and tipped half the glass into his mouth, followed by a sigh of satisfaction.

'What's the story?' I asked, nodding around. 'Got this on a gas man's salary, or did you win the pools?'

'No chance of either. Me gran's. Her old man made a mint from selling shares, or was it in the white slave trade? They never did say, and I was always her favourite. She died last year and left it to me. The charges are shocking! An arm and a leg to change the light bulbs in the hallway.'

'Shocking. Just surviving, then.'

'With the death duties – trust me, it's a hard life,' he joked and swooned a small display of theatre sinking into the leather settee opposite me. He rested a socked foot on a knee and pointed to me with his glass. 'You can handle yourself. You was giving as good as you was getting. I wasn't going to interfere, but Pongo said I should. It'd help them blokes out with their story down the pub later, Pongo said. How can they tell they got spanked by a woman? Here's to you, Genghis Raven.' He took a sip of his drink.

'You didn't do too bad yourself. How's the nose?'

'Not broken. I still got me good looks. If that ladder in your stocking's bothering you, by the way, I can always help you take them off.'

'I'm a big girl; I'm sure I'll manage on my own. But thanks for the offer.'

'Well, don't say I didn't ask. Ever the gentleman is Charlie. Why was you down there in the park?'

'That's what I've been asking myself.' I sat back, and the chair wrapped itself around me like comfortable arms. I stretched my stockinged feet out to the fire, wiggling my toes in the heat. 'I was meant to meet someone who didn't show.'

'Can't blame them. Well, I hope your friend's okay – we could have looked for them if you'd told us.'

'Not a friend.' He gave me a curious look. 'Someone who had some information for me and arranged to meet me there.'

'Eh? Information?' The curious look became curiouser still. 'You're kidding me, ain't you?' He grinned, this time showing his teeth as he leaned forward. 'What are you, a lady copper?'

'Yes, yes, you can arrest me anytime, said the bishop to the actress, blah, blah, blah. And the rest,' I said with a smile, and his face and body creased up into laughter.

'I wasn't going to say that.' He winked. 'Honest! Was that why you was at Mr Greenberg's flat? There was I joking about you turning it over.'

I fiddled with my handbag, found one of my cards, and passed it to him. He whistled a soft note.

'I am impressed! Not a lady cop, but a private one. *Alexandra Raven, Private Enquiry Agent.* Posh, I'm sure.' He tucked it into his breast pocket and patted it. 'So, who was it you were meeting? An informer?'

'I don't know. I think she decided to swap places with the three goons who attacked me.'

'A set-up!' He nodded. 'You should have shot them.'

'It's against the law to carry a gun.'

'Come on,' he said, and he eased himself further forward so he was perched on the chair. 'Not even a cute little .22? Kept in a holster in your garter?' He tipped his head sideways, pretending to look up my skirt, grinned, and then fell back again laughing.

'Yeah, yeah, and the rest. You watch too many movies, Charlie.'

'Well, I can't say you look like a *gumshoe*.'

'I'll take that as a compliment, shall I? Do you know many? What about you? What were you doing there?'

'Pongo and me had a job in the flats where the van was parked. A leak. I was curious when I saw the crowds. Soon as I knew what it was about, I knew there'd be a fight.' He swallowed the rest of his drink and rose to pour himself another. I'd only taken a few sips of mine. 'There's no love lost between me and those Nazi bastards. I didn't get torpedoed twice for nothing.'

'No love lost with me either,' I said.

'You never got torpedoed as well?' he said in mock amazement.

'Of course not, you twerp.' I flicked my eyes at the ceiling. 'I just got something against people who drop bombs on me. God, you're fresh, aren't you?'

'Life's too short, Alexandra, and someone once said you're dead a long time after.' His face had lost its grin. 'Seriously. There's a good show at the Empire… if you fancy it?'

I screwed my face up in a friendly *I'm not sure* sort of way, and he sighed in the same way, looking like a lost little kid.

I checked my watch. 'Can I make a phone call?' I asked.

''Course. Help yourself.' His eyes flicked to where the phone was. 'I'll go and fix my make-up,' he said, leaving me alone.

I called my messenger service. What had happened in Victoria Park occupied my mind. There was always the possibility that I wasn't set up after all. What do they say about flying pigs? I was hoping to speak to Polly, who'd taken the message, but this time, the voice that answered was older and spoke a no-nonsense King's English.

'There are two messages, Miss Raven. A Mrs Geller said to tell you Mr Blau would like to see you when you have some time. And a Mr Marx has asked for you to ring him at his home number,' and she gave me it.

I called Marx, and his breathless voice answered.

'Alex, I was worried,' he said. 'Things got a bit dicey back in the park. I hope you're okay.'

'I had a spot of trouble, but I'm fine.'

'Good, good, good. I'm glad to hear that. Now, we are going to pay your good friend, Captain Otto Grunwald, a visit later today. He's addressing a meeting of businessmen, and we are going to see him, if you know what I mean?'

I did.

'You work fast, finding him.'

'We have our ways. Now, can you be there?'

'I'm not sure. Let me have the address, and I'll see.'

He gave it to me, and I wrote it down on a pad Charlie kept beside the phone, and he rang off. I wondered if Marx would be dressed in black when he met with the good captain.

I placed the phone down, chewed my cheeks, and spent thirty seconds thinking about why Ginny Bright hadn't contacted me rather than what Marx had said. I began to wonder why she'd set me up. If she hadn't, and the pigs were flying again, what had she to show me, and why couldn't it be in my office?

I heard Charlie come back.

'Problems?' he asked. He was fiddling with his nose, the cotton wool no longer there, and practicing breathing through his damaged nostril by placing a finger against the other one and making a snorting sound.

I tore the sheet of paper off the pad and folded it into my hand.

'Just the usual,' I said. 'A man I'm curious about is going to get a visit from some friends of mine today. Who's on at the Empire?'

'Let's see. George Formby might do a turn, that's the promise, with Flanagan and Allen, a sort of wartime tribute show… *I'm going to hang out the washing on the old lamp post* sort of thing. Is the ice melting? Do I detect a thaw? Listen, I can get us into rehearsals – don't ask how! I have friends in high places,' he said in a mocking, pompous way.

'I could do with cheering up. So maybe.'

His face brightened, and his eyes seemed to sparkle.

'I'm good at cheering people up,' he said. 'I used to be in the cheering-up detail in the navy. Tomorrow. What says you? We can get in tomorrow.'

'Only if you can keep your hands to yourself. Otherwise, I'll shoot you.'

'Promise.' He crossed his heart. 'Might be worth it, though, just to see you take your gun out from your garter.

So, tell me about this case you're working on. What it's like being a private investigator.'

'Another time, Charlie – it's all too bloody depressing at the moment. I ain't thanked you, by the way. It was a good thing you and Pongo turned up when you did back at the park. I didn't fancy another black eye so soon after the last.'

He dipped a hand inside his trouser pocket and brought out a pack of cigarettes and a lighter.

'Then tell me about that then, and I'll make us some omelettes. I'm a good cook. You have to be when you live alone. Then I'll drive you home. You'll have to sing for your supper, though. Deal?'

'Deal,' I said. I was hungry and could use company at the moment.

''ere, I thought you was washing your hair,' he said suddenly.

'It'll keep.'

'Mum used to do hers in beer. She said it was good for its lustre. Dad drank it afterwards.' He grinned.

'You were that poor. I suppose you lived in a shoe.'

'Don't you get me started.' Charlie gave me a severe stare. 'It was a boot, actually.'

Charlie flicked the top of the pack open and shook out a cigarette with one hand, the other still holding his glass. He brought the pack up to his lips, pulling one out. Throwing the pack onto the table, he clicked the lighter. His eyes had narrowed, showing the creases at the corners as he studied my face. He inhaled and exhaled a full breath of smoke across the room, away from me. His smile had returned as he left to go to the kitchen.

# Chapter 21

I resisted Charlie's charms and declined his offer to drive me home after we ate. Instead, I caught a bus and then another to reach David Blau's house. The surprise was to see Inspector Dickens. The car he was in, driven by Sergeant Brown, was about to pull away when he saw me. It stopped, and Dickens wound down the window. The look on his face wasn't pretty. He greeted me in his usual friendly way.

'What're you doing here, Raven?'

'You're forgetting, David Blau's my client. More to the point, what are *you* doing here?' I asked.

He mumbled something incoherent, then stabbed a finger at me.

'You tell the old git the next time he reports a burglary he better make sure there is one. The only reason I'm not doing him for wasting police time is because his daughter's missing. But the next time, I'll haul his arse to the nearest nick.'

'You're all heart, Dickie.'

'And for tuppence, I'll haul yours in as well.'

'Look, this is me trembling.' I started to walk away.

'What're you staring at?' Dickens barked at Brown as he wound the window up.

David Blau answered my knock. He did it as if he thought it was Dickens knocking. Anger, which could have been fear, left his face when he saw it was me.

'What did Dickens mean there's no burglary?' I asked.

He led me to the sitting room, where Miriam Geller was seated. She stood up when she saw me.

'Mrs Geller.' I acknowledged her with a nod. 'What's all this about a burglary?'

She looked across to Blau. 'I don't know exactly. But David thinks there was one.'

'*Thinks* there was one? What does that mean? What was taken?'

'That's the point, Alex,' she said. 'Nothing.'

I glanced around the room. There was hardly anything of value to take, and from what I remembered of the rest of the flat, it was the same.

'It's just that David thinks someone was here, inside the house. Things have been moved and rearranged, especially in Anna's room.'

'Did you tidy up since I was last here?' I asked Blau.

He shook his head and eased himself wearily down into the old, battered armchair. He placed his hands, palms down, on the coffee table and stared at them. From my angle, his head was all skin stretched tightly across hard bone. The fight had gone from him.

I went to Anna's room. Mrs Geller followed.

I couldn't detect anything different from when I last saw the room. It was only when I opened the drawers and checked inside the wardrobe that I noticed they were a little untidier than I remembered. The money box was still on the mantelpiece; it still contained the pound note and change. If it was a burglary, it was an odd burglary. Mrs Geller saw the look on my face.

'He thinks someone has been here, Alex,' she said again. 'David doesn't understand why nothing's been taken. Nor do I.'

'He reported it to the police?'

'It was me that called them. I felt he ought to. He didn't want to, but I insisted.'

'I can see why Dickens wasn't pleased.'

I spent a half hour with David and Mrs Geller. I kept my thoughts private, unsure what to make of them. Anna's room had been searched. Saul's room also. His room, for what he'd taken from Goel Hadam. I wondered if Anna's was for the same reason. Were Saul and Anna working together? I shook my head. Saul was spending the money he'd made. If Anna was working with him, she wasn't spending any. The thought that my flat had also been searched came to mind. I had the distinct feeling that someone had been inside; nothing looked disturbed – it was just a feeling. But I had no files from Goel Hadam to hide.

I left David and Mrs Geller and headed back to Soho and my office. It was dark by the time I arrived. I briefly considered meeting Marx. He was a curiosity I'd like to know more about, especially how he operated. For the little I knew of him, I suspected Hauptmann Grunwald was in for a nasty shock.

At that hour, the street was quiet and bathed in shadow. The building was more or less empty; only a few lights remained to show someone was still there. The plain-clothed policeman waiting beside the entrance of the building took me by surprise. I knew who he was even before he opened his palm to show me his warrant card. He indicated for me to go to a car parked across the road. It was a gracious invitation. I saw no need to refuse it.

I don't know how long the black Worsley had been waiting, but it'd been there a while. On the ground by the back-passenger door were the butts of a half-dozen cigarettes. Someone was patient. The window rolled down when I got there. The gentleman inside tipped his hat but didn't invite me in.

‘Miss Raven; working late?’ he asked. It was a polite way to begin a conversation, if that’s what we were going to have.

‘I’m a busy little bee. Buzzing here. Buzzing there.’

‘That’s good to hear. Don’t buzz where you shouldn’t. Anna Blau is your concern; why don’t you keep it that way?’

‘I’m not sure what you mean.’

‘Then let me be clear. The past really is the past, and it’s the future you should be thinking of. People like Otto Grunwald, for instance, aren’t anyone’s concern and you should just forget him.’

‘Who’s this Otto Grunwald?’ I asked.

‘See, that’s the spirit; you’re picking it up already.’

‘I only know a Nazi by that name. A particularly foul little man who might look good wearing a rope as a tie. Did he have a good day, today?’

He gave a tired sigh and tipped his hat politely.

‘Stick to what you know and what you’ve been asked to do; there’s a good little detective.’

The window was wound up, and the car pulled away. He wasn’t in the mood to talk anymore.

I’d seen the gentleman before. He was looking out of the window of the League’s office the day Jack and I passed by. And he’d come all that way to tell me to back off. I wondered why.

# Chapter 22

I should have gone home. That would've been the sensible thing to do. Take Jeff's dog for a walk, feed the neighbour's cat, have a drink, listen to some music, or take a bath and go to bed. But too many things troubled me.

I went up to the office instead, locked the door to shut out the world, and sat brooding at my desk. Then I added up all those things that troubled me.

Number one: Saul's death. It wasn't so much that he was dead as it was that Anna wasn't, or if she was, why wasn't she at the bomb site with Saul? It didn't make sense to kill her elsewhere.

Then, Natalia Popov, or Hildebrandt, or Meyer, or whatever her bloody name was, and Wilfried Ash's interest. She was dead. Saul knew about her; why else have her file?

The Greenberg break-in was a search disguised as vandalism. Only whoever Saul worked for would do that. He was hiding it from them, or hadn't yet handed it over.

Since Anna and Saul's rooms had been searched, it only tied them closer together. That brought me back to Popov, the car which Ginny Bright said I needed to find, and the piece of paper, the front sheet with her name on it, a part of a bigger file.

Latimer, saying Special Branch denied any knowledge of surveillance of the Fascist League, threw me off. Who then was spying on them – assuming the Branch hadn't fobbed Latimer off. Ginny was right. I needed to find out. I was determined to do so tonight. Hopefully, I'd get some answers.

But I didn't trust Ash, even less Ginny Bright. I knew they used people, despite their good manners. It's all part and parcel of their *business.* But why would she set me up? Why did I get the feeling I was being played?

And then there was the gentleman in the car waiting for me, warning me off Otto Grunwald. Too many things were connected with Goel Hadam and Marx's little hobby.

Things would move apace, said Wilfried Ash. What things? What did he know?

I made coffee and called Ash before doing anything else. It was time to get some of the mess out of my brain and into the open.

'It's nice to hear from you so soon,' Ash said. His genial voice sounded full of surprise.

'Ginny called my messenger service. She wanted to meet in Victoria Park. What did she want?' I asked. My voice was hard, and I didn't want him to miss my indignance.

'*Want*, Alex?'

'Yes, want. What was so important she couldn't tell me over the phone?'

'Meet you?' He went quiet in his confusion. Almost half a minute of silence followed until I heard Ginny Bright's voice on the telephone.

'I never called you, Alex,' she said.

It was my turn to fall silent. Then I explained what happened at the park.

'No, it wasn't me,' she said. 'I've been here all day. You're well, aren't you?'

'Just some bruises, that's all.'

'Yes. I expect,' she said enigmatically.

There was little else to say after that. If it was true, then it left a whole lot more to think about. Then the truth would always be a moveable feast with people like Ash and Bright.

It took me two phone calls to reach Marx. He sounded none too pleased. The meeting Grunwald was due to attend had been cancelled at the eleventh hour. Marx arrived only to find the hall empty but for a few businessmen who hadn't received notice it'd been called off. It worried him that his source, the one who informed him that the good captain would be there, now had a bed in the local hospital for the next few weeks. Like I said, he wasn't pleased. Maybe I should have told him about my visitor outside my building, but I didn't.

I called Theo Drakas's neighbour. The little Greek taxi driver had done several favours for me over the years, and I asked him to pick me up from the office. He said yes with no hesitation. One day, I'm going to have to get a car. I couldn't keep relying on favours, even if they were given easily.

With that done, I spent a few minutes looking out of the window. A slight mist was forming. Lights were burning in odd windows where the odd person worked late, and below me, the street was quiet. I checked my watch. I had some hours to wait.

There's a camp bed in a small side room in my office. Occasionally, when I have to, I use it. In a small dresser, there's a change of clothes. Curling up on the bed, I drew a blanket across me, determined to give my mind a rest. The alarm was already set. My sleep was on and off; I wasn't tired enough, and at ten, when the alarm sounded, I got up, dressed in a pair of black slacks, a black cable-knit sweater, and black sneakers. There was some bread and cheese for a light snack, and I made some coffee. I ate seated in front of the electric fire. I felt chilly, even though the night was warm.

When I finished eating, I found my black leather gloves, a roll of halfpennies, a small torchlight, a small black plastic case of lock picks, and a Minox Riga camera with a 50mm lens. I tied my hair back, found a black balaclava, and went downstairs. I slipped out to meet Theo, waiting in the shadow of the doorway. Ten minutes later, right on time, a London black cab swung around the corner and parked beside me.

Theo looked me up and down with sharp eyes before reaching a hand out the driver's window to open the passenger door. I climbed in.

'*Yassou*,' he said. 'You look good in black.' His eyes glinting mischievously as he watched me.

'Red's more my colour,' I said.

'Don't you believe it. Where to, *m'lady*?' He was looking at me through the driver's mirror; wide, brown cow eyes large in his thin, bony face.

'You know where the office of the Fascist League is?'

His eyes widened, then narrowed, and steadied on me. He raked his fingers through his jet-black hair, flattened across his head with Brylcreem. 'A bit late to call on those bastards, isn't it?'

'The later the better, but it's not them I'm seeing. Drop me a few streets away and wait.'

Theo considered me for a moment, and then his hand delved inside the glovebox and took out something. He slid back the dividing glass between us and held it up over his shoulders for me without looking back. He clicked something, and a six-inch steel blade sprang out.

'Useful?' he asked.

I shook my head.

'Not tonight.' I patted the roll of halfpennies in my trouser pocket. 'I brought my own friend. But thanks for the thought.'

We drove away with the meter off.

We'd gone a little over a mile when Theo turned the cab sharply north. He stopped at a crossroad, indicated left, lingered a while, and turned right as if he'd changed his mind. At the lights, he dallied up, and as it turned from green to orange, he accelerated through the red, turning sharply right once past the junction. I was thrown about in the back.

'You lost?' I said.

'You expecting company?' he asked.

I glanced through the back window.

'A black sedan.' He called out a number plate. 'Can't make it out properly. I turn right, and he turns right. I slow down, he slows down. Get the picture?'

I couldn't make it out in the darkness; all I could see were its headlights bumping up and down behind us. When I did get a view, the street lights reflected off the windscreen and shielded the passengers.

'Take us on a tour and then lose him,' I said, and I sat back.

Theo took him north, away from the Fascist League's headquarters. We drove sedately for a mile. Suddenly, he floored it. The taxi was old and struggled to gain speed, but once we'd crossed the road, we were in the back doubles of Bloomsbury. Several sharp turns later, we were back in Soho and the narrow streets. You can turn a London black cab on a sixpence; that was the boast, and that's what Theo did. Once he turned an impossible corner, he slammed on the brakes, reversed, and we parked up amongst some other cars in the shadows with all the lights out. We both ducked and waited.

Half a minute later, the sedan slid past, its tyres screeching as it rushed along. Theo waited five minutes in case the car doubled back. It didn't. He calmly pulled out, turned, and headed towards Clerkenwell and all points east at a sedate pace. He didn't have to say anything as he looked at me in the driver's mirror; his smug smile spoke for itself. I was glad I could provide him with a little entertainment.

A few streets away from the League, Theo cruised with his lights out and parked. He swivelled back to see me.

'You sure about this?' he asked.

I nodded.

'Wait for me,' I said. 'If there's a problem, you'll know. Then you leave and tell Jack Brody. Clear?'

'Crystal. But I'll be here regardless.'

I didn't doubt him. Theo was loyal, if nothing else.

At half past eleven in the evening, the streets were empty. A full April moon hung in the sky. The van Jack and I had seen outside the house with scaffolds wasn't there, just as Latimer said. I walked quickly along, passing a few dark buildings. Gaps between the curtains of several windows left a yellow strip of light. Between every ten or so of the houses, a narrow alley divided the terraces. I slipped down one and into the utter blackness that lay between the sides of the houses. At the other end, on either side, were garden fences. I climbed the first, then the second, and then the third. The fourth fence I climbed was the garden of the house Jack said had the camera.

The back of the house was just a shadow and the windows were dark. The garden's dirt path, overgrown with weeds, led to the back door. From somewhere, there was the sound of a dog barking, followed by the hiss of a cat. I quickly dropped down. I was jumpy. Maybe I should have called Jack after all. It had been on my mind, and I could have used the weight of his support if nothing else.

I crouched by the lock of the back door, about to pick it when I noticed it was ajar. I shielded the light of the torch, so just a small, narrow beam touched the lock. It was busted.

The dog was barking again, louder and closer. Someone shouted, 'Shut up,' but it continued barking, punctuating the silence with its staccato rhythm.

I pulled on the balaclava and crept through the back door. Once inside, I crouched low again and listened. The silence was thick but for my heart beating the blood through my ears. It sounded too fast and too loud, like my intake of breath. This is a bloody stupid thing to do, I thought. If I were smart, I'd have figured that out earlier.

The roll of halfpennies felt comfortable in my right hand as I went through the kitchen and into the hallway. In front of me, the door to the front room hung off on one hinge. I flicked the torchlight around inside. Empty.

Next to it, some stairs led upwards into absolute blackness. Taking each tread, one at a time, testing my weight and waiting for a creak, I climbed them. When I reached the top landing, someone grunted loudly and wheezed from behind the door of the front room. I froze. My eyes were glued to the slightly open door in front of me. I squatted low, resting on my haunches, one hand supporting my balance on the floor. A pale-yellow light from within fell on the threadbare carpet.

What felt like an hour passed until I heard a snore. It stuttered and stuttered and started again, deep and regular, guttural, drunken, and snorting.

I was sweating as I gently turned to the back bedroom. The door was swung fully back. Nothing in the room but furniture. Okay. One person maybe, in the front room. I went there and peered around the half-open door.

The blinds were drawn shut, and a twenty-watt bulb lit the room in a sickly yellow light of shadows. The snorer lay on a sofa, one foot on the floor, shoes off, a coat wrapped around him like a blanket, his head on a cushion. Several empty bottles of beer were on the floor beside him, along with a screwed-up newspaper with uneaten fish and chips, a half-empty bottle of spirit, and some glasses. A telephone rested on a chair. The room smelled of unwashed bodies. But it was just him alone.

On a tripod by the window, a 16mm cine camera with a big lens peeped through the dirty, dusty net curtains. It was aimed across the street, probably at the front door of the

League. Jack was right. The van had been for show. This camera did the real work.

A reel-to-reel tape recorder sat on a table. I'd seen them before, but I was used to a wire recorder. Something sophisticated was attached to it – a switch of some sort. Someone had spent a lot of money on the best equipment.

I went towards it, working my way around the sofa where the man slept, careful to avoid his foot on the floor, when a loose board creaked.

The man grunted awake.

'What the hell!' he said sleepily, and a hand grabbed my sweater.

I shone the torch fully into his startled face. His eyes screwed up tightly. At the same moment, I swung my right hand, the roll of halfpennies in my fist, and caught him on the side of his head. He didn't make a sound and fell backward, unconscious.

I untangled his hand from my jumper and returned the torch to his face. A dribble of blood ran from the corner of his mouth and down his cheek. One of the men who attacked me at the park earlier today.

None of this made sense.

I knew I'd been set up in the park, but by whom? I wondered again if it was by Ginny Bright. Yet she and Ash were just as curious about who these people were. At the same time, I thought they already knew.

I searched through his pockets. A handkerchief, some loose change, a fob with a Yale key – nothing else. His coat pocket yielded just a packet of players and some matches. He carried no wallet, no ID, nothing. Alarm bells were ringing. Shining a light on his face, I took his photograph.

Then I took some more pictures of the room and the equipment and of the loose photographic prints lying on a table – mainly stills of faces. There were several shots of me and Hugo Latimer talking at the bomb site, and one of us outside the Charing Cross Hospital. That one showed an irate Chief Inspector telling off the photographer. These were photographs of people of interest – people to look out for. Why was I one of them?

I went around taking some more photographs wherever I shone the torch.

What I thought was a switch box beside the tape recorder looked instead like a radio-receiving device. I'd never seen one as small and sophisticated as this one before. A cable plugged it into the tape recorder.

There was nothing to say who had set this up, but it didn't bear the hallmark of the police or even Special Branch. Surveillance warrants were a nightmare. Anyway, wouldn't Latimer know if there was a warrant? Unless he was in the dark as well. In which case, that narrowed the field down quite considerably.

I glanced at the sleeping man and stopped wondering why he carried no identification. Instead, I listened to the alarm bells ringing in my head. He'd have hell to pay when he awoke in the morning. I didn't hold out much hope that he'd think he'd fallen and hit his head.

I slipped back down the stairs and out of the back door. Once I had crossed all the gardens, I walked quietly and quickly down the alley and back into the street. The dog was still barking. I climbed into Theo Drakas's cab. He turned around and looked at me.

'Well?' he asked.

I took off the balaclava, wiped my face with it, and shook my hair loose. I raked my fingers through it and then sat back, chewing my lips.

'Strange,' I said. 'Bloody strange.'

'You got what you wanted?'

'More than I figured.'

'Home?'

I shook my head.

'No. Down the road is Goel Hadam. Approach from the opposite direction and park behind the church.'

‘Why don’t you quit while you’re ahead?’ Theo asked.

‘I need to know something first. One more throw, Theo. Then home.’

# Chapter 23

The church had been bombed during the Blitz. The whole front had gone, now just a pile of bricks and mortar. What remained, a solid piece of Victoriana, wasn't going anywhere in a hurry. Abutting the church was Goel Hadam's building. The grass surrounding the church had overgrown the path. It was damp underfoot, and I left a trodden-down trail behind me. But that didn't matter; it blended in with the others that led to the stone floor and the rubble.

Once inside, I flicked the torch around, not too worried that anyone would be here. You needed someone to operate a camera, and any camera here aimed at Goel Hadam would be looking at a brick wall. A tape recorder operator would be a waste of manpower; at a quarter past midnight, the offices had been empty for hours. And I knew there would be a tape recorder, remembering what Jack had said about Marx's office being bugged.

Tucked in a corner, hidden from view, a workman's tent had been set up. It was the sort engineers put up around a manhole to keep themselves dry and give them privacy while they have their cups of tea and play cards. It looked like a makeshift confessional. It also appeared innocuous, as if it had always been here. I slipped inside, closing the canvas flap behind me.

Two crates that served as chairs, another as a table with two tin cups on it, an oil lamp, and a box of matches sat in one corner. A bottle to pee in was tucked away in another corner. It was about as salubrious as the house overlooking the League, but this one didn't smell of anything. On another crate sat the reel-to-reel tape recorder, the same make as the one down the road, with the same kind of receiving device. An electrical cable that powered it ran towards the offices. They were a cheeky lot, drawing power from those they were listening to.

I didn't need to see more because there was nothing more to see. Whoever set this up also set up the other one. I slipped away and found that Theo had moved the cab into a more shadowy place. He flicked the headlights once when he saw me.

'You don't look amused,' he said as I climbed in. He'd turned around; his right hand, resting on the wheel, was clutching the closed flick knife.

'It's a big jigsaw. There are lots of pieces. I don't even know if they all belong to the same set.' I sat back and removed the balaclava and gloves.

Theo returned the knife to the glove compartment and produced a silver hip flask from somewhere. He screwed off the top and passed it to me. I took a sip of brandy and passed it back. He wiped the mouthpiece and took a draught.

'There's a game being played, Theo, and I don't know my part in it.'

'You have one?'

'That much I'm sure.'

'Where to now?' he asked. 'West Hampstead or Soho?'

I looked at my watch. It was too late to go to Jack's, and I had things to do at home. I didn't want company, at least not tonight. I wanted to wake up in my own bed and in familiar surroundings.

'West Hampstead. Bill me tonight's fare,' I said, and he nodded, knowing what I meant. 'Give me a sheet of paper. Got something to write with?'

He passed me a clipboard with a stub of a pencil on a string dangling from it. I took the camera, folded a sheet of paper tightly around it like a parcel, and wrote on the side, *Martha, develop and print for me, Alex.* I gave it to Theo.

'On your way home, Theo, drop that into Brody's letter box.'

# Chapter 24

Before going to bed, I telephoned Latimer at his home. He was an insomniac. His wife answered. I wondered if she was an insomniac as well. A minute later, he came to the phone. I gave him the number plate of the car that followed Theo's cab and asked him to trace it. He wanted to know more. I lied and said I didn't know more, but I had some leads that I didn't want to discuss yet. I didn't want to tell him anything else, I needed to sort a few things out first. And I certainly wasn't going to tell him I'd broken into a house and knocked someone unconscious.

I wasn't an insomniac. Once I put the phone down, I went to bed.

I'd have slept in late but for the little devil nagging me and telling me time was running out. Anna Blau was watching me from the foot of the bed. I got ready quickly and got out of the house.

I found a seat on the Tube sandwiched between a thin man with a runny nose reading Milton's *Paradise Lost* and a prim young woman working her way through *Ulysses*. I felt out of place with the *Daily Mirror*.

Popov was front-page news still. The Soviets had the body now and seemed dissatisfied. The Soviet ambassador demanded to know why an American destroyer left hurriedly that night. His Majesty's Government cited the USS *Winfield Scott* as being on a seven-day goodwill tour, and the seven days were up. They left because the tides were right, and that happened to be at midnight. 'Well, wasn't that convenient?' the Russian ambassador commented, especially as it had an engine and a propeller – or was the US Navy reliant on sail these days?

Charlie Mathers rang as soon as I got into the office. He had two tickets to the rehearsals, and reminded me I'd agreed to go. Though I didn't feel like it, I felt I ought to. Charlie was persuasive, especially when he put on his little, lost, disappointed child's voice. Anyway, Martha wouldn't be up yet, so she wouldn't develop my prints until after lunch.

Before leaving, I called my messenger service. Polly answered. It was she I wanted to speak to. I asked her to describe the voice that left the message for the meeting in Victoria Park.

'It was nothing remarkable, babes,' Polly said. 'She sounded more London than anything else. As for *posh*? Don't give me that, my darling. My aunt Emma from Hoxton sounds posher.'

Somebody set me up and I guessed that ruled out Ginny Bright.

I got to the Hackney Empire at ten, and we sat through an hour and a half of hilarity. It seemed the rehearsal mistakes the actors made were funnier than their polished performance, and they themselves were enjoying it. No one wore costume; people sat on stage watching, and that added to the surreal nature of it all. Charlie held my hand tightly.

'You know something, Alex,' he said, 'you've made my day. But those bags under your eyes say you need to get some more sleep. What you been up to?'

'Wish I could say.'

'This case of yours, I suppose.'

'It's taking some interesting turns.'

'Indeed. Like?'

'Come on,' I said, 'they've opened the bar as well. Fancy a tot?'

Despite the hour, the downstairs bar heaved with people. The noise of the crowd was all around me, punctuated by the occasional laugh rising sharply above the drone. I ensconced myself in a corner on a high stool while Charlie went to get the drinks.

Five minutes later, having weaved his way back through the throng, Charlie exhaled a long breath. He handed me a bitter lemon; he was clutching a pint.

'Cheers,' he said, touching my glass with his. He sipped his drink and returned his gaze to me. I could see the mischief in his eyes. 'Seriously, you look tired, Alex. All work and no play make Jill a dull girl, you know.'

'Long night,' I said.

'What you need is a partner. Take some of the weight off your shoulders.'

'You?'

'Why not? I'm pretty good at finding things.'

'And give up your gas man salary? How will you manage to pay the electric bill for your flat? Anyway, shouldn't you be working?'

'All right. I can take a hint. You don't want to discuss it. But I'll keep nagging you until you tell me your secrets. As for work – bunking!' he said. 'Pongo's covering for me. Shouldn't *you* be working?'

'Nothing to do until later.'

'Like I said, you should have me on your team.' Charlie reached over and held my hand. 'I did all right yesterday, didn't I, protecting you? I could be your partner. I can help you break into the suspect's house. I can wear Pongo's overalls and his dirty cap, carry his tool bag, and pretend I've come to check the gas. *Hello, madam, gas man. Can I check your pipes?*'

'You'll have to say that in an Irish accent. The Irish charm is what you need for bald-face break-ins.'

'You mean my go-lucky cockney's not good enough? *Faith, bejaysus, and begorrah, and there I was thinking I was the bees!*'

'Shut up, idiot,' I said rather loudly, and several faces turned towards us.

Charlie put on his surprised look for their benefit. 'Did you hear that?' he continued in the same Irish accent and loudly. 'And the part's ideal for her, Olivier said.'

I pulled him around to face me.

'Anyway, it's against the law to break in, or didn't you know that?' I said softly.

'I heard that somewhere.' He grinned.

'Can't break in; can't carry a gun; where's the fun, eh, Charlie?' I checked my watch and saw his smile drop.

'It's meant to be before midnight, Cinders, not midday.'

'Playtime's over, Casanova. I really need to go.'

'Finish your drink at least, before you go and save the world,' Charlie said, and I agreed.

'So how did you get into this business?' Charlie asked. 'PI Raven, the sleuth of Soho.'

'My dad. It was his agency. Until 1938, he worked as a Metropolitan Police detective. Then he tackled a young gunman – Billy Shanks?'

Charlie nodded and muttered the name in reply. 'He shot your dad, didn't he?'

'A couple of times. Enough to invalid him out of the force. They'd have taken him back during the war with all the shortages, but Dad had opened the agency by then. I took it over at the end of the war.'

'I remember the Shanks case. A nasty piece of work. They didn't hang him, locked him up in Broadmoor with all the other lunatics they can't hang.' He looked me up and down as if assessing me, and he nodded his approval – of what, I wasn't sure.

'Where did you get your experience?' he asked.

I shrugged, not shyly, but simply.

'Ah! I see. One of them, were you? What do you speak? French? Dutch? German, maybe?'

'French. How come you know what all that means?'

'Ah, well, there's a long story, Cinders,' Charlie said. 'And you ain't got time to hear it.'

I cocked my head to one side and furrowed my brows in mock annoyance.

'I met some of you buggers – dropping you barmy bastards off from a sub on the Adriatic run. The sea was five hundred miles long and a hundred wide. Sounds like there's a lot of space to get lost in, but the entrance to it is too damn narrow.'

'I thought you said you got torpedoed… Not in a sub, I take it.'

'No, I was with destroyers, escorting the Atlantic convoys, then. After the second time, I decided to see what it felt like from the torpedoing end.' The smile that had left his face returned after a few seconds. He nodded. 'Well, here's to you, Alex. If ever there was a crazy thing to do, you did it, and you have my respect for doing it.'

Charlie drank his pint all at once and didn't say anything else. Outside, he held both of my hands in his. The day had brightened.

'I enjoyed myself, Cinders,' he said.

'Me as well. Thanks, Charlie. I needed that. I can get too tied up in my job at times.'

'Then you need to meet me for a drink tonight.'

I sighed. He was good company – funny, entertaining, and kind – and quite frankly, I could use the company. But as enjoyable as the distraction was, it was Anna Blau who was nagging at me. At the same time, my father's face rose up in front of my open eyes.

'My dad would have liked you,' I told him. 'Maybe I'll take you to see him one day.'

He gave me a curious stare, and before he could reply, I kissed his cheeks and turned away.

* * *

I caught a bus that dropped me off in the West End. The pavements were busy as I strolled towards Soho to see Martha and Jack. I weaved in and around knots of pedestrians, crossed the road, and decided to get off the main street, as progress would be quicker through the back ones. At this time of day, the cafes were bustling with the lunchtime crowd of secretaries and other office workers enjoying their hour of freedom. A few of the trenchcoated men, hats pulled low, were wandering the streets, pausing before, and then disappearing into open doorways. None carried cameras that I could see, and I didn't think they were interested in French lessons.

I caught sight of him – a small, thin, bald-headed man in an oversized raincoat – reflected in the shop window. He'd been in the queue behind me at the bus stop outside the Empire. On the bus, he'd been reading the *Mail* while seated on one of the bench seats at the back by the luggage rack, which was ideal for observing who got on and off. Now, several miles from where I first saw him, he was walking through Soho behind me.

Just to satisfy my curiosity, I turned down a street, and he turned with me. When I stopped to admire something in a window, he stopped and did the same at another window. I went inside the shop, looked around a bit, and came out again. The thin man was still there; he'd only moved across the street.

I stopped beside a news vendor. We chatted for a minute as I bought the evening paper. The headline was old news; nothing had happened, and the early edition was doing the best it could with what it had. The thin man gazed steadily into the window of a restaurant, pretending to study the menu while looking at my reflection in the glass.

I walked on. He walked on. I hurried and heard his footsteps quicken as I rounded a corner, and then I stopped. He almost collided with me when he came around the corner. By then, I'd spun around. I kicked his shin and he screamed. I pushed him back into a doorway and pressed my forearm against his throat, leaning hard into him. My other fist was balled up and in his face. I could smell the soap on his skin and feel his breath against my face.

He was trying to reach down and grasp his shin where I kicked him. I pressed my forearm harder, preventing him from doing so. He grunted and stopped struggling, suddenly going limp.

'Who are you? Why're you following me?' I said angrily.

Sallow, white skin clung to his sunken cheeks, the type of skin that sunburns easily; he grimaced in pain. His eyes, though, were bright, intelligent eyes, and they were staring into mine. There wasn't a hint of fear in them.

Slowly, he dropped his gaze, almost as if he were looking down my blouse; only my raincoat was tight around my neck. I followed his gaze like I felt he wanted me to. Between our coats, I saw the point of a knife pressing into the material of my coat.

'If you would be so generous, Miss Raven, and permit me to breathe, I would see it as an act of kindness,' he whispered hoarsely in a soft, emotionless voice.

I agreed to his polite request, released my forearm from his throat, and stepped back and away from the point of the knife. As I did, the blade vanished from where it came. That was the second flick knife I'd seen in less than a day. Somehow, I expected to see such a thing in Theo Drakas's hand. In the hands of this small, unprepossessing gentleman, like snow in July, it looked a little out of place.

'Okay, why are you following me?' I asked.

'I wanted to make sure we were alone, before I approached you,' he said. He lifted his leg as much as he could and gave his shin a healthy rub. When he placed the leg down, he practiced leaning his weight on it as if it were broken.

'I have an office and a telephone,' I offered up.

'Yes,' he said.

'Well, we're alone now. What do you want?'

'Tea and something sweet, if possible.' He adjusted his coat. 'I have a blood sugar problem and had a busy morning. Normally I have a midday snack, and that sorts it out, but today I've been too busy to do that.'

'I meant, why are you following me?'

His hands patted the pockets of his trousers, searching for something.

'No. I usually have some barley sugar, but, no, not today,' he mumbled to himself.

He looked up at me. He said nothing. His eyes said nothing. His face said even less.

'Why don't I buy you tea and a cake and we can talk?' I said. 'Nico's nearby.'

'Will they have doughnuts? They have the right amount of sugar, I find.'

'I'm sure Nico's will have doughnuts.' I indicated the way. 'If not, I'll ask if he can make some.'

He walked in front of me slowly so I could catch up, and together we went along. From behind, we must have appeared to be an odd couple, with me nearly a head taller. From the front, I'd guess we'd look just as odd; only you'd be able to see the smile on my face.

'I take it you've got a name?' I said.

'Several,' he answered.

# Chapter 25

I took him to Nico's, a small cafe off Wardour Street, towards the Shaftesbury Avenue end. The coffee was good, and they had doughnuts. I was going to sit by the window, but the small man found a gloomy corner and sat with his back to the wall, facing the door. Angela, Nico's wife, served us. She had a pretty but unassuming face and a demeanour that said if you sent her your waifs and strays, she'd look after them no matter what. How they made money eluded me.

An eclectic bunch surrounded us.

A couple of students from the nearby Central School of Art were holding forth on the merits of Wassily Kandinsky. A mousey-thin girl with unhealthy black hair was saying he was a genius and losing ground against her weightier friend, who bemoaned the lack of figurative representation in his work. *It's abstract, abstract, abstract*, she argued with wild gestures, *of course there's nothing figurative.*

Two workmen sat in dumb silence, reading their *Daily Mirrors*, while eating with their forks only. They reminded me of an old married couple, devoid of conversation that the years had sucked out of them.

Across from them sat an old man, his eyes bright in anticipation of a conversation that would never happen.

His gaze followed anyone who walked past in hope. Angela wouldn't throw him out until they were ready to close, nor would she charge him for all the cups of tea he drank.

Angela brought us two coffees and two doughnuts. I watched as the thin man spooned four teaspoons of sugar into his coffee. He stirred it for a half-minute. I figured at least that much stirring was required to dissolve that much sugar.

'You left me any?' I joked. He looked perplexed. 'Which one of your several names shall I use?'

He took a bite from his doughnut, chewed it thoroughly, and swallowed it. It could have been my imagination, but I thought some blood entered his cheeks, and his face softened slightly.

'Hawkins,' he said as he took a second bite. It seemed as if he'd thought hard before answering.

'That's today's name, is it?'

'No, that's my name. Hawkins.' His expression was a slightly puzzled one, but only slightly.

'Right.'

He'd devoured the doughnut and was eyeing mine. I pushed it across to him. He smiled a thank you, and he immediately started into it. I waited patiently, sipping my coffee and listening to the students argue. *How can a canvas painted red with an orange line drawn down it be called art?* They had moved on from Kandinsky. *In the same way that Malevich can paint one black and call it art*, one said. Their argument was getting heated. I waited for the sound of a slap across the cheek with a glove and the challenge of a duel on Hampstead Heath in the morning mist.

Hawkins finished the second doughnut and half his coffee when he finally sat back and seemed to relax. I worried his blood sugar was now a lot higher than it should be.

He brushed sugar off his fingers and onto the floor, and his hand slipped into his pocket. Rather than the switchblade, he brought out several devices with wires attached and laid them on the blue Formica table. He patted his chest, and his hand delved into the left side of his coat. It appeared a second later, clutching a blue pamphlet. That, too, went on the table. He hesitated a moment, then his hand went inside his jacket, and a pair of horn-rimmed spectacles ended up precariously perched on his nose.

'Ready?' I asked.

'Sorry, Miss Raven… Yes, I do know your name, as you've already gathered.' He spoke in a monotone. 'I know all my clients' and charges' names. I take great pride in doing so.'

'I'm your client?'

'Oh, yes.'

'How remiss of me not to know.'

'Do you know what these are, Miss Raven?' he asked, pushing the wire devices across to me.

Even though I did, I turned them over in my hand for a few seconds before replying in a sort of vacant way. 'Bugs, I think the Americans call them.'

'This one was attached inside your phone in the hallway of your house.' He said it in the same bland way as before, not sounding surprised, concerned, or anything. His matter-of-factness was disturbing, especially as he'd have had to break in to remove them, and he didn't seem the kind of man that would or could do that. 'And this one was from the phone in your office.'

Now I was concerned. I watched him with furrowed brows as he sat in unmoving, unresponsive silence. Okay, so maybe he was the type of man who could have done it. It didn't seem possible, but there it was.

'I removed this one before you'd woken up.' He tapped one of the bugs. 'I wanted to check on your flat but didn't want to lose sight of you when you left for work. However, I was satisfied that your flat itself would not have been bugged. It's an expensive business monitoring them, and the phone is the best one for quick results.'

'You broke in…?' I stopped speaking.

His face gave nothing away, like a gambler's poker face, blank and unperturbed. He tapped the other bug.

'This one I removed earlier this morning, before the sun was up, in fact, from your office. But don't worry, I replaced them with damaged ones; one with an internal fault and the other with a loose electrical connection. I guessed the type, and it was correct. Anyway, they'll look as if they've failed when they are taken back and tested.'

'Two failing at the same time, long odds don't you think?'

'Very. But it happens. Mr Ash suspected something of the sort and had prepared me for the eventuality.'

'Ash? Wilfried Ash?'

'Yes, yes, Ash.'

'You're a man of surprises, Mr Hawkins. You know Ash?'

'We've' – his eyes blinked several times – 'worked together for a number of years.' They settled into their normal rhythm again.

I was a little stunned.

'Did Ash send you? Do you know who bugged me?'

He could have nodded, but he didn't; instead, he assured me, 'Your office, by the way, has no *bugs*.'

The feeling I had that my flat had been broken into came back to me. It was the same feeling David Blau had. Only in this case, it wasn't by Hawkins. I should have been grateful; instead, I said, 'You'd better explain yourself.'

'Just that Mr Ash was impressed with you.' He had taken off his glasses and was polishing them with his tie. 'He's seldom impressed with anyone. But you, he was. I think he may have made some enquiries about you when you saw him. You did see him, didn't you? Yes, of course you must have. He never leaves Orford anymore, so he couldn't have seen you. Miss Bright leaves on occasions, but Mr Ash never.'

I was forced to take another look at Hawkins. Now I was slightly amused. He was a most unlikely burglar. He was the type of person you'd see sitting in a corner of a pub until closing time. You'd feel a little sorry for him; you might even buy him a drink, but you'd never speak to him. And you'd never suspect he carried a flick knife.

'Is he still writing his book?' he asked.

I gave a slight laugh, just enough to say yes. If further proof were needed that he knew Ash, he'd confirmed it.

'You can use your phones freely,' Hawkins said. 'But every now and then, check to see if the device inside is the same. That is, until all of this is over. However, whatever calls you made up until this morning would have been listened to.' He smiled at me, a broad, ungainly smile from lips that weren't used to smiling.

'Until all of what is over? You seem to know what's going on, Mr Hawkins. So, until just what is over?' I asked.

'Whatever it was you discussed with Mr Ash, of course.'

'I see,' I said without seeing. 'Does Ash know who bugged me?'

Hawkins shook his head slightly, thought for a second, and then nodded. 'He probably does. I would suggest, however, that whatever your business was with him, would be the reason for it.'

'I was asking him about–'

'Ah-Ah-Ah!' He held up a hand to quiet me, and his eyes went away and back again. 'I don't wish to know. My business is this only.' His glasses went on again. 'Mr Ash also asked me to give you this.' He handed me the pamphlet. It was old, the cover was creased and dog-eared, and the pages were yellow at the edges. *Quotes by Sun Tzu* was written in black capitals. 'He has found it useful and hopes you will as well.'

Hawkins finished the last dregs of his coffee and stood up. His glasses went back inside the soft case and into his inside right pocket. He found his gloves and slipped them on, adjusted his scarf, and then the top button of his coat, readying himself to leave.

'Mr Hawkins,' I said, 'I'm impressed. But you know I did spot you following me.'

'The reason you knew was because I wanted you to know.' He looked at me as if what he was telling me was obvious. 'I have been following you all morning, Miss Raven. When you left your flat, when you left your office. You sat on the top deck, the third row from the front of the bus that took you to Hackney. You met a gentleman at the corner of Wilton Way before going to the theatre with him. You were seated in the stalls, row 9, seat 12. When we boarded the bus to the West End, it was then I was sure you weren't being followed, and I could reveal myself.'

He'd said it in his factual way, with no hint of smugness or conceit, just straightforwardly, as if reading it from a list.

'Why should someone follow me?' I asked.

'Whatever your business is with Ash and what he does is the reason.'

'Yes, of course; what else could it be? That business you don't want to know or talk about,' I said sarcastically. 'Would you have stabbed me, by the way?'

'Only slightly,' he answered.

'Just enough to get my attention,' I confirmed, more to myself than to him.

'I had several messages to deliver, and I have done so,' he said. 'To your satisfaction? Perhaps when you next speak to Mr Ash, you will communicate that. He's a valued client.'

'How long have you known Mr Ash?' I asked.

He thought for a while, and in the same mechanical manner, he replied, 'Since August 1937.' He checked his watch slowly and deliberately, the way he did everything, as if he were calculating the exact time of their meeting.

He started to leave, but stopped and turned back.

'In the book, he has indicated certain passages that he said will be of interest.' He hesitated, perhaps unsure of himself, before asking, 'If the bugs are of no use, Miss Raven, may I be permitted to have them?'

His face looked expectantly; at least that's what I thought it looked like. Hawkins had one of those faces that could look like anything it wanted to without too much trouble.

'I have no use for them. I'm sure you'll find one.'

He gave a slight nod that passed for a happy acknowledgement and scooped them up into his coat pocket.

'It was nice to meet you, Miss Raven. It's always nice to meet new-found *friends.*' He lingered on the word *friends* and fixed my gaze with his. I wanted to tell him we weren't friends, but as he turned to leave, he accidentally barged into one of the arguing students. If Hawkins had been wearing a hat, he'd have taken it off.

*How can you be so naive?* the figurative artist was saying, ignoring Hawkins's apology. *Duchamp?* he barked; *it's something you piss in, for Christ's sake.* That brought a haughty folding of the arms from the black-haired girl and a giggle from their friend.

I flicked through the booklet. It was small; twenty-four pages, if that. Page fourteen had been folded back. There were two quotes on that page that had been circled in red. I flicked through the rest of the book quickly. No others had been highlighted.

The first read, *Pretend inferiority and encourage arrogance.*

Sergeant Bignall, my self-defence instructor during my time in the forces, once said, *There are times to act stupid, to act like you don't know what's going on. Your greatest asset is that you're a woman, and we all know how brainless they are. Never let on that you're not.*

*To know your enemy, you must become your enemy*, was the only other one highlighted.

I went to the door and watched Hawkins as he walked unconcernedly along and merged with the crowd. If I had asked anyone in Nico's who I was with, I would have gotten several different answers and descriptions. Hawkins was the perfect blank slate.

I stayed in the cafe for a few more minutes, trying to make sense of everything. Wilfried Ash had asked to see me, and I knew afterwards it was in connection with Anna Blau. The reason he was interested was only hinted at. He'd also hinted that he'd help me. If his help was Hawkins, then I should be grateful. However, I remembered Ginny's words: *Much of it is in the shadows.* I was beginning to understand… or at least I thought I was.

# Chapter 26

I arrived at Martha and Jack's shop to learn that something had happened to Theo Drakas. At first, I feared he'd been in an accident. That changed when Martha Evans barked at me.

'What happened last night?' she growled. Before I had time to say hello, she was all over me. 'Well, what happened?'

'What do you mean?' I asked.

'Theo got duffed up good and proper. I know he was with you because he dropped this off.' She showed me the camera I'd asked him to bring. 'So, what happened?'

'Where is he?' I asked.

'At home,' Jack said.

I started to leave, and Jack took my arm, stopping me. 'We'll see him together,' he said, and he grabbed his coat.

'I'll have them, Alex,' Martha said. 'I like that little Greek sod.' She pointed a finger at no one in particular, but then I wouldn't be too surprised if it wasn't at me. 'You'll see, Alex. Just you see.' Her face had turned ugly.

We drove across Waterloo Bridge, past the station and towards Elephant and Castle, and turned onto Walworth Road. After a half-mile of depressing grey shops, we turned off onto a side street. The whole journey had been one of silence. Jack was giving me space and time to think. By the time we arrived at Theo's, I knew what I had to do. I opened the door, and as I was about to get out of the car, Jack reached over and pulled it shut.

'Don't play games with your friends, Alex. That's not like you. What ain't you telling us?' He lit a cigarette, announcing his intention to sit there until I told him.

'I'm being played, Jack.' I leaned back and stared aimlessly out the window. 'I don't know exactly why, but I think I know by whom. Last night, I broke into the house that overlooked the Fascist League, the one we saw that day we passed by. Theo picked me up and gave me a lift there. It wasn't the police or Special Branch watching the Nazis, but the cloak-and-dagger boys from Whitehall. They knew about Theo because they were following us when he picked me up outside my office. They'd also bugged my phone; that's why they knew to be there. Theo lost them. But they'd have known it was him.'

'Why are they so interested in the League? And why in you?'

'What happened to Theo had something to do with Hauptmann Grunwald. Him and people like him. Marx called them the *chosen few*, remember? A car was waiting by my office yesterday. They warned me off of Grunwald. The gent who did the talking was the same one I saw at the headquarters of the League the day we went past it. He's with the government.'

Jack twisted around, one arm on the steering wheel and the other over the back of the seat. He seemed to have forgotten the cigarette he'd lit, and he held it loosely between his fingers.

'People like Grunwald are now working for us,' I continued. 'It wouldn't do to let it be known who last employed them.'

'Not after the bloody war we fought.'

'Marx was going to confront Grunwald but he vanished. He was warned. And then I was warned to keep away. After that, I got a call from Wilfried Ash for a meeting. You don't know Ash, but he was part and parcel of what we did during the war. He knew I was trying to find out who a name belonged to–'

'What name?'

'Hildebrandt,' I answered. 'You'd know her better as Natalia Popov, the missing Russian who has been in the papers.' His brow furrowed. 'Yes. The one they fished from the Thames.'

Jack bit his lip in contemplation. His brain was working, so I told him the rest, about the break-in at the Greenbergs' flat, what I'd found there, and then, 'Anna Blau's house was broken into. Nothing was taken, but it was searched.'

'That ties Anna in with Saul Greenberg, surely?'

'I think people might think she and Saul were working together. But my flat and office were broken into. Nothing was taken. It was to bug my phone. Not by Ash. No. I'd guess it was the gent who warned me off that bugged me. Ash made sure the bugs were removed.'

'What's he got to do with things?'

'He was interested that I was looking for Hildebrandt. But something else is going on, Jack, that I don't understand. The thing is, I don't think it's Popov in the mortuary.'

'Why?'

'I don't know why. There're just a few things that don't add up. Anyway, I'm pretty sure Popov was in the car that broke down beside the bomb site the night Saul was killed. But why Saul was killed, I don't know.'

'You sure she was in the car?'

'As sure as I can be.'

'If Saul recognised her, if that's what you think, they'd not hesitate to kill him.'

'But why not kill Anna?' I said. 'She was there with him. She would have seen what Saul saw. She would have witnessed the murder. Why not kill her as well?'

Jack shook his head slowly.

'So, I'm assuming she's alive.'

'If she's alive,' he said, 'I can't leave you alone for a minute, can I? If any of this is true, you know you've just crossed the street. This isn't a police matter anymore, not if the glory boys are involved.'

'I'm not stupid, Jack.'

'Just what have you disturbed, Alex?' Jack asked, not expecting to get an answer.

'I'm not the problem, Jack. I'm being protected.'

'What, you've got some bloody guardian angel hovering over you? You're sure you're not that stupid after all?'

'Trust me, Jack, I'm not the problem.'

'Yet!'

'Yet, then. I was attacked in Victoria Park during the demonstration. I went there to meet one of Ash's associates who'd have information for me.'

'So, you were set up by the Ash you trust?'

'No, not by him, but by someone who knew I'd seen him. I didn't know why, but now I think I know. I'm sure that's what Ash was telling me through a friend of his, the one who found and removed the bugs.' I shook my head again, unable to explain why. 'I'm just getting paranoid in my old age, I guess, but I don't trust his friend. I don't think he means me harm, either. Anyway, one of the attackers in the park was a man I found in the house I broke into.'

'Is he still there?'

'With a sore jaw.'

'I see,' Jack said. 'Where does that leave you with Anna Blau?'

'I think she has absolutely nothing to do with any of this. But people are trying to make me think she has. I think I know what Theo is going to say, so I want you to do something for me. Contact Nat Pepper–'

'The housebreaker?'

'I've got a fast turnaround job I need done tonight. Tell him it'll be as safe as I can make it. But use a public phone and tell him not to contact me directly, but to meet me in the Coach and Horses. I'll brief him on what I want done. He'll need a lookout. Maybe you or Martha. I don't trust anyone else for this. Nat will fill you in on the details when he knows the job. And you give him a lesson on how to use my camera; he'll need that.'

Jack nodded and didn't ask for more. He leaned across me, opened the door, and I stepped out.

Hindsight is twenty-twenty vision, as the saying goes. I wasn't that stupid, was I? Or maybe I was. Last night, I hadn't expected to be followed, just as I hadn't expected my phone to be tapped. I hadn't anticipated things getting this complicated. I should have known – Saul Greenberg was dead, after all – and that should have warned me.

# Chapter 27

Theo Drakas lived in a two-up, two-down Victorian terrace with an outside toilet. His family had lived here since before the First World War. His father, a merchant seaman who settled in London after he married a Serbian immigrant, was killed on a wet January night in 1941 during the Blitz.

Aella, Theo's wife, answered the knock on the door. She gave me a tight-lipped stare. I knew she was angry at me for what had happened to her husband. She made me feel dirty. She invited us in, and a warm cooking smell greeted us. Two young boys eyed us from the open door of the living room, where a radio played quietly. We went up a narrow dog-legged staircase that led to the room at the front of the house.

Theo began to rise as we entered his bedroom, a small, compact room where the Madonna shared wall space with the Arsenal football team. Aella pushed him down again. He looked a sorry sight. His face was bruised; the black-blue patches surrounding one eye were swollen, almost closing it. His other eye was bloodshot. He smiled tightly and waved a hand for us to sit. He wore one of those washed-out, grey-blue striped pyjamas. He was so thin, it made him look like a concentration camp inmate. The top was open, and Theo's ribs were bandaged. His prominent Adam's apple, which made him look like he had a crooked neck, bobbled as he swallowed.

Aella gave me another harsh stare but said nothing except that she'd make some coffee. She was angrier at the men who had worked her husband over than at me, but that would change when she had time to think properly. I couldn't blame her. I felt it was my fault.

Theo shook his head at the coffee and pointed to the dressing table and a bottle of ouzo that was beside a crucifix.

'Get some glasses, woman,' he said.

She glared at him. 'You call me that again, Drakas, and I'll close that other eye.' She shook her fist at him, mumbling something unflattering in Greek. His smile widened in glee, and he winced as it opened up the cracks on his lips. She shook her head and left.

'You don't want to get on her wrong side,' he whispered to Jack, laughing.

'I wonder if she's taken lessons from Martha?' Jack whispered back.

Theo licked his lips clean of blood and mopped up the remainder with a handkerchief.

I sat on the chair beside him and hunched over. 'Theo, I'm sorry–'

'Nonsense,' he said. 'I've had worse.' He smiled tightly and then the smile slipped from his face. 'There were two of them, Alex. Big bastards with big bastard boots. They showed me some kind of ID, but what it said I couldn't tell you.'

'What did it look like?' Jack asked.

Theo shook his head. 'I've never seen ones like it before, Mr Brody. They weren't coppers' ID – I know what they look like.'

'Special Branch?' I asked.

'No, it wasn't them, either. They knew who I picked up, Alex. Don't ask me how. One of them mentioned you by name.'

'My phone was bugged,' I told him. 'They knew who I called, and they would have gotten your number plates when they followed us.'

'Bob's your uncle!' He nodded in understanding. 'They wanted to know where we went. I told them they should go forth and multiply.' He grinned at Aella, who'd returned holding four small glasses.

She shook her head, unimpressed. 'Tough guy,' she murmured under her breath.

'That wouldn't have pleased them, Theo,' I said, shaking my head as well.

'But I did a good job losing them, didn't I?' He said it proudly, like he'd just won a prize, and the prize was the kicking.

Aella filled each glass with ouzo and handed us one. All the time, Theo grinned at us.

'*Yiamas!*' he said brightly, and he drank half the glass. We did the same. 'I didn't tell them, Alex. Then they went to work on me. The big one had fists like Aella's iron. Then…' His eyes dropped, and he swallowed the rest of the ouzo. 'Alex, they threatened Aella and the kids. You know, I'd have taken the beating, but not when they said they'd do the same to them. If they touched her or the kids, I'd have gutted them.'

His stare told me, given half a chance, he'd have done it.

'There wasn't much he could do,' Aella said. 'The big one had a face like a monkey and the manners of a pig. He talked in a funny way–'

'Everyone talks in a funny way as far as you're concerned. Especially if they've not a "saaf" London accent.'

At Theo's imitation, she flicked her eyes to the ceiling. I thought he might be pushing his luck.

'You dumb little–' Jack smiled a big, rugged smile at him. 'You should have told them and spared yourself a beating. But you're just a mean little bastard, aren't you?'

Theo grinned and winced.

'Mr Brody, you grow up around here, and you learn two things. You learn to know when someone's going to give you a beating just for the hell of it. They would have kicked me around even if I'd told them right out. Then they would have said it was to teach a wop like me a lesson, but they wouldn't have told me what the lesson was. So you learn to shut up until you're ready to speak. That way, they believe you when you do.'

'And the second thing?'

'Friends are like family, especially the good ones.'

'I'm just sorry I got you mixed up in this, Theo. I didn't know these boys would cut up rough,' I said.

'I'll heal. But if I see them again and I'm in my cab, I'll run the bastards over and say it was an accident.' He held out his glass, and Aella filled it, then made sure ours were topped up.

'I told them we went to the headquarters of those fascist devils. But I never told them where we went after. They asked, but I said I took you home. You see what I mean, Mr Brody? They believed me. I never told them about the camera, either.' He looked over at Jack. 'I didn't tell them I came to you after, Mr Brody.'

'You should have told them,' Jack said. 'I'd break their legs.'

'I did good, Alex?' he appealed to me.

'You did,' I said. 'I just wish I knew what the good was for.'

We left Theo with his bottle of ouzo, and Aella took us downstairs and said we were going to eat something. Her eyes dared us to say no. I think she needed to do something and have people around for a while longer.

'You know who did this to Theo, Miss Raven?' she asked.

'I'm not exactly sure, but I have an idea,' I said. 'I won't call on Theo again, if that'll help, Aella.'

She gave a small, humourless laugh.

'Theo wouldn't like that, Miss Raven. He listens to Dick Barton with the kids on the radio every Saturday, then they go into the garden and shoot up the place. He tells them he drives a private detective around, and he has to come and rescue you every now and then. He saves you at least once a week.'

'And twice on Sundays, I'd imagine,' I said.

'He's a big kid,' Jack said.

'You ought to see,' she said, smiling kindly at Jack.

I reached across to my handbag and took out four five-pound notes, then handed them to Aella. She refused to take them until Jack took them off me and wrapped her fingers around them.

'Theo was doing a job for Alex,' he said. 'It's his wages, and he's earned it.'

Her eyes lingered on the money, and she rose and pushed it into a teapot that was on the mantelpiece. She sat down again and didn't say anything else until we had finished the meal.

'I have to make a telephone call, Aella,' I said when we'd eaten.

After she asked her neighbour for permission to use their phone, I called Sergeant Brown. I thought it pointless to call his boss. I wasn't in Dickie's best books, and I needed a favour.

Brown sounded depressed, or perhaps lost; I'm not sure which – he didn't sound like life was a bed of roses, and if it was, he'd been sleeping on the thorns. I arranged to meet him at a place I knew in Soho. He had to think about it like you'd think about committing a crime, and I could hear the reluctance in his voice when he agreed. I didn't need to tell him not to tell Dickens.

I made a second call, this time to Charlie Mathers at his home. I wasn't surprised that he was in. If anything, I was a little disappointed that he was.

'Alex!' he said loudly. 'What a surprise. 'ere, missus, how'd you know my number?'

'I made a call from your phone last time I was there; remember?'

'And you made a note of it. Clever thing. Well, things are looking up for Charlie boy if you took that much trouble!'

'Still on for a drink tonight?'

'Just tell me where and when, and I'll be there. I'll even wash my hair.'

I made the arrangement, replaced the receiver, and came back to Theo's house. Jack was drying his hands on a tea towel while Aella wiped and dried the dishes. We sat and talked for a while, and then we said our goodbyes. Theo was a little drunk and slurred his happily.

# Chapter 28

Jack went back to the shop, and I met Brown in a small Turkish coffee shop on Greek Street, of all places. I wasn't sure if the owner, Mehmet Yilmaz, ever considered the irony. It was populated by dark-skinned men, several of them smoking hookah pipes. The pungent smell in the air wasn't French cigarettes. There were also no women, so I was the anomaly to be stared at. It was like one of those scenes from a B-movie western: as the bad guy enters, the piano stops playing, and everyone looks up. I didn't have my gun with me, and I'm not sure I'd look good in a black Stetson. The sound of jangling spurs was replaced by the sound of spoons stirring glass cups.

The coffee, strong and black, sat like mud in a glass; the sweets were deliciously sweet and dripping with honey; and Brown, who looked like a policeman as well as a fish out of water, was ignored. The chatter around us was in Turkish, and they could have been talking about anything, knowing that Brown didn't understand a word they said. We sat in a corner, and I gave him the wall seat so he could keep an eye on the clientele. He liked that.

When Hugo Latimer's substantial frame filled the doorway, I knew why Sergeant Brown looked nervous.

Once again, the piano stopped playing. Ignoring everyone, Latimer came and sat beside us.

'You telling tales outside school, Sergeant?' I asked.

Brown flicked an awkward smile at me at the same time Latimer flicked his head at Brown. He took the hint and left to stand outside like a scolded dog.

'You've got him well trained,' I said.

'I want this conversation private.' He motioned for coffee and returned his attention to me. 'What else do you know about Popov?'

'Only that she's dead, and nothing else I haven't told you already.' I kept my suspicions to myself.

'Hildebrandt, Meyers, Popov.' He nodded, lost in his thoughts for a moment.

'Tell me, has there been any noise coming from Special Branch recently?' I asked.

'Apart from the usual?' He shook his head. 'Why are you asking?'

'Just to confirm, it wasn't them outside the Fascist League or at Goel Hadam?'

'Goel Hadam? What's Bruno Marx got to do with any of this?'

'Hildebrandt, Meyers, and Popov. He has a file on her.'

Latimer eased himself back in his chair, took out his pipe, and noisily tapped it out into the ashtray as if calling a meeting to order. It opened a few eyes around us, but they quickly returned to sleep.

'That means some of our friends from the old days are involved. That's why they're keeping a close eye on him,' he said as he filled the tobacco bowl absent-mindedly.

'Why are they interested in the League?' I asked.

'It's all about making friends who have a common enemy.'

'Even when they were once the common enemy?'

He gave me a wry smile. 'The more you know about your friends, the more they stay friendly. How do you know it's the cloak-and-dagger boys involved?'

'It doesn't leave much choice if it's not Special Branch. I paid them a visit last night. And earlier today, a friend of mine who was with me got beaten up. They wanted to know where I went. Then someone told me my office and home phones had been bugged. He even showed them to me. I felt as if he knew who did it. He also passed on a bit of advice from Wilfried Ash.'

Latimer's eyes rose slowly to meet mine, and, for a moment, he stopped fiddling with his pipe. Then he placed the pipe in his mouth, found a match, and lit it.

'You're full of surprises today. What's Ash got to do with the disappearance of a girl?'

'Nothing, I think.'

'Then why's he giving you advice? He's not usually that kind.'

'Maybe he's mellowing in his old age?'

'Maybe I'll win the football pools.'

I told him what prompted me to visit Ash – the name I'd found in Saul's room. I didn't tell him what Ash told me about Popov wanting to defect. Neither did I tell him that Ash thought Anna Blau was dead, and if not, would be soon. Maybe I should have, but in my experience and in my dealings with Latimer, it was always good to hold something back. I knew he'd ask his own questions. The circle he and Ash moved in was small and intimate. The people he would ask would almost certainly be the same ones Ash asked. In which case, Ash would soon find out Latimer was interested.

'Why did you want to see Brown?' he asked.

'I need something checked out. I need it done quickly.'

'And quietly, no doubt. Why?'

'Let's leave that answer for later, Hugo. I don't feel much like talking about them at the moment.'

His stare said, *Not too much later.* 'What's the name?' He'd taken out a small notebook.

I gave him several names, and he wrote them down.

'Check the military, as well,' I said.

Latimer sat back in his chair and considered me for a few moments before he waved Yilmaz over. The owner had been waiting patiently with a coffee, not wanting to disturb the chief inspector until asked.

Yilmaz was a stout man in a striped shirt who belied the myth that stripes made you look thinner. He placed down the coffee, then ran his fingers through his jet-black hair that was greying at the temples and wiped one across his small bushy black moustache, something clearly on his mind.

'It's all right, Mehmet,' Latimer said, understanding his worry. 'I'm too important to get out of bed for a little bit of hashish. Just keep the chatter about gunrunning down while I'm here.'

Mehmet's face flushed. 'You joke with me, Mr Latimer.'

'I joke with you, Mehmet.' Latimer waved his pipe towards the door, pointing to Brown, who looked like a waif in an oversized raincoat standing in the cold outside the shop. 'Ask him to come in.'

Brown came and stood nervously in front of Latimer. The chief inspector tore out the sheet he'd written on and passed it to Brown.

'Get on to criminal records. See if they've got cards on these names. Speak to Jenner, and Jenner only, understand? Ask him to check with the Central Registry as well – the armed forces, especially. And to do it on the QT. It's urgent. If you get any jip, give them my name.'

Brown left with some relief – I knew the weight Hugo Latimer's name carried from experience, and Brown would be more than happy to use it to its full effect.

'How's this friend of yours?' He was being polite. I don't think he really cared.

'He'll live. The ones who roughed him up showed him some IDs he didn't recognise.'

Latimer nodded. 'The people you mix with would recognise several, I suppose. Okay. I have some of my own questions to ask back at the Yard. Keep in touch, Alex. I know you. So, you keep in touch. You're not telling me everything, and I don't like or appreciate that.' He gave me a hard stare to emphasise the fact.

'The car that followed me last night. Did you manage to trace it?' I asked.

'Not yet. After what you told me, I'd hazard a guess that it doesn't exist. But I'm guessing it belongs to whoever bugged your phone.' He downed his coffee in one gulp. 'In which case, you be careful, Alex.'

'Oh, I am, Chief Inspector. Especially now.'

He turned and left, and the chatter in the room increased in volume.

I waited patiently for Brown to return. It took an hour and a half for the policeman to come back.

'There's nothing on any of the names,' he said. 'No green or white cards according to Mr Jenner.'

'So not suspected criminals with or without a record.'

He shook his head in confirmation.

'Jenner made some other checks, but lots of records were destroyed during the Blitz.'

'Did he check with the military?'

He paused, as if it were something that needed careful consideration when a simple yes or no would suffice.

'That's proving a bit more difficult. Jenner thinks he's getting the runaround, but he can't be sure.'

'Yes, I guessed as much. I suppose you've passed this all on to Latimer?'

He smiled apologetically.

'I don't suppose you'd care to tell me what's going on?' he asked.

'You don't suppose correctly, Sergeant.' I stood up to leave. 'Oh, pay the man for the coffee; there's a dear. It seems as if the good Chief Inspector forgot.' I smiled, and he smiled back.

I left him and walked deeper into Soho, towards the Coach and Horses. I had to see a man about a burglary.

## Chapter 29

Nat Pepper had two boasts. The first: he'd never been nabbed. The second: as far as housebreakers go, he was the very best. Nat never lacked gall. The first was a lie. Nat's defence of the lie was that at the time, he wasn't a housebreaker, so that arrest didn't count. The second was debatable but generally accepted as true. He put his success down to careful planning and the fact that he was such an ordinary looking bloke, no one would suspect him of anything illegal, the perfect camouflage in his line of work.

He sat comfortably in the lounge bar of the pub, reading a novel with a glass of port on a table beside him. The lamp shone on his pockmarked skin, which looked to have the coarseness of leather with the texture of cottage cheese. A fine spray of white bristles, like silver dust on his chin, betrayed his age. His eyes brightened when he saw me, and his teeth glimmered white behind his smile. He took off his round wire-framed glasses and pinched the bridge of his nose before placing the spectacles into a case he had resting on the table.

'Alex, girl, it's been a while; I thought you was dead,' he said and laughed. 'An' here you are, pretty as a picture and truly scrumptious if I may say so.'

'You may, Nat, and if you want to add more, don't let me stop you.'

'Oh, girl, if I was twenty years younger…'

He wrapped his arms around me, almost lifting me off the ground. His smile was infectious, and I was smiling along with him. We might have turned a few heads in the pub, either case, Nat ignored them, and I did the same.

'Girl, you losing weight?' he asked. 'You need a proper feeding; otherwise you'll just waste away. Now, what about dinner at this nice place I know in Brixton?'

'As much as I'd love to, Nat, it'd only turn into a drinking session – and I'm definitely not in your league. Rum's for the big boys. Another time, maybe.' I nodded to a corner that was empty of people, and we went there. I refused his offer of a drink.

'I'm sorry about the timing,' I said, 'but I need this done quickly.'

'Brody mentioned.'

I gave him a note with an address. His eyebrows rose as he read it.

'I want you to go there tonight and tell me what you find.'

'Tonight don't leave me much time to case the place.'

'I know how you like to work, Nat. I can't help it. I won't be offended if you say no.'

His tongue bulged his cheek and his mouth screwed up.

'Care to tell me why the hurry?' he asked.

I shook my head.

'You don't want to know. Look, Nat, I'll not kid you; this is serious stuff. More serious than breaking into some toff's house, stealing the diamonds, and getting done by the police. That's why you take nothing. Understand?'

'Nothing? What kind of burglar you think I am?'

'One with brains. Nothing. Don't worry, I won't grass you up to the burglars' union. You're in and out, and no one knows you've been there. Then you vanish for a while.'

'Brody said it was serious. He said something about the little Greek guy as well.' His brow furrowed in thought and then he nodded, slowly and deliberately, and he folded the paper into his wallet. 'Okay, Alex, for you. Brody said Martha will be lookout. There's something about a camera.'

'Martha will explain it, just don't take any pictures of yourself in case you lose it.'

I told him what I wanted done and the set-up. His face gave little away as he listened, but I knew he was curious. Nevertheless, he didn't ask any more questions. I was glad. I didn't want to lie to him. Then we parted ways; he for his home to gather what he needed, and me for my office.

When I got there, I curled up in my clothes on the small camp bed. I drew the blanket over me and dozed through the afternoon. I didn't want to think. Thinking was giving me a headache. It was blissful to have a blank mind. Even so, my thoughts inevitably strayed to Anna Blau. And in the way of things, to some others I'd not thought about for a while.

I got up several hours later, washed my face, straightened my hair, and made myself presentable with some powder and lipstick. Then I left and took the Tube to Ladbroke Grove, where Charlie and I had agreed to meet.

# Chapter 30

I met Charlie at a pub near Ladbroke Grove. It was a barn of a place, populated by men in rough-knit sweaters and smart jackets, drinking pints from knobbly glasses. Their better halves, as they constantly referred to their wives, clutched neat, straight ones. A fug of grey-blue smoke hung unmoving in the air, surrounding everyone and everything. A pianist smashed out a melody to triumphant cheers, and the barrels were rolled out again as if the war had never ended. We found a corner and shouted at each other; there was no other way to be heard above the ruckus.

'You look down,' Charlie said, leaning in close to my ear.

His breath smelled of mint, and his skin of a lemony cologne. How he was dressed, his gentle, sedate manner, maybe even what he'd been through in his life, the few bits I knew, I couldn't help thinking, he'd be an easy person to fall for.

'A friend of mine's had an accident,' I said.

'He's not hurting too badly, is he?'

'He'll survive,' I shouted back.

'Life's not fair, Alex.'

I nodded. 'He has two kids and a lovely wife. It makes me angry.' I looked Charlie squarely in the eyes. 'God help whoever did it, especially if Martha Evans finds them before I do.'

He clasped my hands in his, pulled me closer, and kissed me. I was taken by surprise.

'Sorry,' he said, 'I couldn't help myself. You just looked too cute.' I started laughing. 'I said I was in the cheering-up detail in the navy, didn't I?'

'You're right,' I shouted back.

'About the navy or looking cute?'

'No, about life.'

He looked at me curiously, before he lit a cigarette and contributed his share to the smokescreen around us.

'What's really troubling you, Genghis Raven?'

'Oh, just maudlin thoughts. I have them every now and then. The past is never that far away, is it, Charlie? My father, my aunt. Some of the people I worked with. What happened to them. Sometimes they come back to haunt me.'

His face was thoughtful, and the smile, when it came, was a sad one.

'Yeah. I know what you mean.' Charlie drew deeply on his cigarette. 'I get them as well. I tell myself it's stupid, blaming myself because I survived when others didn't. After all this time, I still don't know how to reconcile it.'

I can't say I did either.

'What do you do, Charlie? Just pick yourself up and start again?'

'Just think about the future. It's got to be a damn sight better than what went before.'

'Then to the future.' I raised my glass and touched his.

A couple of hours of passive smoking and several drinks went by quickly. It was past nine when we left the pub, giggling like schoolkids. The air outside smelled fresh, and my eyes were stinging. Charlie had his arm around my waist as we made our way to his car.

'Come on,' he said, 'let's go back to the flat. I promise I'll be a gentleman. Scout's honour.'

'You've never met my dad, have you?' I said.

'I can honestly say I haven't.'

'Come on. Let me introduce you.' I grabbed his hand and pulled him along and away from the car.

'What?' he asked, confused.

'Come on–'

'You're pissed,' he said.

'Pissed? Is that the way to speak to a lady? I'm a little cut, yes. I might even be three sheets to the wind, as you sailors say–'

'Only three?'

I laughed, saluting him.

'I walked into that one, didn't I?' He laughed along with me. 'Where is he, your dad?'

I pointed across the street and dragged him along.

A brick wall ran the full length of the road, broken every now and then by iron railings. I found the lowest part of the wall and tried jumping up to reach the top. My hand slipped off, and I tried again. The same result.

'Now what are you doing?' Charlie asked.

'Come on, give me a bunk-up,' I said.

'Up there?'

'Of course up there. Where else?'

He shook his head and cupped his hands together. I stepped into them, and he eased me up so that I could sit atop the wall. I reached an arm down to him.

'You crazy?' Charlie asked.

I grasped his arm and leaned backward to counterbalance his weight as he pulled himself up. Once on top, he glanced left and right. A few cars passed us by in the otherwise empty street. They didn't pay us any mind. Behind us was Kensal Green Cemetery.

'We could get arrested for this,' he said.

'Stop being a wet blanket,' I said, lowering myself to the other side. 'Come on. You're my knight in shining armour, my rescuer, the scourge of Victoria Park. Pretend you're off the Dalmatian coast dropping off an agent, and we're on a recce.'

'When you said you wanted me to meet your dad, I didn't think he'd be here.'

Ragged clouds slipped across the sky, the moon played hide-and-seek, and we danced ghostlike across the damp grass following the yellow pool of the flashlight I held in my hand. The silence pressed the great weight of the night down on us, heavy and oppressive. The shadows, solid and unmoving, grew and embraced us as we walked on silent heels.

'If anyone sees the light, they'll think we're vampires,' Charlie said.

'Vampires? Devil worshippers are more likely.' I placed the torch under my face and leered at him. 'This way, Igor,' I said in my best Boris Karloff impersonation, limping along.

'Oi! I thought we was devil worshippers!'

I knew exactly where I was going and could probably find it in the dark. Charlie held my hand and followed. After a minute, we were standing in front of my father's gravestone. I shone the light on it.

'Hi, Dad,' I said, wiping my mouth and dripping nose on my sleeve like I used to when I was a kid. 'I know, I know. It's late. But what the heck, right? I thought you'd like to meet Charlie Mathers. No, we're not dating, and no, we're not gonna get married. We're just friends, and no, not friends like that, so get that thought out of your head.' I whispered to Charlie, 'He's so bleedin' suspicious!'

'You're so bleedin' drunk,' Charlie said.

'It's rude not to say hello,' I admonished him loudly, and he shushed me.

'Sor-ry. Hello, Mr Raven. How are things?' Charlie glanced at me. 'Well, what else do I ask him?' Charlie whispered.

I waved the light around.

'That's Marie, my big sister,' I said, and suddenly I felt deflated.

Charlie knelt and gazed at the stone, which was also my mother's.

'Four years old,' he said, looking up at me. 'With her mum as well.'

'Not fair, is it?'

Charlie stood up and took my hand. 'Let's go, Alex,' he said.

'No, no, not yet.' I said it harshly and pulled my hand away petulantly. I shone the torch on another stone. 'Meet Aunt Katherine.'

'And who is she?'

'The lady who taught me French and lived in Paris, where I spent every summer, Easter, and Christmas holiday until the war began. She's the reason I speak French so well.'

Charlie stood still with his hands in his pockets to keep them warm. I stepped closer to him and wrapped my arms around my waist and hugged myself. Then I stepped back, straightened up, and took a deep breath. I switched off the torch, turned slowly around, and began walking away. Taken by surprise, Charlie had to skip to catch up with me.

'You know something, Raven; you're a crazy bitch,' Charlie said. 'It's past ten in the evening, and here I am with you in a cemetery of all places – which we've broken into, I'll remind you – meeting your parents. I reckon I must be crazy as well.'

'Let's go,' I said.

We walked back in silence, just the sound of our steps dragging the gravel behind us. We clambered back over the wall, and when we reached his car, I allowed him inside and stood on the pavement beside the driver's door.

'Get in,' he said.

I shook my head.

'I can't leave you like this.'

'You go on, Charlie; I feel like a walk, if that's okay?'

'On your own?'

'I've got an awful lot to think about.'

He looked at me for a while and then he nodded his head. 'I enjoyed the evening, Alex. Even meeting your dad. We should do it again. Not meet your dad, I mean… Can I call you tomorrow? I know a small restaurant up west you'd like.'

I nodded; he smiled, and drove off. I waited several minutes. Shaking off the drunkenness with several deep breaths, then I walked briskly to the main road and flagged down a taxi.

# Chapter 31

The door to Martha's shop was on the latch. I walked in, flicked it off, and closed the door behind me. I walked through the semi-darkness and into the back room. A blackout curtain draped the floor in front of the kitchen. Nat Pepper was seated in a comfortable chair, dressed in black, and reading the same novel he had been reading in the pub. A small standard lamp was next to him. Opposite him, Jack, who had also been reading, closed his newspaper. They both looked up at me.

'How did it go?' I asked Nat.

'The front door was easy.' Nat placed the book down, having folded back the top corner of the page he was on. 'You'd think a man like him would have better locks – especially in a rich man's place like that. The wall safe was older than the Ark and took five minutes. It took me longer to find the damn thing.'

'And?'

'Martha's printing the shots,' Jack said.

'Nat?'

'He's no gas man, nor an electric man, and he doesn't work for the council, even though he's got their IDs – he's not a union rep, either,' Nat said.

I stared blankly into space. 'It figures he'd have a lot of ID papers.'

'That's the thing! The IDs ain't forgeries, I'm sure of that. But they ain't his. One's in the name of Burroughs; another is Philbert. His passport is for Paul Thursday. The gas board one is Charles Mathers. Your guess is as good as mine for his real name.'

Jack handed me a glass of port; I took it and placed it down on the table and gazed at it.

'Good-quality clothes hanging in the wardrobe,' Nat continued. 'Some jewellery that's worth a bit. I reckon eight hundred pounds in used ones was in the safe.'

'You didn't take anything?' I gave Nat a stern stare.

He sipped his port, sat up in his chair, and shook his head.

'Man,' he said, 'it was hard leaving them behind. And there was a small automatic, one of those little Belgian things you ladies keep in your purse, a .25-calibre.'

'Not Martha,' I said. 'She'd want something that'd do the job.'

Nat laughed softly. 'She would, wouldn't she!' he whispered to me.

'Oi! I heard that,' Martha shouted from a room behind a blackout curtain. 'Is that you, girl?'

'Are the prints good?' I shouted back.

'Nat did all right for an amateur. A few blurred ones, but all right.'

'Man, that's a nice little camera, Alex,' Nat said. 'I gotta get me one just like it.'

'What else, Nat?' I asked sharply.

'He's careful. Professionally careful, I mean. It nearly caught me out.'

'That takes some doing.'

'There was a fine dusting of talcum powder on the combination dial of the safe. If I hadn't noticed the white dust on me gloves, I'd not have noticed it at all. So, that got me thinking.' He tapped his temple to show he'd been thinking. 'A careful man, all right. I checked under the rug by the door. The damn thing looked wrong when I first sees it. There they were, perfect impressions of me plates. He'd sprinkled powder under the rug. Anyone stepping on it, their weight would have left a shoe mark. Now, who does that and puts talcum powder on his safe if not a careful man? I put everything back as it was. I re-powdered everything, even blew away the spots that fell on the table below the safe, just as he'd done. Nothing looked disturbed. I was in and out in an hour.'

'How did you know?' Jack asked me.

I sipped the port he'd given me, swallowing it with some of my annoyance.

'Someone asked me if I'd made any friends recently.' I screwed my lips up, so that's what Hawkins meant, *new-found friends*. Then my *friend* saved me in a staged fight, and I was too dumb to notice.

The blackout curtains parted, and the room behind them was bathed in a red light. Martha carried a tray with her.

'Clear your junk, Nat,' she said, nodding to the table. Nat collected his book and spectacle case along with his drink, and Martha placed the tray down under the light. It was filled with wet photographic prints. 'You're in vogue,' she said to me.

There were several copies of prints there. Some of me and Jack taken the day we were standing outside the League's building. We were captured when we waved at the van, and there was a print of me taking one of the leaflets from the dispenser outside their door. There were a few more, this time of me and Hugo Latimer talking together at the bomb site where we found Saul Greenberg's body.

My service record was there – a photographic copy of it anyway – but it was incomplete; it was only the front sheet with some minor details. I looked absurdly young in the picture that was taken of me almost eight years ago.

I peeled them apart from the others and placed them on one side.

'You take a good shot, girl,' Martha said in a quiet, unimpressed monotone. She searched through the prints and found what she was looking for.

'The papers were in a folder,' Nat said, recognising what she held.

He'd taken pictures of the front sheets of various documents. There were faces. Some wore stiff peaked caps, while others wore foraged ones with the spread eagle clutching the swastika pin. They looked like the document Bruno Marx showed me, only these were neater. I recognised only two of the dozen shots Nat had taken: Natalia Popov and Hauptmann Otto Grunwald. There was a different name under each of their names.

'Naughty, naughty,' Martha muttered, recognising them for what they were. 'These are things he shouldn't have. He's going to catch merry hell if they find out he's got copies of them.'

'He's either overconfident or…' I picked up Popov's print.

'Or what?' Martha asked.

'She got a new name,' I said to Martha.

She flashed me a *so what?* face. 'That's important?' she asked, and I nodded.

'These ones,' she said, laying down some dry prints, 'were the ones you took at that place you broke into. Nothing remarkable. I'll ask around to see if anyone recognises the one you clobbered.'

'Don't bother. You won't have any luck,' I said.

'The tape recorder's the latest make,' Jack said, 'and that's money.'

'The same type was in the church behind Goel Hadam.'

'And him.' Martha handed me a print of a hatted man exiting the League. 'He's Inspector Moncrief. He was in Special Branch, but he's not anymore.' She huffed. 'Truth is, I don't know what he is now, but judging by all of this, he's gone up in the world.'

'Yes, I met the man.' I studied the picture of the face I'd seen through a car window. 'He's the one who warned me off.'

It made sense now. Martha shook her head.

'I called Marx from Charlie's place,' I said. 'Marx said he'd found where Grunwald was having a meeting. The meeting got cancelled at the last minute. I wrote down the address when I was there.'

She nodded slowly. 'Your boyfriend must have checked the sheet under it and put two and two together.' I didn't like how Martha said *boyfriend*, and I gave her a stare to show it. It didn't worry her. 'That means he and Moncrief are working together.'

She was right. Not only about Charlie discovering what I'd written but also about Moncrief, who'd indeed gone up in the world.

'None of this stuff smacks of police, Alex.' Jack had read my mind. He sat down and tapped out some cigarettes from a packet. He passed them around to Nat and Martha. 'Not even Special Branch. It smacks of what we used to do during the war.'

'I hate to say this, girl, but the big ape's right, and you need to speak to Latimer.'

'And tell him what? That the Secret Service have got eyes on the League and Goel Hadam? That ex-German officers are working for us and lunching at the Savoy? What exactly do you want me to tell him that he doesn't already know?'

'Maybe tell him that the car that broke down at the bomb site was an official off-the-record car,' Jack said. 'Like the one that followed you and Theo last night.'

'He knows about the one last night. I gave him a number plate. How do you know about the other?'

'A woman called at the shop for you,' Martha said. 'Fifty, maybe, prim and proper with butter-wouldn't-melt manners. She'd a message for you. The car that broke down was an unregistered black Wolseley, she said to tell you. It had two passengers and two others. She was adamant about the passengers – two! She said that it was no use trying to find it as well.'

'Virginia Bright,' I said.

'The one who set you up?' Jack asked.

'She didn't. Someone who knew I visited Ash did. They figured it all out after bugging my phone. They used my messenger service to set me up at the park.'

'And Charlie boy came charging up, right on cue,' Martha said.

'He was charming,' I said flatly but I didn't look up. I just stared at the prints on the table, not really looking at any.

'I bet he was.'

I flicked my eyes to her, then looked away.

'I don't know entirely what I've got myself into,' I said. 'Three things are going on – what happened to Anna and what's going on with Grunwald.' I picked up the print of Popov's face and looked at it some more. 'And this.'

'What's Ash's interest, Alex?' Jack asked.

I didn't want to tell them Ash had found religion, partly because I didn't believe it and partly because I knew he'd have another agenda. I was blundering into things, making waves, and stirring up the mud, and I couldn't help but think that suited him. And Anna Blau was caught up in it all, more by accident than design.

I sat down as Martha cleared away the tray of prints.

'How many people are in this circus of ours?' Jack asked.

'Far too many,' I said. I picked up my drink and sipped it.

Nat stood up and slipped on his jacket. 'Looks like you lot have your problems.'

He collected his stuff. He placed a pair of black silk gloves in the bag, along with a cloth cap and a chemise leather duster.

'If that's all, I'll be on my way,' he said. 'I'm not sure I like what you people are talking about. I'm not sure I want to understand. I'm just a simple housebreaker.' He laughed, leaned backward and rolled his shoulders, working out the crick in his neck. 'You know you getting old when you like your bed. So, goodnight, sweet ladies; it's been a pleasure as always. Brody, my man.' He nodded.

'Go on holiday for a week,' I said. 'If anyone calls saying it's us, it won't be.'

'I could use a rest. Me sister lives in Glasgow. It ain't Monte Carlo, but it'll do.'

He tipped his hat and left. The bell above the door jangled, and then the lock clicked shut.

'What now?' Jack asked.

'She's got a new name,' I repeated.

'So, Popov's got a new name,' Martha said.

'You don't give a dead woman a new name, Martha,' Jack told her.

'I'll make us some tea,' Martha said, 'then you can tell me what's going on.'

* * *

I called Wilfried Ash. To be safe, I did it from the telephone box at the corner of the street. It was past midnight, but Ginny had said he'd be awake. He wasn't surprised to hear from me.

I told him about the break-ins. He acknowledged my words but said nothing; he only listened. I told him about Charlie Mathers and what we'd found. He did the same, merely murmuring yes or no as was appropriate – but I sensed he was interested. I told him about Hawkins, and I thanked him both for his gift of the pamphlet and for how Hawkins dealt with the bugs. Ash was silent. The silence hung in the air, thick and heavy like a blanket, suffocating any sound. I thought we'd lost contact for a moment until I heard his voice muffled in the background, speaking to someone. I couldn't make out what was said or to whom he was speaking; other than that it was a man's voice – I don't know what made me think it was Hawkins, but that's what I thought.

'Good, I'm glad he found you,' Ash said eventually.

'Will you thank him for me when you see him?' I asked.

'I shall, Miss Raven.' I heard Ash laugh. 'I shall, but it might amuse him. It's not often he's thanked. Hawkins is an odd man, isn't he? Where are you?' I told him. 'Will you be staying there tonight?' I said yes. 'The leaflet, by the way, wasn't sent by me.' Then the phone went dead.

# Chapter 32

I slept in the spare room above the shop and awoke early. The conversation with Ash nagged me. I knew when I mentioned Charlie that I'd said something that piqued his interest. I sat up in bed with the thought that the man he was speaking to last night was Hawkins. I didn't know why I had the thought. It wasn't so much that I recognised the voice as the rhythm of the few words I'd heard. It awoke that paranoid part of me that saw shadows everywhere.

I left Jack and Martha asleep, popped out to a cafe at the corner that had just opened, and sat down to breakfast. I was its only customer. Benny, the proprietor, was a talkative individual blessed with the good sense of knowing when to shut up and leave his customers alone with their own thoughts. Mine was about my day and where it would lead. Last night's revelations weighed heavily.

I'd just finished the bacon and was halfway through my tea when a thin, pasty-faced, dishevelled fellow stood before me. His mottled cheeks had liver spots, and he looked old before his time. He could have been twenty; he could have been forty; hell, it was difficult to tell, and I couldn't be bothered to guess. I decided to ignore him. He didn't go away. Instead, he scratched under his arms like he needed a delousing spray of DDT. I saw the needle marks on his forearm, and I gave him a *keep your distance* stare. Taking the hint, he sat on the opposite table from me but still stared at me.

'Your name Raven?' he asked eventually.

'Someone taught you to speak, did they?'

'Fuck you!'

'You'll be lucky. Who wants to know?'

'Charlie would like to see you.'

'Charlie who?'

'Mathers.'

'Why?'

'He don't tell me nothing.' His eyes were fixed on my plate. Two toasts remained. His lips parted, revealing cracked brown tombstones. His eyes bobbled left and right and back to my plate. They were constantly moving, unable to keep still.

'Where?' I asked.

He tapped his pockets and found a slip of paper. It had an address written on it – the house number of a street off Gray's Inn Road, near Farringdon.

'How did you know where to find me?' I asked.

'Just told you'd be here or in your office.'

'Charlie said that? He must be psychic.'

'He told me what you looked like. An' I seen you through the window.'

'You sure he didn't point me out?'

Something that could pass as a smile moved in his face. I'd lost my appetite.

'Here.' I passed the saucer of toast over to him, and he snatched it before I'd placed it on the table.

He mumbled what might have been a thanks, but it could have been a line of a Keats poem. It was difficult to tell.

'Benny,' I said, 'give him a tea.'

Benny gave me a sour look. So, I left a decent tip. The look didn't change.

Jack was in the kitchen when I returned. I told him I was going to meet Charlie. He shook the sleep away.

'You want company?' he asked.

'No,' I said. 'This is to do with last night. If Charlie's who I think he is, then Nat didn't catch all his tricks.'

'Then it's best I was there.'

'Don't worry, Jack. I'd have had to have this conversation with him at some point. The sooner the better. Maybe now, I'll get some answers.'

'It'll be a two-way street. What're you going to tell him?'

'Let's see what he asks.'

* * *

It was a pleasant enough morning for a stroll – not too cold, not too warm, dry, with no wind. The sun, fed up with the clouds and rain, pretended spring was here. Great shafts of it shone between the buildings like solid chunks of amber. It was warm whenever I crossed through one. I walked down Oxford Street; there were no shoppers yet, just the shop girls making their way along. I went past Tottenham Court Road station, then Holborn, and turned into Gray's Inn Road at Chancery Lane station. A hundred yards along, on a small side street, I found the address I was given.

The building was derelict. Several nameplates of now-defunct companies still hung beside the door. The Destiny Employment Agency had the second floor. The street door was open, so I went in and walked along a short corridor to a set of stairs that led upwards into gloom. The dark-green paintwork could have been a trend during the thirties, and the place had the quality of being last lived in then. On the second-floor landing, a mottled sign said I'd found the Destiny Employment Agency. I had no need to knock. The door had no handle and was ajar. I went into a small reception of bare wood and dust, an empty free-standing bookcase, and another door at the end.

'Charlie?' I shouted.

Pongo's voice shouted, 'Alex, in here.'

The room was empty of furniture except for a desk piled with junk. The floorboards were bare and creaked as I walked. There were two dusty windows with only shapes visible through them. Pongo stood beside one of them. His hands were in the pockets of his greatcoat; he hunched his shoulders as if cold. The room was warm.

'Where's Charlie?' I asked.

'He's not happy with you, Alex,' Pongo said as he approached the desk. Once there, he perched his behind on it, his hands still in his pockets.

'Why's that?'

'He fancies himself a lady's man, and generally he does okay. But not with you.'

'Shame. He'll get over it.

'Probably. But not the hassle and the fallout. They don't go away easily.'

'So, where is he?'

Pongo looked at his watch. 'Explaining himself to the headmaster, I should imagine.'

'Who are they?'

'Since you rumbled us, I think you know.'

'If it wasn't the talcum powder on the safe or the powder under the rug, what was it?'

Pongo smiled. The first real emotion to cross his face since I'd entered the room.

'Your man replaced the items in the safe incorrectly. Charlie always leaves something overhanging the others. It's small, but big enough. Hats off to your man, though; he got most of it right.'

'Charlie's a clever man.'

'Not clever enough. He didn't appreciate the irony of being played by you. Taken to a pub, then a cemetery, and kept away so your man could do his bit. He's done it too often enough to others to like it done to him.'

'I guess I over-clevered things. A straight burglary might have been simpler. So, what happens now?' I went to stand by the mantlepiece, across from the desk. 'Does Charlie know you're here?'

'Whose suggestion do you think this is?' Pongo spread his feet and scuffed his heels, making marks on the dusty floor. He looked at them as if they were some sort of writing to be deciphered. 'What did you find last night?'

'From his safe? Nothing.'

He gave me a knowing nod. 'Did you photograph something? That's what I'd do.' His smile was brittle.

When I didn't answer, Pongo sniffed a laugh.

'Who you working for?' he asked. 'Ash?'

'Why him?'

'Well, you know him, at least. He's been a busy boy of late. Asking questions here and there.' Pongo screwed up his lips. 'I guess you saw the files. The question is, Alex, what did you make of it all? And what did you tell Ash? You have told him, haven't you?'

I stood quiet. I didn't like the way the conversation was going. The menace in his eyes was clear. I knew what that meant. He was nearer the door than me, and I'd never make it before him.

'They made me think. They weren't something Charlie should have, were they, Pongo?'

He sighed rather loudly while shaking his head. It wasn't a happy sigh.

'Oh, Charlie boy, how you messed up this one. He was always greedy. I told him to park his ambition and copy one file at a time, not the whole bleedin' lot at once. But not my boy – he had to take them home as well.'

'So, you and Charlie are freelancing. Doesn't His Majesty pay you enough? Who are you moonlighting for?'

'Does it matter?' he asked.

'I guess not. It's just money, after all. There would be plenty of buyers as far as those files are concerned, but it's the Russians who are interested in Popov.'

'Popov? What do you know?'

'That she's not dead, despite what the papers say. Everyone's playing a game in which she's the prize. She was in the car that broke down where we found Saul's body. The body in the mortuary is a smokescreen. The American destroyer, the other body; who was that one?'

'A shmuck who smuggles people.'

'Fodder, in other words, just to convince us she's dead and eating hamburgers in New York at the same time. Getting the Americans involved by passing the blame off on them… I bet they're not pleased. And all the time she's being debriefed somewhere by your cloak-and-dagger friends. Where's Anna Blau?'

'Everyone thinks they know better than the professionals. The saying was always *keep things simple*. The more complex they are, the more can go wrong.' He shook his head. 'This has been a balls-up since day one. First getting a flat tyre, then that boy turning up and dying on us, then Popov getting all righteous with us about the girl that was with him. The stupid bitch, it would have been so simple to kill the girl there and then.'

'Anna,' I said. 'The girl is Anna. The boy who died on you is Saul. They've got names. So they were just in the wrong place at the wrong time – they weren't mixed up in any of this?'

Pongo gave me a hard stare. 'That's the point, Alex. They are now, and there's no denying that – accident or otherwise.' He stood up, and the desk he'd been leaning on creaked with a complaint that echoed in the empty room. 'The thing, Alex, is that you've figured out most of *"this"* already. Ash's no fool. He'd have hinted something to you – is that how you figured out Charlie?'

'I didn't know about your freelancing opportunities. Maybe Ash does, maybe he doesn't. And Charlie made some mistakes,' I said.

'I've seen Charlie work. He's good. No, you needed some help to figure him out.' He shuffled from one foot to the other, like a greyhound waiting in the traps to be released. 'Brody and the woman probably know, and that complicates matters.'

'I guessed. And Popov?'

'She's the goldmine.' He rubbed his thumb across his index and middle fingers. 'If things had gone to plan, we'd be set up for good. Then you and Ash came along and spoiled everything. Now it's all going to hell in a handcart. It's all about confusion now, Alex. Charlie and I will need a bit of time before Ash comes calling.'

'I see,' I said.

'I don't think you do, Alex.' He reached behind him, and a length of lead pipe appeared in his right hand. 'I'd prefer to shoot you; it's a damn sight simpler, but Charlie says it has to be this way.' He patted the pipe into the open palm of his left hand, and it made a dull clap. 'You've stirred up a lot of trouble for us these past few days.'

I nodded, my eyes fixed on the pipe, rising and falling into his palm.

'Who's the prime candidate for my murder? Is there one?'

'There will be one by tomorrow. There are a few I can choose from who'd fit the bill.'

'Including the junkie I just met. In fact, he'd be ideal, wouldn't he? Just the sort who'd beat a girl to death with a lead pipe. Where will he be found? In the basement or the bottom of the stairs with his neck broken?'

'I like the bottom of the stairs. Charlie's for an overdose.'

'With the content of my bag in his pockets. But this isn't just about what was found in your safe, is it?'

'No. Not just that. It's also about a particularly nasty little German who doesn't want his past dug up. Marx's done a good job there.'

'Ah, I wondered when Grunwald would crawl out from the woodwork.'

'You and the Jew boy have stirred one pot too many. Mr Grunwald likes his new role as defender of the West. His special friends will deal with Marx. I'm here to deal with you. He doesn't want anyone to get in his way.'

'What about Brody?'

'He's only a problem if he gets curious.'

'Oh, he will. And Ash?'

He gave a wide smile. 'Ash is one of the untouchables. He's far too much trouble.'

'He's no fool,' I said. 'He'll put two and two together–'

'You know, I think he has. That's why we'll be gone before he can do anything. Long gone. In the old days, he could have had us hung, drawn, and quartered on a whim. Not these days. These days it takes a while longer than he's got. As for Anna Blau, when the others get their acts together, she'll vanish. Popov's too much of an asset to jeopardise by keeping Blau alive.'

'So, she's alive?'

He stood up straight, but his body hung loose. 'No hard feelings, Alex. But Chas and I have been planning this for too long to have you mess it up.'

Pongo stepped forward, quickly taking up the space between us, the pipe ready to sweep down across my head. I stepped in close, cramping him up. He swung the pipe, and I raised my arm, deflecting it. It caught me a glancing blow, making my ear ring. My momentum carried me forward, and I kicked hard with my knee into his thigh. He grunted in pain and pushed me away. I reached to grasp at his arm but missed and crashed into the wall behind me.

He was twisted around, half bent, his dead leg collapsing under him, and he leaned entirely on his good leg. Cursing, his hand slipped inside his pocket, only to reappear clutching a revolver. He'd gone for the simpler option. I came forward again. His face curled into a nasty sneer. I dodged sideways just as he fired. In the small, empty office, it sounded like an explosion bursting in my ear.

Pongo pitched forward. A red hole had appeared in his forehead, and his eyes gaped in wild surprise. They were looking at me, but they were dead eyes. His ankles, bending awkwardly like they shouldn't, like his legs were made of rubber, gave way and I grabbed and caught him as he toppled over me. He was a dead weight, and I spread my legs, trying to hold him. It was like stopping a piano from slipping down a flight of stairs. My legs folded under me as we sank to the floor. His head pitched forward and came to rest on my shoulder, his arms hanging loosely on either side. The gun in his left hand fell with a clunk, and the pipe rang with a dull rattle and rolled away, stopping against the wall under one of the windows.

I pushed the dead man off me in a wild panic and scrambled backwards until I struck the wall behind me.

Standing in the doorway, Hawkins was calmly unscrewing the silencer from a pistol. His eyes were focused on the task at hand. The small, innocuous man seemed not to have noticed either me or the dead body on the floor.

I clambered on to my knees, and there was a long silence. My ears rang with the concussion of the round that came from Pongo's gun, fired the instant Hawkins had shot him. I'd been splattered with his blood and brains and felt physically sick. I watched in shuttered silence the surreal way Hawkins walked across the room, wiped his pistol clean with a handkerchief, and placed it on Pongo's back for all to see and find. Just as calmly, he pocketed the silencer. He then walked around the body and reached a hand down to me. He was looking at me kindly.

I fenced his hands away and struggled to stand. My legs trembled but held me upright.

Pongo was lying on his front, his legs twisted sideways, his head resting the opposite way from his legs, his arms to either side, and his palms facing up to the ceiling. The revolver seemed to lie just out of reach of his hand.

'If I may take your coat?' Hawkins said softly, holding out his hand.

'My coat?' I stuttered.

'Please, Miss Raven, your coat.'

I slipped it off, realising that the left shoulder was stained with Pongo's blood. Hawkins gave me his handkerchief.

'There's a washroom along the corridor. If there's running water, it may be a good idea to wash your face.'

'My face,' I mumbled.

'Yes, your face.'

I made my way to the door, glanced back, and stopped.

'You shot him,' I said dumbly.

'He was about to shoot you,' Hawkins said. 'I should have acted earlier.'

It wasn't the regret of having killed someone but of miscalculating a situation. He seemed to be a man who seldom did that and would worry over why it had happened, not its consequence.

A small square window allowed just enough light into the washroom so I could see myself in the cracked mirror. I leaned on the sink on extended arms and examined my face. I looked pale and sickly, the spit of Pongo's blood like dark spots freckling my skin. I'd aged since this morning. I washed my face and the front of my hair, taking deep and deeper breaths as I slowly came to myself. Then I dried my face on the handkerchief. I checked carefully to see if I'd rid myself completely of blood.

When I came back to the room, Hawkins held my coat. He'd turned it inside out, hiding the bloodstain. In one hand, he clutched the contents of the pockets which he swapped for his handkerchief. That included my name tag from inside the coat and the laundry label it carried. Now it was just someone else's coat and not mine.

He left for the washroom, and I saw him wiping all the surfaces that could carry a fingerprint with them. The same had been done to the room where Pongo lay. Hawkins carried an air of professionalism that demonstrated none of this was new to him; he was doing it all by the numbers as if he'd done it all before.

When he was satisfied, he came back. I knew he'd searched the body and taken anything that could identify it. It was all about delaying things and making the police's job hard. It was all about confusion. That only made me wonder even more about Hawkins. He stood next to me, surveying the room one last time to see if he'd missed anything.

The room was quiet and still. He was quiet and still. And Pongo was quiet and still.

# Chapter 33

'Why are you following me?' I asked Hawkins.

'I was instructed to help you,' he said.

'I must remember to thank our mutual friend.'

'He asked me to keep an eye on you this morning. Our friend suspected something of this nature. He's quite perceptive.' He glanced down at Pongo. 'I don't kill people unless I have to, Miss Raven. I had to kill this gentleman. Judge me if you wish.'

'I wasn't going to. You saved my life, and I'm grateful. I'm sorry you had to. But only a bit.'

I spent a few minutes asking questions – just who exactly he was? What did he know of what was going on? What my part in it all was? I'm sure he knew that – only for Hawkins to politely dance around each question and say nothing. So I spent a few minutes gathering my thoughts together.

'If you would consent to wait here for a few minutes,' Hawkins said, 'I have a phone call to make. Will you wait?'

I was curious and confused, and he'd asked me nicely, and he knew what he was doing, so I said yes. He gave a slight bow of his head and left.

With my gloved finger, I wiped a circle in the dust on the window and watched Hawkins cross the street to a red telephone box opposite the building. He spent a minute and a half speaking on the phone. Then he walked down the road to a second-hand clothing shop a few doors away. I turned away and turned my back on Pongo. A few minutes later, I heard footsteps on the stairs, and Hawkins came back carrying a women's coat and what looked to be brown parcel paper. He handed me the coat, and he took a minute to wrap my bloodstained one in brown paper before securing it with twine.

The coat was a little too long for me and a little old-fashioned. It smelled musty. Even so, I wouldn't stand out wearing it, as I would without it in the cold morning outside.

'Are we going to just leave him here?' I said.

'It is what we will do.'

I didn't know what to make of his matter-of-factness. It was all practical: a straight line between two points.

'I was hired to find Anna Blau,' I said, 'I guess you don't know her. I don't know her, either. But I understand what's happened. Why they didn't kill her then and there, like Saul, I don't really know. But they didn't. By now, she may well be dead. But I have to believe she isn't.'

He listened patiently to my ramblings, perhaps understanding them, perhaps not; I couldn't read the mask that was his face.

'I want to find her, Mr Hawkins. I don't know where to look. But I know who to ask. Now, what is it you want?'

'To help like I have been asked to do,' he said it without caring whether I believed him or not.

'Then I need to see a man named Mathers.'

'And he will be of help to you?'

'I think he will.'

Hawkins did not take his eyes off me. He considered me for a full minute, weighing what I didn't know in his mind, before pouting his lips.

'Then, shall we find him?' he said.

I nodded.

When we left the building, he tucked the brown-paper parcel under his arm. I followed him out and onto Gray's Inn Road. He stopped me from hailing a cab and instead directed me to a bus stop, where he waited with me but not with me at the same time. He was unhurried, nonchalant, and invisible.

It took me the bus ride to come to myself, along with the fact that we'd left Pongo's body lying in an empty office for someone to find. The anger in me, though, simmered. Not because Pongo was dead, but because of Charlie, the game he'd played with me, and the fact that he'd sent Pongo to kill me. And because I'd been taken in. I might not have been any the wiser if it hadn't been for Ash. If it weren't for Hawkins, I'd be dead.

And, also, because of Anna Blau, a total innocent caught up in a game that would kill her – if it hadn't already.

When we alighted the bus at Oxford Street, Hawkins made to hail a cab. I stopped him. I wanted to go to my office first. He hadn't spoken a word to me since leaving the building, and he didn't now.

It was ten o'clock. I ignored Arnie, who tried to speak to me from the entrance of his sandwich shop. Once inside my office, I unlocked the steel filing cabinet and pulled open the bottom drawer. It mainly contained files stored flat, some old clothes, and what I was looking for: a .32-calibre automatic pistol wrapped in a cotton shawl.

'Is that wise?' Hawkins asked. He stood quietly in the doorway, still clutching the parcel.

'I just don't want any more surprises,' I said.

He nodded and did not say anything else. Somehow, I thought he agreed with me.

I found two magazines, checked that they were full, and pressed one into the handle until it caught. With the safety on, I slipped the gun and the spare magazine into my handbag.

# Chapter 34

I left Hawkins at the entrance to Charlie Mathers's flat. He'd seen me in, having picked the lock. He was a surprising man. Hawkins had knelt to tie a shoelace and had risen with a small, ugly, black automatic pistol in his hand. The flat was empty, and when Hawkins was satisfied, he left, but not before asking me if I was sure of what I intended. I told him I was. He asked how long I intended to wait. I told him as long as it took, but said it wouldn't be too long. He left and didn't look back.

I chose a comfortable Parker Knoll armchair to wait in; it was situated in a dark corner of Charlie's living room. A standard lamp was next to it, along with a small, polished table. Behind it, in a well-stocked bookcase, I found a volume of Wordsworth's poems. I rested the .32 on my lap; the safety was off and a shell was in the breech, the book and my right hand covering it. I waited.

The room fell quiet, and soon I became aware of the silent noises, the ones you never hear unless you really listen, and we seldom do that. The chatter of people passing by the building from three floors below rose and faded, as did the sounds of cars on the street, an aeroplane in the distance, the kiss the pages made when I turned them, the evenness of my breathing, and the muffled thud of my heartbeat.

I read the words of the poems but didn't take them in. I slipped in and out of my thoughts, my mind moving quietly through the days since Mrs Geller asked me to help David Blau. I thought of the blank eyes of Pongo and the surprised look on his face. It'd happened so fast that he didn't even know he was dead. I thought of Saul Greenberg and was glad that Farmer didn't show me the rat-eaten body. *They go for the eyes first*, he'd said, as if it were common knowledge, something we all should know, useful stuff to fill a gap in a conversation at some dinner party – *by the way, did you know…*

I thought of Solomon Greenberg, what he must have gone through in his life, and how he looked, with bright eyes trapped in a broken body, and of Ruth, whose devotion knew no bounds. I wondered if she'd be thankful when he finally gave up the struggle, if she'd be free, or if the past was something she'd never be able to discard. Would her dead son allow her that luxury? I thought about Anna Blau, someone I didn't know but felt I'd always known. And about Theo Drakas, who had taken a beating for me.

And I thought of lots more things, besides.

In the cold and dark room, midday came and went. Outside, the clouds had thickened and snuffed out the light. There was hardly enough left to read, but I wasn't reading. The darkness felt comfortable. A few times I heard the sound of the lift and footsteps clacking across the linoleum from somewhere inside the building – the grating and slamming of the wire door, the hum of the mechanism, raising or lowering it. Some raised voices carried into the room.

My anger had long since subsided. It had been raging beneath my mind for some time, and it was now hiding somewhere within me, waiting to be summoned. I felt calm and rested. The dull ache on the side of my face where Pongo had struck me was no more than a memory. I got up, went to the bathroom, threw cold water over my face, and returned to my vigil, my eyes fixed on the door.

Time moves slowly when you wait.

The whirr of the lift came to me again. I heard it as a soft noise and heard the jerking clank of the mechanism as it stopped. Then came the grating of the wire gate and the sharp noise it made as it was slammed shut. Footsteps approached the door, the sound of keys fiddling with the locks, and Charlie Mathers stepped in, looking a little dishevelled. He took off his coat, tossed it aside, loosened his tie, and went to the liquor cabinet beside the living room door and poured himself a whisky. He turned and was about to take a sip when he saw me. He stopped.

'Alex,' he said. I heard the surprise in his voice.

'What's the matter, Charlie? No cute remarks today?' I asked.

'What can I say, Alex? I've had a hell of a day.'

'Me too.' I sat back deeper into the chair. 'Mine began with a message to meet you. A nasty little man with rotten teeth delivered it. But then you know that.' I nodded my head towards the chair opposite. Charlie moved quietly over and sank into it, sitting stiffly like a mannequin in a shop window display. 'Imagine my surprise when I got to the Destiny Employment Agency and you weren't there.'

I saw the look in his eyes, the uncertainty that lived there before they dropped, and he was looking at the floor. I could hear his brain thinking. He'd been holding his glass in both hands, and, as his right hand quietly slipped off, I allowed Wordsworth to fall to the floor. The clatter brought his eyes up. I crossed my legs and held the .32 flat on my knee, aiming at him in a somewhat casual manner. He drew in a slow and long breath, held it for a second, and let it out silently. We stared at each other for what seemed like an eternity.

'We both know I can use this.'

'Pongo?' he asked.

'You might read about him in tomorrow's newspapers if you live that long, assuming they find him before then. Both hands around the glass, Charlie.'

He gave a soft smile that wasn't a smile and held the glass in both hands.

'So, what happens now?' he asked.

'That's up to you, isn't it?'

'Are you seriously going to shoot me? In cold blood? I don't think so, Alex. I know you.'

'You don't know me, Charlie. You might have read some reports on me, but you don't know me. I'm no doe-eyed innocent, fresh from prep school. I've done things I'm not proud of. If I live long enough, I'll probably do others. But it's not me I've come to discuss. It's Anna Blau.'

He sipped his drink, spying me over the rim of the glass.

'*Am I blue?*' He hummed with an awkward smile. I didn't smile, and his slowly slipped away and vanished. 'What if she's dead?'

'Is she? Pongo seems to think she's not – at least not yet.'

'She will be by tomorrow. Maybe I can help you get her back before then?'

'Maybe. Where is she?'

'Well, where is she, indeed?'

'You're not holding the cards, Charlie. So, tell me a story. I think I know most of it, but help me out by filling in the rest.'

He sat back in silence, just looking at me. His smile had returned, but it looked forced, and it wasn't the happy, carefree one he usually wore. It was the sort of smile to convince someone you were confident while hoping you weren't overdoing it.

'That could take some telling,' he said.

'Then let me help you. I know you and Pongo were involved in Popov's disappearance. But I don't care about her. What happened with Saul Greenberg?'

Charlie made to place the glass down, and I flicked the gun at him to keep hold of it.

'He was in the wrong place at the wrong time,' he said.

'So were you, I guess. A nice place to get a flat.'

He hunched over as if to confirm how unfortunate a place it was.

'We didn't exactly plan it.'

'Then Saul and Anna came along,' I said.

'He recognised her. That was the problem, Alex. He recognised her. He'd gone to one of her lectures and knew who she was. He'd read her works and understood some of them. He tried to speak to her; there was a struggle; the man I was with panicked. He punched him. I was changing the tyre at the time; I didn't even see him coming towards us until it was all over. The boy fell and struck his head on the fender. He was dead when we put him in the cellar. That's the truth. It was an accident.'

'No, Charlie. He died from shock and a broken leg after you threw him into the cellar.'

He fell quiet and bit his lip. 'Ah, I didn't know that,' he said softly.

'How did you know him?' I asked.

'Saul Greenberg? I didn't?'

'*Read all her works. Understood some of it?* How did you know that? Did he mention that when he bumped into you that night? *By the way, Charlie, I know Popov and her research. It's all tough stuff, but I understood it…*'

Charlie gave a ghost of a laugh and took a sip of his drink.

'He recognised *you* and Popov. Was he working for you?'

'Since you know, why are you asking?' he said.

'Curious, that's all. All the time, Saul's been passing you information about the Nazis Marx found, and you've been paying him to get it.'

'He wanted the money; he was no innocent.'

'No, probably not. You don't spend your youth in a concentration camp and emerge all innocent. With the files he gave you, along with the ones from your other friends, you've built up quite a little nest egg. But it wasn't Popov's Nazi past that attracted you. Just her Russian present. Was that why you arranged the break-ins? To see if you missed anything, and to make sure he didn't have anything linking you to him? He must have been surprised to see Popov in the car since he had Marx's file on her.'

'She's the golden egg-laying goose.'

'It was a nice scheme hatched by your friends for her defection. A body identified as Popov, the way you tried to suggest the Americans were involved, and it was a kidnap. Who were they, the two you burnt on the boat? Shmucks, Pongo said.'

He hunched his shoulders and sighed tiredly.

'Just a couple of West Germans who were in our business.'

'But didn't understand their part.'

His look said what his mouth didn't.

'But you knew the Russians would see through the fake body and who they would point to – you left them enough clues, maybe too many. Maybe that was the point, because all the time, she'd be safely working for us. I get that, Charlie. It was well done, I'm sure.'

'It was, Alex, even down to the American destroyer rendezvousing with a submarine the day after she left. We just let things hang. And while everyone talked about it, Popov would just disappear off the map.'

'I'm sure you're very pleased with yourselves. Now, about Anna.'

Charlie puckered his lips, inhaled, and exhaled heavily.

'We debated what to do with her. Popov insisted we bring her back with us. She grew a conscience. That surprised us. But what could we do? Only when we got Anna back, we didn't know what to do with her. If we'd let her go, she might have told the papers that Popov was alive. And if we got rid of her, we risked Popov shutting up or being difficult. You see the dilemma?'

'So you'd wait until you debriefed Popov, get her settled, and then deal with Anna.'

Charlie glanced over to the drinks cabinet. 'You know the game we're in. We have to keep her alive until we're sure we have what we want. Can I get another drink?'

I kept the gun on him and told him to remain seated, and he sat back.

'Pongo told me all about your freelancing opportunities. I didn't figure it out at the time when I saw the pictures my friend had taken.' I flicked my nose to where his safe was.

His face hardened; it had lost all its playfulness. A mask had fallen away, and his look was mean and nasty.

'I fought a war, Alex, to rid this world of those Nazi bastards. And what do I find? I find that after all the fighting, here I am, protecting them. I'm looking out for them. I'm living with them; having supper with them; I'm laughing at their jokes; I'm reminiscing with them… *my, they were good old days*, they confided, and we'd sing a chorus of *Lili Marleen* to get us into the spirit of things. There they are, living in luxury, driving their fancy cars if not having people drive for them, and it's like nothing ever happened. There's a bigger enemy, and we need friends like them, I'm told. We need their expertise if we're going to win this one, I'm told. Let's get into bed with them, I'm told. Let's forgive and forget.'

'I bleed for you, Charlie. Life's a bitch. What can I tell you?'

'I bled enough for them, Alex. Didn't you?'

‘This isn’t about me, Charlie. I’ve got no problem with the past that I can’t deal with.’

‘Then you’re lucky.’ He dropped his gaze into his lap, and slowly his eyes rose back up again. ‘Well, Pongo and I were after some of that, some of what they had. If the edges are that blurred, who’s to say that next year they won’t revert to being our enemies again or that the Russians won’t be our friends? They’ve made it a dog-eat-dog world.’

‘Just like you rescuing me, let’s be friends, and then later, let’s not. Yes, Charlie, the edges do blur, and they do so quickly. You almost fooled me.’

‘Only because of Ash. I still can’t figure out if you and he are working together. But you visited him.’ He furrowed his brow. ‘Pongo and me couldn’t be sure; we needed to know.’

‘Know what? About your scheme? If he recruited me into helping him?’

Charlie hunched his shoulders and lost the smile.

‘I’m not working for Ash,’ I said. ‘I don’t even know his real involvement, but I suspect that when he told me he had a problem to fix, that problem was you. I’m working for Anna Blau; no one else.’

He leaned forward, leaning his elbows on his knees.

‘How do you know he ain’t using you? That’s what Ash does. That’s what he’s good at doing.’

‘Sit back, Charlie; I’d hate to have to shoot you.’

‘You won’t shoot me, Alex; you’re not that type.’

‘You don’t want to find out.’ I flicked my gun at him, and he settled back. ‘But yes, I’m sure he’s using me.’

‘Is Pongo really dead?’ He looked at me morosely. ‘Did you kill him?’

‘So, you started your collection,’ I said, ignoring his question. ‘Faces from the past. Who were you going to sell them to?’

‘Ah, Alex, that’s the thing. We’d only just started to explore that.’ He was smiling again. ‘The Americans were interested, the Israelis, the French – you'd be surprised. Some wanted to hang them, and some wanted to employ them. Some wanted to give them medals. There's no justice, just what there is.'

'Then Popov came along.'

'That was for later. When things settled down. Then Pongo and I would retire. South America. Argentina. One of the big cities.'

'Where you could live as kings, I suppose, amongst the other Nazis hiding there.'

'Kings, princes, the lot.' There was a long silence as he considered me. One foot tapped out a slow rhythm on the carpet as if he were listening to music, and a finger of his right hand echoed the beat in syncopation. 'Alex, there's money here,' he said in that *let's all be good pals* voice. 'Lots of money. Enough to keep us in luxury for the rest of our lives. We could go anywhere, do anything, buy anything without worrying whether we could afford it. The world would be our oyster, as they say. I have twenty-odd names; each is a gem. Some of them can just be sold; some can be auctioned to the highest bidder; and some, like Grunwald, will even pay to keep their secret hidden. What do you say, Alex? Now that Pongo's dead, his share could be yours.'

'Anna Blau–'

'Damn her!' he shouted. He ground his teeth. 'Don't you see–'

'I see a pathetic little man with a gripe. So, why's it taken you so long to discover the world's unfair? What gives you the right to make it more unfair than it is? Money? You're a grubby little man, Charlie. For that, Anna's got to die to keep a sordid little secret that you'd expose in a year's time anyway?'

'And what are you going to do about it? Shoot me, and you'll never find out where she is. Not before tomorrow. Then it won't matter a damn. She'll be dead, and it'll be all over. Popov will be controlled so tightly that she'll never know what happened. Why do you think we agreed to bring the girl along in the first place?' He banged the glass down on the table, and rose from his chair. His face, damp with sweat, glistened in the light. 'I've been planning this for a long time. I've taken all the chances, and I'm not asking you to take any. It's a shame Pongo's dead, but there it is. It makes things more difficult, nothing else. But I'm going to have my cake and eat it, Alex, and if you want a share, it's yours if you'll let me do what I have to do. For God's sake, be sensible.'

'Sit down, Charlie,' I said. 'I'm not telling you again.'

He spread his arms wide. 'Shoot me then. Go on.' The smile returned to his face as he lowered them. 'I can use you, and we can set ourselves up for the rest of our lives in comfort. Think about that. And who's gonna miss another fucking Jew?' The smile had turned into a sneer. 'I'm going to get another drink.'

He'd turned to walk to the drinks cabinet when I pulled the trigger. The shot echoed around the room. Charlie howled in pain and crashed against the chair, slipping off of it and onto the floor. He grasped his fleshy thigh.

'Bitch! Bitch!' Charlie screamed. 'You shot me, you fucking crazy bitch!' He twisted around, his face creased in pain.

'I for one am going to miss *another fucking Jew*,' I shouted. 'I swear, Charlie, you're going to tell me where she is.'

'Go to hell,' he screamed.

I began to speak then stopped. Ginny Bright was standing in the open doorway of the living room. She came in and calmly slipped off her gloves. I wasn't surprised to see her. I thought my guardian angel would have told her or Ash where I was and what I was planning. I half expected Hawkins to be here as well. I suspected Ginny had been waiting until Charlie returned. She, too, wanted to hear what he had to say.

'If she won't kill you, Danny boy,' she said, 'I will.'

Charlie's head spun around, his eyes widened, and he became quiet. Ginny came to stand between us. She reached inside her bag and took out a small automatic pistol.

'And you know I will. And I'll do it without qualms, or compunction, or regret, and I'll get away with it because no one's going to arrest me. Like Ash, I go back a long, long way. Long before you even wore short pants, Danny. Long enough to make friends who'll turn a blind eye to whatever happens here. And when I tell them about you selling secrets, they'll give me a medal and might even make me a Dame. *Lady Bright*… It has a nice ring, don't you think?'

She dragged a stiff back dining chair and placed it several feet in front of Charlie or Danny – his real name presumably – and sat comfortably on it.

'You can put your gun away, Alex,' she said. 'Mr… Hawkins… appeared concerned about you. I told him he didn't need to be. But he insisted.'

'He's been looking out for me,' I said.

'That's kind of him.'

'I'm glad you sent him,' I said.

Maybe it was a smile she gave me; I couldn't tell. She returned her gaze to Charlie.

'So, Danny, I shouldn't be surprised it was you freelancing, and I'm not. In many ways, I agree with you: you don't fight a war and expect to – what was the term you used? Go to bed with them? But we have, and I'll not comment on it anymore. But, Danny, Ash wants to know where Anna Blau is. And this is the deal.'

She placed the gun on her lap, took out a cigarette, and, placing it between Charlie's lips, she lit it. He took it greedily. She leaned forward, the gun pointing at Charlie's face.

'If you don't tell me, I'll kill you,' she whispered. 'I agree, it's not much of a deal. But you see, time is of the essence, and, as you said, she'll be dead by tomorrow. It's been long enough for your people to have done the initial debrief of Popov, and you'll be moving her soon. Then, as you said, Popov will be controlled so tightly, there'd be no need to keep Anna alive. So, understand, if Anna dies, then there's little point in keeping you alive. Yes, you could argue that you have other information we need. But at this moment, in this room, Danny boy' – she swept her head around – 'you're only as important as I think you are, and if you don't speak, that's not very important.'

She leaned back, giving Charlie a moment to process what she had said, then resumed speaking.

'You may not even get prison, Danny. Did you think of that?' She leaned forward and tapped the side of his head with the muzzle of her gun. 'There's a lot in there that you know, and a prison sentence would cause us some difficulties. Of course, we could just blow your brains out, and that solves that little problem. But no one needs to die, Danny, least of all you, least of all today. So, where is she?'

'I thought you'd know that.' Charlie grimaced and groaned. He laid his head back against the seat of the chair. His fingers clutching the wound were red with blood.

'You need a doctor, Danny, and you're making a mess of your carpet. You're never going to get those stains out, no matter how much you scrub. But back to Anna Blau. I know several places that'd be suitable; only I'd be guessing. She's in the same place as Popov, I'd warrant.'

Charlie flashed a glare at me. 'You crazy bitch,' he said. 'You threw it all away over a nobody.'

'That's a matter of opinion, Charlie,' I said.

'Crazy bitch,' he mumbled. 'Okay, Ginny. But I want guarantees–'

'Danny,' Ginny hushed him. 'Anna first.'

There was a moment of hesitation before he said, 'Howden House. She and Popov are there. Forrester is debriefing her. Yes, he's almost done.'

'I see,' Ginny said. 'Where is she being kept? From what I remember of the place, the basement would be ideal.'

He nodded.

Ginny took out a notebook and pen, and she wrote the address down, tearing off the page to give it to me. She took out her car keys and passed them over as well.

'The red Ford parked by the letter box. Leave the car anywhere,' she said. 'It's like a bad penny; it always turns up.'

'There's a lot going on here, Ginny,' I said. 'I don't suppose you're going to tell me all of it.'

'Official Secrets Act and all that. Remember that little gem we signed? Get Anna Blau back, and don't worry about the rest. I wonder what that makes us if she's allowed to die, Danny?'

'Stupid.' He scowled. 'One girl… for all we could gain…'

'Suddenly become a patriot, have you, Daniel? It's become "we" again, has it?' She slipped out of her shoes, wiggled her stockinged toes, and sat back in her chair, making herself comfortable. 'On your way out, Alex, go to the bathroom and get me all the towels there are. Danny boy and I will have a chat. It's likely to be a long one. I wouldn't want him to bleed out on me.'

'Is he your *information problem*?' I asked, remembering her words, when she dropped me off at Ipswich station that night.

'Not a problem anymore.' She considered me for a few seconds and said, 'I know what you're planning, Alex.'

'Do you? Me, I wish Ash could just make a phone call. But I guess it's not like the old days when he could do that.'

She shook her head.

'We can't guarantee who's on our side and who isn't. There's a lot of jealousy.'

'And lots angling for knighthoods at Anna's expense.'

'Far too many cooks.' Then she shook her head. 'No. Latimer can't help either. He's clever, but the people who have Anna will tie him up in so much red tape, he'll never hack through it in time.' She glanced at the carriage clock on the mantlepiece. 'It's late; you'd better go. Like I said, I have an idea of what you're thinking. If I were ten years younger, I like to think I'd do the same. If Danny lied about where Anna is, you ring me here and let me know.'

'At least tell me how I got involved in all of this?' I asked.

'This part? By accident. You mentioned a name you shouldn't have to a man you shouldn't have.'

'Otto Grunwald – Pongo told me.'

'Our Mr Marx can be a tenacious bulldog. One that can't be bought or threatened. Lots of people, including the good Hauptmann, doesn't want his past known. Did Moncrief visit you?'

'Is it his job to look after him?'

'Amongst other things. It suited Danny's purpose to help him and the captain out. Yes, far too many cooks.' She smiled at me. It was goodbye.

'Well, Danny, what shall we talk about?' I heard her say when I was leaving. I'd done what she asked, and he was trying to staunch the bleeding with a towel. 'Let's get the small talk out of the way first, shall we? The weather is cold, and it looks as if there may be snow in April. It'll delay the cricket season, they say. Won't please Hutton, but there it is. He'll have more time to practice his off-drive. Now, let's get down to brass tacks.'

# Chapter 35

If you drew a straight line from the headquarters of the Fascist League to Goel Hadam and extended it twenty miles or thereabouts, you'd arrive at Howden House. Lord, Chief Marshal So-and-So Howden owned it, and when he died intestate and heirless, the government owned it. You were in the country now, and the dirty old London air was behind you, though the smell of freshly manured fields from the farm opposite would make you wonder. Somehow, it still smelled fresher than Charlie Mathers's Pimlico flat.

Howden House, a sprawling mansion over three floors and dozens of bedrooms, stood back from the road, peering over a thick border of trees. A long, exposed gravel drive led from the main road to the imposing front door. A high brick wall surrounded the grounds, and it was difficult to gauge the length of the perimeter; several miles would be a good guess. One end was a wood of mature trees with thick undergrowth; the other end was composed of dense scrub. At intervals, signs informed you that it belonged to the Ministry of Defence Training Establishment and you were to Keep Out. To make that clear, at the entrance to the drive, a grand affair of solid stone masonry pillars stood a sentry box behind iron railings.

I drove past it at a sedate twenty miles per hour. The sentries looked bored and were too busy talking amongst themselves to notice another car driving by. A quarter of a mile further, where the road twisted around following the walls, was an area covered with foliage. I pulled up off the road and parked out of sight of any traffic. I walked around the wall, away from the gate, every now and then, scaling it to get a view inside.

I didn't think the grounds would be patrolled, and there were no signs that they were. A clear glimpse of the house showed it lay in an open field; fifty yards of clear space separated it from the trees. I caught sight of a few army types doing nothing in particular other than smoking. Even though it could accommodate half a battalion, I thought most of the rooms would be empty. More of a worry was the searchlight on the roof.

Walking further, I came across the main telephone line and the pole connecting it to the others in the district and all points beyond. I made a note of it. Then I walked back to where I'd parked.

After three quarters of an hour, I set out back to London. I knew what I had to do.

At four o'clock I arrived in Soho.

I told Martha and Jack my plan, as crazy as it was. I'm not sure what they made of it. But I've never had to ask either to trust me. I've never needed to. I was glad I didn't have to this time.

'If we're going to break in–' Jack started saying.

'*I'm* going to break in,' I interrupted him.

'If you're going to break in, then we'll be needing some more help.'

'Especially if the place has security,' Martha added.

I nodded.

'I've thought of that already,' I said. 'Bruno Marx. I need you to call in a favour from him, Jack, and tell him about the bugs.'

'Good thing I kept it a secret then, wasn't it?' Jack said.

I had some good news for Marx and I had some bad news for him too. I was going to disappoint him. I was going to make him angry.

I drove Ginny Bright's car with Jack and Martha inside. At five o'clock we pulled up in front of the Goel Hadam building. It was emptying out; people were calling it a day and going home. Marx was still in his office, supping from a glass filled with brandy.

He was about to speak when I placed a finger across my lips.

'It was quite a dust-up at the park,' I said. 'I suppose you expected that?'

He took my hint with a curious look and started speaking about what happened that day, saying only what was reported in the newspapers. Jack went quietly to the drinks cabinet and carefully and silently lifted it up a quarter of an inch and swung it a little away from the wall. He motioned Marx nearer.

The bug was a grey box with wires leading into it, affixed to the wall with tape.

'You look famished, Miss Raven,' Marx said smoothly.

'I've not eaten since breakfast,' I replied.

'Good. I'm hungry as well, and I did eat after breakfast,' he said, waving us out the door with an open palm.

The kitchen was one of those sterile tile affairs that could serve as a hospital or a mortuary in a pinch. Marx went about making scrambled eggs while Martha boiled a kettle and toasted bread.

'That explains the break-in,' Marx said. 'Special Branch must be getting worried.'

'The cloak-and-dagger men,' I said. 'MI5, not Special Branch. They've got surveillance down the road at the

League as well. The bugs are being listened to in the church at the back of your building.'

He nodded.

'You worry them. Every now and then, you dig up someone they want buried. Otto Grunwald's one.'

'We'd begun looking into him immediately after you left us,' he said. 'Some interesting things came to light.'

'I'm sure. Only he's made new friends.'

'Indeed. So we started a file on him. Then he vanished.'

'That was my fault. I didn't know I was being played.'

I explained, as best I could, what had happened. I told him about Saul's death and Anna's kidnapping. I told him about Charlie and how he'd been keeping an eye on me, but not why – he already guessed why. For the moment, I left Popov out of it. I told him where Anna was and what I intended to do. I told him I needed his help. And I told him it might all be too little, too late, and Anna might be dead already.

Marx listened quietly, and we sat and ate quietly. Then I told him what I knew he wouldn't want to hear.

'Saul planted the bug,' I said. 'I'm guessing only.'

'She's a good guesser,' Martha said to Marx. 'I'd trust her guesses.'

He used his fork to move the scrambled eggs around his plate for a few moments.

'How do you know?' he asked.

'Just a few things that didn't make sense. He had more money than he should have had. He was knowledgeable in terms of electronics. He worked late when the building was empty. He knew where your files are kept and what they are worth. The man called Mathers paid him for the files. Saul needed money for his father, Bruno. I can't say I blame him.'

'It was a Jew who betrayed Jesus,' Marx said with quiet anger.

'You ain't Jesus,' Martha snapped. She'd fixed him with a hard stare that made him look away.

'What about the break-in at his place?' Marx asked.

'Saul knew the value of the files, so he hid them, maybe even copied them before passing them on,' I said. 'He'd fallen into bad company–'

'This Mathers person?'

I nodded.

'Then why did he kill Saul?'

'He did and he didn't. But he was there when it happened. The break-in and vandalism were excuses for them to search Saul's room. They did the same at Anna's place, thinking she and Saul were working together. They didn't want any connection found to them or what they were doing.'

'I cannot see Anna working with Saul. Tell me she wasn't.'

'She wasn't. Anna's involvement was to be in the wrong place at the wrong time. No more than that, I'm sure. But Charlie and his friend have their own collection of ex-Nazis, which they were planning to sell to the highest bidder. You had a file they wanted that Saul probably got for them. Someone they wanted to vanish. Julia N Hildebrandt.'

Marx nodded after a brief moment of reflection. 'She's of interest to MI5? We more or less cleared her.'

'How did her name come to your attention?' I asked.

'It was no more than routine. Several months ago, we came across a document of a meeting she had with a Colonel Messner in 1942. He was seconded to a branch of the Abwehr – German Military Intelligence, sort of your MI5 equivalent. It warranted investigation. But as far as we know, it was a meeting to discuss codes and ciphers and nothing else. Why is she of interest?'

'Because of the codes and ciphers.'

Marx sat back and crooked his head slightly.

'She is someone they don't want to exist, is that it?' he asked. 'Then just who is she?'

'Natalia Popov, the Russian scientist who disappeared.'

His eyes brightened, and he leaned forward. 'Tell me,' he said.

'The Russians swept her up at the end of the war, particularly because of her expertise in cipher analysis. At some point, Popov must have decided she'd prefer British austerity to Russian hospitality. The fact that her husband is dying from radiation poisoning might have helped her decision. She'd been courting British Intelligence and their chance came with this symposium. Only things went wrong. On their way home that evening, Saul and Anna came across a car that'd broken down. Popov was in it. Saul made the mistake of recognising her. His death was something of an accident. They took Anna because Popov didn't want her dead.'

Marx pushed his scrambled eggs around the plate.

'So, what about Anna?'

'As I said, she's alive because Popov didn't want her killed along with Saul that night. Why? Who knows? But she won't stay alive after tonight. When things come out, everyone will want to cover their tracks. They won't need Anna then.'

'And they are about to, I suppose. This *bad company* Saul fell into…?' Marx asked.

'One's dead; the other may be dead. Either way, they're not important anymore.'

Marx's face became pensive. He'd gotten his appetite back and was busy finishing his eggs.

'All right,' he said. 'How can I help?'

'I'm going to break in and free Anna,' I said. He didn't raise even an eyebrow. So I did it for him. 'I agree; it's not much of a plan as it goes. But it's all I've got. Just have your men ready and waiting at midnight. Three is all we'll need. If it all goes according to plan, then there'll be nothing for them to do, and they can go home and catch up on their sleep.'

'They will need to be armed, of course.'

'With blanks only,' Jack said, leaning across to Marx to show he was serious.

'That depends on who we are going up against, Mr Brody.'

'A platoon at the most,' I said. 'Maybe not even that. They look like regular squaddies who're on to a cushy number. They're lightly armed. The problem is the open ground. It'll be dark, but there's a light on the roof. I want you to deal with the phone lines initially.'

'We can do that. But I'm worried if it all doesn't go well.'

'Let's understand each other, Marx,' Jack said, cutting across me. 'We're not storming Gold Beach. Leave your beef about the Secret Service at the door. After we're done, you can do what you want about them bugging you, but tonight, I'm worried about Alex's safety first–' he looked at me '–Anna's second,' he finished unapologetically.

'Don't worry, Mr Brody, I can take orders as well as give them,' Marx said. 'We'll be ready before midnight. Dead soldiers would raise far too many questions. So, blanks it will be. We'll deal with the communications and help create a crossfire so they don't know which way to turn. If things go *belly-up* – that is the expression, yes? Then I think this is all about making a lot of noise and making it seem as if we are storming Gold Beach, yes?'

He'd said it with a sort of glee in his voice, as if hoping there would be trouble, and I remembered that look in his eyes in Victoria Park when he had spied his prey.

We went back to the shop to get ready. To the disappointment of the men in raincoats with turned-up collars that populate Soho in the evenings, it would be closed tonight.

## Chapter 36

An hour before midnight, Jack roused me. I dressed in black slacks and a thin black jumper. He'd made sandwiches and tea. I ate with little appetite while seated at the table, where he sat quietly pushing bullets into the magazine of a Sten gun. He'd already filled five magazines with ammunition he kept in a biscuit tin. There were two tins. One contained blanks. Two of the magazines, which were wrapped in red electrical tape, had been filled from the other tin. I said nothing. It was better to be prepared than not. In that spirit, I felt the butt of the .32 nestled in a pocket. Fifteen minutes passed, and the muffled sound of a car pulling up broke the silence between us.

'Martha,' he said without looking up.

Jack slung a large bag over his shoulder, and we left the shop immediately. He placed the bag on the back seat of the car, a run-down black sedan, and I sat beside it. Jack eased himself into the passenger seat. Martha glanced back at me. Her eyes were uneasy.

'I could use a tot,' she said, and she turned back to the road.

The traffic was light, and we drove in silence. Martha drove around a little, making sure we didn't have company. Satisfied we were alone, and half a mile before reaching

Goel Hadam's headquarters, we parked up and waited. Less than five minutes later, a car drew up behind us and flashed its lights twice. Marx had arrived on time as agreed. I glanced at him through the back window. He gave me a sharp nod, and we set off.

We drove sedately, observing all the rules of the road. I cleared my mind of any thoughts about what we were about to do and gazed out the window at the countryside, or the little I could see of it lit by a hard April moon. At this time of night, only a few cars passed us going the other way. Behind us, the headlights of Marx's car illuminated the inside of ours, casting swiftly shifting shadows. The engine hummed, the air inside warmed up, and I was sweating under the thin jumper.

The drive was uneventful, and as we passed Howden House, we could see the sentry smoking by the gate. He was on his own. He probably didn't even notice us passing. We drove on for a quarter of a mile, and when we rounded a corner, we parked beside the perimeter wall under a copse of trees.

We got out, and I went to the other car. Bruno Marx wound down the window. Maybe it was the worry on my face that prompted him to say, 'It's okay, Miss Raven. We know what to do.'

I didn't doubt him or his men. I was doubting myself. Suddenly, the plan, for what it was, seemed stupid.

'If we hear shots, we'll deal with the searchlight, and Obi will take out the telephone lines. We can't do much if they use short-wave, but I can't see them doing that, can you?'

I shook my head.

'It's a good, isolated place. If we shoot, no one will hear.'

I doubted that and he nodded and drove off to get him and his men into position.

I went back, and Jack handed me a small bag. I knew it contained a jemmy, some lock-picking instruments, and a few other items that would be useful.

'Jack can go instead,' Martha said. She was holding a Sten gun and squeezing a magazine with electrical tape around it into place.

I shook my head. 'Don't kill anyone, Martha,' I said.

'Don't worry, girl, I'm a good shot,' she said, smiling at me. I didn't know if she was boasting or being reassuring.

I walked towards the outer wall, a dark barrier extending to either side, surrounding Howden House. Jack made a stirrup with his hands, and I placed a foot into it. I thought of Charlie Mathers as he eased me up. I sat crouched on top of the wall as he passed me the bag. He pulled himself up beside me.

'I'll give you thirty minutes. I'll hang the lamp on one of those trees.' His eyes showed me where. 'If you're out earlier, shine a torch to tell me, and I'll switch the lamp on to show you the way back. If things get ugly, it'll be on anyway, so look for it. Martha and me will give cover fire if needed.'

'Let's hope it doesn't come to that.'

'I'm willing to hope,' he said, and he eased me down into the grounds. 'Between us and Marx, we'll create merry hell for a few minutes. Hopefully that'll give you enough time to get back.'

A lazy curtain of trees was in front of me, beyond which I could see the open ground leading to the house. The sky was broken up by clouds, the moon wasn't yet full, and stars twinkled frostily above, not ideal for sneaking about. A light, cold breeze wound through the trees, rustling the branches and leaves. A small car was driving towards the house from the gate, its lights bouncing in front of it as it negotiated the uneven gravel drive, the rev of its engine a low, grating hum in the quiet night air. The building itself was dark, except for a few windows on the top floor that glimmered yellow. I looked back. Jack had found where he wanted to be, and I could only just make him out. Martha was concealed under some branches on the wall, oblivious to me, concentrating on what she had to do.

I wound my way around the bushes and trees as quietly as I could until I came to the edge where the grass of the open ground began. I crouched and swept my eyes over the area. There was nothing to see, and, keeping low, I began a slow trot towards the house. The grass was sodden, and soon I could feel the dampness penetrate my shoes and socks and hear the soft squelching noise of each step. The moon dipped in and out of the clouds, and the shadowed walls ahead of me shifted with the subtle changing light every few seconds. A searchlight flicked, weaving aimlessly across the grass, illuminating nothing in particular.

The fifty yards from the trees was a long and lonely distance to manage before I reached the wall of the house. I leaned against the bricks and glanced back the way I'd come. I made a mental note and a guess at where Jack would hang the light. In the dark, I'd already lost my bearings. I'd need a light to find my way back to where we were parked.

The searchlight swept overhead, still making a slow crawl across the grass, sweeping left and right aimlessly.

Taking a few deep breaths, I crept along the perimeter until I found a window flanked by a small screen of bushes. The shadows were welcoming, and I took a moment to compose myself while sheltering there.

The window was old, and I peered through the dusty panes. The room behind it was dark and, I hoped, empty. It was unlikely anyone would be sleeping downstairs; the sleeping quarters would be upstairs. I pushed the sharp end of the jemmy into the woodwork between the window and the frame and leaned on it. The frame was solid and would give, but not without a loud crack if I continued to force it. Inside the bag Jack had given me, I found a sheet of paper that I knew would be there. It contained a backing that I peeled off and then I pressed the sticky side firmly against the glass. Using the jemmy, I struck it with a sharp blow. There was a muffled crack and then silence. I held my breath for a minute and listened before pulling the paper away. The broken glass came with it.

Reaching inside, I fiddled the catch open and pushed the window up. I glanced behind me. The wooded area was just a dark mass against the horizon. I eased myself up and through the window.

The room was large, with a threadbare carpet and old, dilapidated furniture. The fingers of the moon, poking through the two windows, tickled the shadows, revealing it as a library. Banks of books covered two walls.

The door was unlocked. I opened it enough to peek into a dark corridor. It was empty. I hugged the wall, making my way to one end. There were stairs going up, but none going down.

I retraced my steps back to the library and then tiptoed past it until I found some stairs going down. A clock chimed the preamble to one o'clock from somewhere above, and a few seconds later, several others joined it. The overlapping sounds echoed unhindered around the upstairs floors and along the corridors. I stopped when I heard voices.

Two men were talking loudly.

'Jumped-up little twerp.'

'Leave it out, Phil. You're a corporal and he's a lieutenant colonel.'

'Waltzing in here like he owns the place.'

'Maybe he does.'

'If I had my way–'

'You'd spend three months in the glasshouse. So, shut it and stop bending my ears.'

I glanced down the corridor, from where the voices and a cold breeze were coming. Two khaki uniforms were by an open door, framed in the soft light of a weak bulb from a lamp on a table. One bent his head as the other offered up a match to his cigarette. Leaning against a wall behind them were two rifles. Through the open door, I could make out the nose of a car. The soldier who was smoking took his gun and stepped outside. The door clicked quietly shut, and then the hushed calm descended again as the other sat in a chair beside the lamp. He crossed his legs, picked up a book that had been resting face down on the table, and began reading, hunched near the light.

The house creaked and groaned in the night, as if easing itself into sleep. I was grateful for the noise.

Returning back along the corridor, I slipped down the stairs and entered a passage with a stone floor. The chill in the dark, enclosed space was biting. I found a torch in the bag and flicked the light around cautiously.

There were various doors along the corridor. The first one opened easily when I turned the handle. It was an empty storeroom. I tried the next. That too was open, and that too was empty. Third time lucky, I thought, and I tried the handle of the next. It was locked. I placed my ears against the door and heard gentle snoring. An iron key was hanging on a hook driven into the solid stone wall. The key turned with a sharp snap, and the door creaked when it swung back into a windowless room. The snoring stopped. I shone the torch inside and caught the pale face and frightened eyes of a shabby girl peeping over pulled-up blankets.

'Anna Blau?' I whispered.

She looked at me with wide, unblinking eyes.

'Anna Blau?' I whispered louder, and shone the torch fully in her face, this time recognising her from the photograph her father gave me.

'Y-yes,' she stuttered.

'Time to go, Anna,' I said. 'Get dressed. And do it quietly.'

'W-who're y-you?'

'Someone on your side. Answers later. Right now, get dressed.'

She hesitated, maybe unsure if I was serious. Then suddenly, she threw back the blankets and began scrambling into her clothes.

I crouched on my haunches, peering through the door. I took out the gun, pulled back the slide as carefully and silently as I could, and clutched it in my right hand. The safety was on. It felt odd and heavy and made me distinctly nervous. I wondered if I'd use it. I'd shot Charlie because he'd annoyed me. When I shot him, I didn't mind doing it, and I wasn't aiming to kill.

Anna came to stand beside me, now fully dressed.

Her hair was uncombed and tangled, and it was obvious she'd not washed for several days, perhaps the whole time she'd been here. She looked drawn; her eyes, sunken in her face, were surrounded by dark rings. She looked frightened, jittery with nervous energy and curiosity, and I felt her tremble.

'We're leaving,' I said. 'Is there a door down here to the outside?'

'I saw one there.' She pointed along the corridor.

'Now listen, Anna,' I said, placing a hand on her arm. 'If everything goes well, we'll be gone long before they know we've left. But if something does happen, then do exactly as I say and do it quickly.' She nodded. 'There's likely to be a lot of noise if that's the case. Don't panic. Just follow me. We're going to leave across the lawn at the back of the building, where there will be a wall to climb. You'll know where to go. You'll see a light swinging where the trees are. Head for it. There'll be friends waiting there. Do as they say.'

'You'll be with me, won't you?' Her voice was tinged with fear.

'If not beside you, I'll be close by. Don't worry about me. Just keep moving.'

‘Thank you,’ she said, grasping my hand, and I could see the tears in her eyes. ‘Thank you.’

We walked quickly down the hall towards where she said the door was, but not before I locked the door and replaced the key on the hook. Ahead of us, a set of heavy blackout curtains concealed an eight-foot-high flight of steps. The door at the top was made of solid oak, and the lock was old. There were two sets of bolts, rusted in place, that held it firmly against the frame. No one had used the door in a long time, and it was no use trying to open it – it’d make a devil of a noise before giving in. We’d have to go the way I came in.

I retraced my steps along the stone passage, up the stairs, and into the other dark corridor. I could feel Anna tremble as her hand reached out to hold mine. At the top of the stairs, my nervousness wasn’t far behind hers. I looked in both directions and eased myself out, beckoning her to come. She followed meekly. As we started to go back to the library, from behind one of the doors came raised voices. I froze. Anna came closer, her hand holding on to me. Someone was shouting. A number of voices came from behind a door. It wasn’t an argument; it was panic.

Suddenly, two shots exploded from one of the rooms. In the quiet of the house, they sounded like the clapping of thunder. A door flew open down the hall in front of us. A solid block of yellow light landed in a rectangle on the floor. Three figures rushed out. A woman in a nightdress was being carried along, stumbling between two men. Natalia Popov had been shot. Her right shoulder was red with blood, and her face was drained and pale with shock. She was trying to look over her shoulders as she was being dragged along.

There was a rattle of a dropped rifle from the front door and the noise of the guard scrambling to pick it up, quickly followed by a clatter of boots across the floor.

Above me came the sounds of shouts and the stamp of more boots on bare wood.

Suddenly, another door in the corridor opened in front of us and someone in uniform dashed out. The two men with Popov carried pistols. They raised them just as two more shots crashed into the confined space. They both fell dead. Popov stood, mouth gaping, seemingly frozen in terror.

Anna Blau screamed. Her hands swept around her ears, and the uniformed figure turned towards us.

Hawkins, dressed as a lieutenant colonel, was looking at me.

Popov ran. In a wild panic, she stumbled awkwardly back inside the room she'd just left, shouting, '*Net! Net! Net! Ne strelyay v menya.*'

Hawkins moved along the corridor after Popov. Just as she slammed her door shut, he fired again, this time emptying the magazine into the door.

'Move!' I yelled at Anna and shoved her so hard that she hit the wall. I grabbed her wrist and dragged her along, feeling her stagger beside me, almost tripping over her feet. I pushed her towards the room where I had entered the building. She screamed and fought me, trying to go back to the staircase that led to the cellar, all the while trying to look over her shoulder. I was doing the same.

I caught a glimpse of Hawkins deftly slipping the magazine out of his gun. He replaced it in a single motion. We'd reached the library. I shoved Anna in and slammed the door shut behind us. I turned the key in the lock. Everything was happening in a frenzy. The clatter of boots and the shouting of orders echoed throughout the house.

'The window,' I shouted.

A single shot came from behind the door followed by a muffled scream of pain. Two more shots crashed and I could hear footsteps running away.

I didn't wait. I pushed Anna to the window. She was acting on instinct as she climbed through. I followed, both of us landing in the shrubs below. Lights were going on everywhere. The windows blazed with them, and lamp posts surrounding the building budded and bloomed with a flickering, cold white glow. The searchlight was scanning the grass, moving purposefully from left to right and back again. A siren sounded.

I took a look at the trees, trying to orientate myself, and saw the gleam of a small torch swinging slowly back and forth in a lazy arc.

'There, Anna.' I pointed. 'Run to it. For Christ's sake, run.'

I had to grab her hand and pull her along with me to start with. As we went, several soldiers came charging towards us from one end of the building. The searchlight caught us, held us, and followed us. Suddenly, there was the chatter of a machine gun and flashes from the woods. Another burst came from the opposite end, where Marx and his men were. There was a tinkling of glass from the high windows, and the searchlight left us and illuminated the trees where the shooting came from. A third burst further on was followed by the crash of an explosion, then another, then one more. The chasing soldiers dropped to the ground in fear of the gunfire that seemed to surround them. Between them, Marx and his men, Jack and Martha, were sowing as much confusion as they could.

'Get up,' a captain shouted as he ran up. Standing amongst the huddle of men, he pointed in our direction. 'Get the fuck up. Get after them.'

A sergeant stood up gingerly amid the din of machine gun fire and motioned for his men to follow him. They rose and quickly fell again as shots rang out around them.

'Get up! Now!' the captain shouted and rushed forward past them.

That did the trick, and they were charging towards us, but now they were a disorganised bunch, and they came haltingly with every clip of gunfire that fell amongst them.

Anna and I weaved our way through the woods when we reached the trees. We stumbled past Jack, who was leaning almost casually against a tree. He stepped out and fired a burst of shots at the leading pack of chasing soldiers. They scattered or fell to the ground. A few returned rifle shots, aimed at nothing in particular and adding to the din.

We made it to the brick wall. Martha reached down, grabbed Anna's hand, and yanked her up without any ceremony, hard and fast. She did the same to me. She eased Anna down the other side and quickly followed her. I remained on the wall.

I shouted for Jack to come, then noticed a car moving along the gravel driveway towards the gate. It was in no hurry. Its headlights flashed up and down, and the instrument panel illuminated only one occupant, the driver, Hawkins. Jack climbed up beside me, the wide grin of a schoolboy on his face. He and Marx were probably the only ones enjoying this game.

'Come on, you two, move your arse and stop playing silly buggers,' Martha shouted.

Jack and I jumped down and ran to our car.

Anna was huddled on the back seat, shivering and crying, and I slipped in beside her. I wrapped a blanket around her and held her hands tightly. Jack, taking one last look around, threw a smoke grenade over the wall, the prearranged signal to Marx that it was over, and settled down in the passenger seat.

'Let's go, come on,' he said, rocking back and forth as if urging the car forward.

Martha pulled away smoothly and, once on the road, turned off and swiftly headed away from Howden House. She turned several times, maintaining a sedate pace, before finding a main road that paralleled the ones we'd taken earlier and heading back towards London. The road was empty and dark without street lights. The two cones of headlights met ahead of us, painting the tarmac with a harsh brush of light. It drained all the colours of the bushes and trees, and left black, fast-moving shadows that slid away into the darkness as we passed.

Jack handed me two Sten guns over the back of his seat. 'Break these apart,' he said. 'Carefully,' he added, and he passed me a bag to put the pieces in.

I knew what he meant. As good a weapon as they were, they were notoriously unreliable. In my nervous state, even though they were loaded with blanks, the last thing I wanted to do was shoot someone. Very carefully, I pulled out the magazines and ejected any bullets left in the breech.

'Come on, Martha, give us a song; there's a young woman back there who looks like she's seen a ghost,' Jack said.

Martha glanced into the driver's mirror and gave a deep, guttural laugh. Her face was flushed red in the glow of the lights from the instruments. A smile blossomed and grew in her face.

''ere, then, let me teach her a song if she don't know this one,' she shouted, and started to sing *I Do Like To Be Beside The Seaside!*

She tooted the horn, and Jack stopped her doing it again in case it drew too much attention.

'All together now, repeat after me,' she said, having sung a verse.

Jack started singing with her. I started singing. I nudged Anna, and soon she started singing, hesitantly at first, then with the same gusto as Martha. Anna looked at me through frightened eyes that quickly mellowed. The realisation that she was safe and free made her smile contagious. Her hair was wild and uncombed; she was no longer shivering, and her voice was raised in celebration.

As we bowled along the road, we were soon singing at the top of our lungs. The music hall was arriving in an old four-door sedan, heading back to Soho in the early hours of the morning. God knows what the coppers would make of it if they stopped us.

# Chapter 37

The adrenalin had drained by the time we arrived back, and the songs had long since died. Silence reigned. Anna was asleep, leaning against me, still holding the blanket around her shoulders. Jack had his head resting against the backrest. His eyes were closed, but he wasn't asleep. And I just stared through the windscreen in the direction we were going.

Martha parked by the front door of the shop, and we climbed out. It was dark, the streets were quiet, and only the black-and-white cat roaming the empty pavement was about. Once inside, Jack sank into a chair. He leaned back with his eyes closed before reaching into a pocket and taking out a pack of cigarettes. His thumbnail flared a match, and the smell of smoke filled the room. Anna Blau stood awkwardly watching, like it was the first time she'd seen us.

'Why don't you have a sleep?' I said to her. 'It's too damn late for explanations.'

Jack stirred and yawned.

'Don't worry, Anna,' he said. 'We'll get you home tomorrow. I know you're anxious to see your dad. But right now, we're all too knackered.'

'We'll get you rested and tidied up first,' I said.

'Has he a phone?' Jack asked.

She shook her head.

‘Then tomorrow, yes?’ he said.

Anna nodded.

‘I’ll get some blankets for the couch, Alex,’ he said to me. ‘Anna can have the spare room.’

‘Come on,’ I said to her, ‘I’ll take you up.’

Martha, standing behind Jack, leaned forward and kissed the top of his head.

‘Good night, sweet prince. Just don’t disturb me when you come up.’

I settled Anna into the spare room. She pestered me for an explanation. I didn’t have one to give. Before I left, I laid out one of Martha’s old dresses that was hanging in the wardrobe, along with some clean underwear. She climbed into bed, was about to say something, then snuggled down and drew the blankets around her neck. She was tired and drained.

When I came back, Jack had made the sofa up and was mixing two drinks. He gave me one and eased back into his chair. He raised his glass in a silent toast, and we drank a sip as I sat on the sofa.

‘What happened back there, Alex?’ he asked softly. He sat quietly and looked at me broodingly.

‘We got Anna back,’ I said. I suddenly felt very tired, with a head stuffed with cotton wool, and I yawned widely.

‘That’s not what I meant.’ He held out his hand. ‘Let me see your gun.’

I placed it on the coffee table between us, and he took it, ejected the magazine, and the round in the chamber. He checked the magazine. It was one bullet short – the one I’d shot Charlie with.

‘I heard two shots,’ he said. ‘Two more, then a whole lot before I saw you and Anna leaving the building.’

‘Hawkins was there.’

‘The little man?’

I nodded. ‘Only, he was dressed in a lieutenant colonel’s uniform.’

He thought for a while, his forehead crinkling up, and he was breathing deeply.

'You never told me how you knew where Anna was being held,' he said.

'Charlie Mathers told me. He didn't have much of a choice; Ginny Bright would have killed him if he didn't. And I'd already shot him.'

'Then it wasn't you who fired in there.'

I told him how Hawkins had shot Pongo and saved my life, and how I had shot Charlie before Ginny Bright turned up. Then I told him what had happened at Howden House. Jack listened without speaking. When I finished, he rose, stretched his arms out wide, yawned, and moved towards the door.

'You've been played, Alex,' he said. 'But I guess you know that already.'

'I'm not complaining. Anna's safe. Hawkins saved my life twice now.'

'You're no fool. People like him do it for a reason, and the reason is not charity. You're alive because he didn't want to kill you. Another day and you'd be dead.'

'Charity or not, I don't have bad news for Mr Blau, and as you say, I'm alive.'

'So, who's this little man if I can't guess? Why did he kill Popov? To keep her from saying anything? The simple solution? Lieutenant colonel's uniform! That takes some front.'

I laid back on the sofa and stared at the ceiling. My mind was washed out and tired.

'I think he's working both sides of the street,' I said.

'You reckon?' Jack didn't quite roll his eyes.

'I think he was sent to kill Popov. He found her through me. But something else is going on. He could have easily killed her.'

'He emptied his gun with her behind the door. I think that qualifies.'

'That's the point, Jack. That's the whole damn point,' I said tiredly.

'I don't know what you mean. But after all that hoo-ha in the papers, doesn't it mean the Russians knew she was alive all along?'

'Especially if they sent Hawkins – I know. It's all a game, Jack, well, you know. Ash was using him as much as he was using Ash – everyone uses everyone.'

'But why did Ash allow Popov to be killed? What did he have to gain?'

I shook my head and, stretching out, wrapped the blanket around me.

'It's all a game, Jack,' I repeated with the same tiredness of before. I didn't know what else to tell him.

'Do you know what you've got yourself into?' he asked.

'I think I do. If I don't, I'll know tomorrow.'

'Would you have killed him?'

'Who?'

'Mathers.'

'Flick the light switch when you go, *sweet prince*,' I said.

I was too tired to think, too drained of energy, too old, I thought, or too long in the tooth to care. Or just too damn stupid – there was always that possibility.

* * *

I slept late. Everyone slept late. When we awoke, there was a strange, sullen silence; perhaps it was a sense of relief, I don't know.

Anna looked refreshed when she'd bathed and combed her hair. Martha's dress was a little too big for her, but she'd pinned the waist with a safety pin, and it was a better option than wearing her dirty clothes. It would do anyway, until she got home. She blushed in embarrassment when she came down for breakfast and realised just what type of shop Jack and Martha owned. Martha's sniggering didn't help. We ate, and the dull chatter became more animated as we slowly came to ourselves.

Anna told us what happened. How she saw Saul being struck and falling. It was Popov who stopped them from hurting her.

'Saul had gone to a couple of her lectures,' Anna said. 'She told me in the car they had spoken. She liked him. He was curious and intelligent, she said, and she thought I was Saul's wife. I didn't know what to say, I was scared, so I said I was.' Anna looked straight at me. 'She said she was sorry he was dead, and she told me about her husband. He's dying… I think she really was sorry, Miss Raven.'

At Howden House, she'd been held effectively incommunicado, unsure where she was and what was happening. That was all she really knew until I came and found her.

I called my messenger service. Wilfried Ash would like me to visit him. I can't say it surprised me. News of what happened at Howden House would never reach the newspapers, but it would reach Ash. I wondered how he would deal with the news of the men Hawkins shot. I wondered if it mattered to him.

The sun was bright when I stepped out of the shop. It had drizzled a little before dawn, and the streets were still glazed with rain. The old black car was gone, and I remembered hearing Jack leave the shop before I fell asleep last night. I went around to a local garage where I'd left Ginny Bright's red Ford and drove back to the shop to collect Anna. Then I drove her to the East End to her father's house.

I parked a street away. We sat talking for a minute.

She'd read the morning paper that had been delivered to the shop as she'd waited for me to get the car. The news was all about the death of Natalia Popov, how an abduction had gone wrong; she had died in a boat fire several weeks ago, and her body had been taken back to Russia. There were hints that the Americans were somehow involved and that the Russians were still angry at the British police's failings in protecting a citizen of the

Soviet Union. It bore all the hallmarks of something that would rumble on and off for the coming weeks, if not months, and go nowhere.

'I don't understand,' Anna said. 'She didn't die in a fire. It was her at that place.'

'She died in a fire, Anna,' I told her. 'Whatever else you saw or thought you saw, never happened.'

'But she didn't–'

'Anna, as far as you're concerned, the last two weeks didn't happen.'

'But Saul's dead. That happened. How can you say that?'

'I just did. And life's unfair and all that guff, but, Anna, trust me on this. You were a part of what went on; now you're not, and you want to keep it that way.'

She sat just looking at me as if I were a madwoman who'd just entered a room carrying a dead horse under her arm. Her lips trembled and her brows creased, and I stared at her with as much sympathy as I could muster.

'Get on with your life, Anna. Forget about what happened, and if you can't, don't talk about it. Not even to your father.'

She tried to speak, but no words came out. Then she drew in a deep breath and chewed her lips.

'But what will I tell the police?' she said eventually.

'I don't think you need to worry about them. I don't think they'll bother you.' If Hugo Latimer didn't know already, it wouldn't be too long before he'd be told to shelve the investigation and bury it somewhere deep and dark. If Latimer was good at one thing, he was good at that.

'Why did a British officer kill her, Miss Raven? Who is she? Why did he kill those other soldiers?'

'Why don't you see your dad?'

'Would they have killed me, Miss Raven?'

She already knew that answer, so I said nothing.

I started the engine and drove the small distance to her house. I would have gone in with her, but instead I dropped her at the door and waited as she knocked. She didn't need me to be there; she needed friends and family. Mrs Geller opened the door and almost fainted. In her joy, she didn't see me, and as the door closed, I heard screams of happiness from behind it.

* * *

It had turned into one of those spring days, boundless with promise, with a sparkling blue sky and a fat yellow sun warming everything its rays touched. I drove north-east towards Orford and Wilfried Ash. The window was open, and the wind whipped my hair into a tangle as the city gave way to the countryside and the air became crisp with spring scents. When I arrived in Orford, I was sad that the drive was over. It felt good to feel the wind in my face, blowing away last night's staleness.

I found Ash in his living room, armed with his binoculars, looking through the French windows at his garden.

'It's moved on,' he said sadly.

'The sparrowhawk?'

He nodded, but that wasn't what he meant. 'Too near people and not enough cover. Tell me what you know,' he said.

'Brody said I've been used.'

'He's a clever man.'

'By you and by Hawkins.'

He paused for a few moments, raised his binoculars to his eyes, seeing nothing.

'Not by me, Alex, if you can believe that. Mr Hawkins, however…'

I didn't believe him, but I wasn't going to argue.

'Hawkins? Is that his name?' I asked and Ash hunched his shoulders. 'Probably not,' I confirmed for him. 'Who is he? You seem to know each other quite well.'

'Does it matter who he is, Alex? But I think you know.'

I nodded. 'Not until I saw him at Howden House, dressed in an officer's uniform, I didn't. A freelancer who works both sides of the street.'

He didn't nod; he didn't shake his head, either.

'I understand my role, Mr Ash. I know what a Judas goat is. I think I understand the whys and wherefores of all of this. And I know I led him to Natalia Popov. Who was I meant to find her for? You or Hawkins? But tell me this, Mr Ash, how can a man who is such a good marksman, good enough to kill three men with a single shot each, miss killing Natalia Popov when she was such a sitting target? Why did he then empty a magazine of shots at her?'

His face hadn't changed one iota – the perfect poker face.

'Who is to say he didn't kill her?' he asked.

'I am. And that's the point, isn't it?'

Ash struggled to stand and found his walking stick. He tottered over to the sofa and the fire.

'As you say, that is the point.'

He eased himself down, and Ginny poured tea for the three of us.

'You were not meant to see what happened, Alex. Hawkins had to do what he did before they moved her again. But you did see, and it's not something you will speak about. You see, Natalia Popov might be an asset; she might not be. Time will tell. If she's genuine, then we'll use her skills. If she's not, then we'll learn just what it is the Soviets are deficient in to send her to us. We are all playing an elaborate game, and that includes Natalia Popov. Either way, she'll not be wasted.'

'And Hawkins' part was to convince everyone Popov was serious in her intention to defect.'

'Serious enough to shoot her and for her to get shot. The games we play… *Deep in my shut and silent heart…*'

Ash shrugged his shoulders.

'It was meant to be a simple defection, Alex. But at some point, a third party was involved and Ash was squeezed out,' Ginny said. 'Whether her defection is serious or not, this third party wanted to make sure we kept her. So they arranged the charade of the burnt bodies.'

'Of course they knew the Russians would see through that sham,' Ash continued. 'So they gave the suggestion that the Americans were involved and it was they who kidnapped Popov. Hence the second body which they knew would be identified as someone known to have smuggled people out of East Germany. The American warship, it leaving when it did, its rendezvous with a submarine, all added to the suggestion.'

'The Americans' denial of having Popov only made it seem as if they indeed had her. It's not something they'd readily admit to,' Ginny said.

'That was why Hawkins was involved. Both to make sure that she was where she was meant to be, with us, and to convince us the Russians wanted her dead, making her defection plausible by attempting to assassinate her.'

'And failing,' I said.

'Of course. And as you've said, that was the point. So what does that suggest? But perhaps they have completely misread Popov. She hasn't forgiven them for her husband's illness.' Ash pursed his lips.

'Or maybe she has. Who knows?' Ginny said.

'But Popov is dead as far as everyone is concerned,' he continued. 'Her body is being flown back to the motherland for an official burial, complete with all the pomp and circumstance, the medals, and the words of gratitude and veneration. Now that the Russians know we have her, we will see where the game leads us.'

'And everyone will continue to play it as if nothing has happened,' I said bitterly.

I understood it now. In time, the real Natalia Popov would slip slowly out of the newspapers and then vanish all together. It would be as if she never existed. But in some out-of-the-way place, she'd work her mathematical magic, breaking complex codes while hiding in the shadows. That, at least, was one scenario.

But there were others.

Who she was, or more to the point, what she was, wasn't my concern. She could have been a defector, a double agent, a triple agent, or any combination of the above. The same could be said of Hawkins. I can't say any of it worried me anymore. Everyone was playing games, and Ash, ever the pragmatist, was playing the long one. I really didn't care. Charlie said it right – life's *too short.*

'Then there's the good captain, Hauptmann Grunwald? What happens to him?' I asked.

Ash gave a small shrug and drew in a deep breath. I knew what the shrug meant. He'd become one of the untouchables and would be fighting the good fight. I wondered what Marx would make of it.

'Am I safe?'

'I honestly don't think you exist, Alex. Nor does Anna Blau. Not officially, not unofficially. I wouldn't worry about any recriminations. Hawkins likes you, after all, it seems.'

'I don't believe I'd like him as a friend, Mr Ash.'

'So, I am *Mister* Ash now, am I?'

'I think so, don't you?'

He gave me a slow smile and nodded his head in a fatherly way.

'The girl, Anna Blau, is okay?' he asked.

'She is. She's just confused.'

'She'll not speak of anything?'

'I've told her it wouldn't be wise.'

'Without telling her why, I hope.'

'The hole's deep enough, why make it deeper? And her friend, Saul Greenberg, is dead. It will probably be an unsolved murder. Isn't that what everyone wants?'

He sighed sadly, spooned two sugars into the cup, stirred it, and then sipped his tea. I couldn't read him.

'Like the person mistaken for Popov and the body found in the motor cruiser,' I reminded him. 'All dead.'

'That was really Charlie's friend's game,' Ginny said in placating tones. 'It wasn't how it was meant to be. It was meant to be just a simple defection. But that's what happens when too many people are involved and things are done too quickly.'

'Tell that to the soldiers Hawkins killed.'

Ginny did not look up. She merely stirred her tea and calmly placed the spoon down on the saucer before sipping it.

'And you?' Ash asked. 'What of you?'

'I've been reminded of the Official Secrets Act several times this past week. I can take a hint.'

I had liked Ash when I first met him. Drunken evenings with AB were always welcome events. Today I wasn't sure how much I liked him. But perhaps my face said it instead, and I didn't need to find the words.

'How is Charlie?' I asked Ginny.

'It's time for Wilf's nap,' she said, helping him stand.

And like that, it was over. Ash was tired; I could see the strain on his face, and he retired to bed even though it was mid-afternoon. We'd run out of conversation, and the questions I wanted to ask would receive no answers. There was little point staying longer.

Ginny drove me to Ipswich railway station. On the journey, she spoke about their summer plans, but I felt she did so out of politeness and no more. It was surreal. A bomb had exploded, and there we were, seated amongst the wreckage, discussing holiday plans.

THE END

## The Book Folks & Joffe Books Story

The Book Folks began in 2013, founded by Erik Empson with a simple but powerful goal — to publish highly readable, compelling fiction that readers would love. With a focus on crime fiction, thrillers and gripping mysteries, The Book Folks quickly built a loyal audience and became known for championing talented authors from the UK, Ireland, the US and beyond.

From gritty police procedurals and psychological thrillers to fast-paced action and suspense, The Book Folks earned a reputation for curating addictive stories at affordable prices — often introducing readers to hidden gems and breakout talent.

In 2025, The Book Folks proudly became part of Joffe Books, the UK's largest independent publisher. Joffe Books started in 2014 when Jasper Joffe published his mum's long-rejected romance novel — which unexpectedly became a bestseller. That spirit of risk-taking and reader-first publishing has defined Joffe Books ever since.

Together, Joffe Books and The Book Folks are united by a passion for page-turning fiction and a deep respect for the authors who create it. We're proud to publish some of the best-loved names in fiction — including Joy Ellis, Faith Martin, Caro Ramsay, Simon Brett, Helen Forrester, and Robert Goddard — as well as fresh voices bringing new energy to the genre.

We never forget that everything begins with the author's story — and that continues with you, the reader.

We love hearing from you, so get in touch any time at feedback@joffebooks.com.

And if you'd like to receive free books and hear about our latest releases, sign up to our newsletter:
www.joffebooks.com/freebooks

Thanks for reading — and for being part of our story.

www.thebookfolks.com

Printed in Dunstable, United Kingdom

73913764R00152